I'M THE TRUTH
MY QUEEN WILL
NEVER *Escape.*

Mine

BEAUTIFUL SINNER SERIES

ELENA M. REYES

SUMMARY:

In Miami, I'm royalty.
The beginning and the end.
I'm the truth my queen will never escape.

Thiago Rivera De Leon doesn't believe in second chances, and I never show mercy to those stupid enough to cross me. Loyalty wins you favors but trying to overthrow the city's king will find you with one of my bullets between the eyes.

A simple promise I always keep while abiding by two rules:

I don't forgive. I don't forget.

And after spending the last five years behind bars, I'm out with two goals in mind...

Kill the bastards responsible.
Reclaim my Luna.

Beautiful
SINNER

I'd burn the
world to
ashes if it
meant I have
your heart
again.

ACKNOWLEDGMENTS

Before we get to the book and its yumminess; I need to thank a few people that I adore:

K.I. Lynn, C.M. Steele, and Mary B. Moore: You guys are such a huge part of my life and I'm thankful to have you in my corner. Thank you from the bottom of my heart for always pushing me when I get lazy, for challenging me to always be better, and loving me as the crazy, loud-mouthed Latina I am. You're my favorite *chicas* and I love you.

Marti Lynch: All I can say is THANK YOU! Seriously, you have the patience of a saint with me and always come through. You are the best editor and friend an author could ask for.

T.E. Black Designs: You nailed this cover. Seriously, I can't stop staring at my pretty. Thank you!

Michelle Myers: I can't thank you enough for stepping in to beta this book for me. I know it's been crazy, a bit delayed, and you've been so patient with me. I appreciate all the help, babe. Love you, Boo!

Elena's Marked Girls: You guys keep me going and always give me a reason to smile. Thank you for everything. For your unconditional support and encouragement. Please know that I love you—that you mean everything to me.

Tiffany Hernandez: Girl, you're the best PA ever! Thank you so much for all the hard work, for keeping me on track, and taking care of whatever I throw your way last minute because I've become the unorganized queen. It's because of you that I'm able to focus all my energy on writing and getting things done. You ROCK my world!

Hubs and Kiddo: You are my heart. My entire world. Everything I do, I do it for you.

GLOSSARY FOR SPANISH & CUBAN SLANG:

Primo/Prima = Cousin

Viejo/Vieja = Old Man/Woman

Mierda = Shit

Bebe = Baby

Cabron = Fucker

Mamajuana =
This Comes From The Dominican Republic And Is Made By
Combining Rum, Red Wine, And Honey And Soaking The Mixture
With A Special Tree Bark & Herbs. The Color Is A Deep Red, And
Some Say It Tastes Similar To A Port.

Pincha = Work

Singao = Fucker or Asshole

Hijo de Puta = Son of a Bitch

Que Vola = What's Up

Acere or Asere = Friend

Dale = Go ahead or Give

Tio/Tia = Uncle or Aunt

Salsa Rueda or Salsa Casino =
This is a style of salsa dancing that originated in Cuba. Here, the couples form a large circle or rueda, and they execute turns, steps, and patterns in unison to the calls of the singer or leader.

Chapter 1
THIAGO

THE SOLE CLOCK on this floor strikes seven a.m. and my eyes snap open, neck cracking as I raise my head and wait. The shift is abrupt, harsh, and yet the rest of my over six-foot-four frame remains in place as I stare at the entrance to this cell.

A solid door made of steel with a slot at the center just big enough for my hands to slip through. It's how they move you. How they demean your manhood, exhibiting for all to see the hold they have on your freedom. How they have you by the metaphorical balls.

I'm coming for you.

It's my reprieve and penance all in one; that thought brings forth a volcanic rush of ire through my veins as a certain memory slams back to the forefront: *You broke us.*

I did this. The sole blame lands at my feet.

My hands clench and unclench, nostrils flaring. My body thrums with the violence brewing as the day before my arrest plays on a constant loop.

It's meant to torture.

Unforgiving in its detail.

It serves as a reminder of two very hard truths:

I've hurt the most important person in my life.

This is the price I've paid for being the heir to Orlando Rivera De Leon. For taking my rightful place as the head of our family.

Staring at the small metal slot on the door, I breathe in and out slowly while fighting to regain control over my impulses. I'm wound tight as the seconds count down to a day five years in the making: *my release.*

I've been a patient man.

I've been playing by a set of rules designed to make others feel falsely powerful. To feel secure. To show me their hands in a game they'll never win.

Something that ends within the next few hours as I retake my crown, because in the city of Miami...

I *am* the law.

The beginning and the end.

I. Am. King.

A second alarm blares through the dirty old speakers of this inmate housing unit, and yet, everything else remains quiet. Everyone but me, and it's as if the entire building is cowering back. Hiding.

More than that, the constant *tick tick tick* of my fingernails drumming against the heavy metal door is proof of my mood. I haven't moved from my place in front of the room's entrance in hours. I'm restless. Counting. Thinking. Angry as I taste the sweet note of freedom that cloaks my piece-of-shit cell inside this federal prison.

My home for the last five years. Where they've put me away with every intention of keeping me inside indefinitely. And yet, I couldn't give a flying fuck about the time lost because everything in my life will always start and end with *her*.

She's the one regret I have. The one I'll lay down my life to make right.

"My beautiful little Luna," I whisper, waiting for the telltale sign of movement outside these doors. I know what's coming. How this will proceed, and my lack of patience is beginning to show as the loud sound of multiple doors unlocking follows.

My muscles further coil and I close my eyes, taking in a deep breath that I let out slowly. This isn't the time to argue or break the neck of the correctional officer in charge, especially when he's under my employ. When he's kept me in the know all these years as the justice department tried and failed time and time again to keep me within these walls, by any means, and failed.

I'm a hot commodity. A known killer with mafia ties is something the United States government hates to see walk out these doors.

They've done everything in their power to pin bullshit on me. To try and take me out.

Moreover, the irony sits in doing time for a crime I didn't commit.

I'm not an innocent man. I've taken more than one life in my thirty years on this earth, but this body doesn't belong to my count. Not that it matters. What's done is done, and I made the decision to accept this as my fate.

Instead, I'm focused on the future. It's time I reclaim what's been taken from me.

"Hands behind your back and away from the door, Leon."

"Done." A lie he will never call me out on, and a few seconds later his face appears in my line of sight. He's alone. Hands shaking as he holds out a small device toward me. "Where is she?"

"At home." Officer Ortiz's voice shakes and he clears his throat.

"This is verified?"

"By your brother not ten minutes ago via her bodyguard on duty." Inmates walk past my open door and their heads are bowed, some even fidget to move faster. The officers herding the state's cheap labor department toward the early morning mass, for those that have found religion while inside their concrete cage, also look away and pretend that mine is an empty room. A cough pulls my attention back toward Ortiz. "He said to warn you. There's something going on at her job and she'll be gone all day—big meeting about a recent case—until late this evening."

I nod in understanding, but she won't be making it in today. "Turn around and stand in the doorway."

"It's a bit risk—"

"I didn't ask you for an opinion."

"I apologize, sir." Ortiz lowers his eyes immediately and follows orders, and once he's in place, I dial the ten-digit combination of numbers I'll never forget. The series is embedded deep into my consciousness. Tattooed into my DNA.

It rings. Three in total before there's a click on the other end.

Then, there's the sound of her breathing: soft and warm from being half-asleep.

It takes her a minute or two to say anything, but when she does, I'm transported back to my youth. Back to the very first time I laid my eyes on her doe-eyed brown ones. How I stopped in my tracks.

How I knew I'd never be the same after that singular moment.

How at just one week shy of my eighteenth birthday, I knew she was special.

"Hello?" *Motherfuck.* One word from those sweet lips and I come alive in a way I haven't since my incarceration began. Every nerve ending constricts and my hand tightens around the small plastic device. It protests, but I remain in place, taking in the curiosity in her tone and then the small gasp that follows as I let out a low groan. "Thiago."

Not a question. Not a single doubt.

Luna knows me like I do her. It's always been this way for us.

4

A few beats of silence linger between us as I wait. Wait for the inevitable question.

"How are you calling? Why are you after—"

"Mine." It's all I say because nothing else is needed. My girl is smart.

Luna has the means to find out where I am and how I'm doing. Something that she'll deny, but we both know is the truth. Something that within the span of the last five years she's done multiple times. On a constant basis. Every four months without failure.

"Thiago, no. *No.* You don't get to—"

"My beautiful queen." My voice is rough. It holds a tinge of the demonic need that courses through my veins for her. I also don't miss the small little keening sounds that come from the back of her throat—a whimper that I'd know anywhere. It's the same one that passed through her lips when I'd part her thighs and slip inside her tight heat. The same one she'd make when I'd tell her how much my world revolves around her. "Today. Tomorrow. Always."

"Thiago, how could you let me think—"

"I'm coming for you." With that, I hang up and drop the phone to the ground, breaking it as I step on the device. Ortiz is there and his body is tense, head shifting minutely from side to side while making sure unwanted visitors to this floor don't force my hand—that I don't unleash the pure thirst for revenge that simmers beneath my skin.

Another alarm rings throughout the unit just then, this one signaling an early morning cell check before breakfast. Not uncommon. I expected this, but there's nothing that can hold me inside.

The release was processed and pushed for earlier than normal by a hefty donation from my family to the governor of Florida's reelection campaign. They need funding, and I want out of these doors before the clock strikes nine.

Because that is how the system works. I'm corrupt, but so are they. Everything done in public is nothing more than a pony show, because behind the scenes we are all dirty.

"Sir, it's time," he says low but doesn't look back.

"Handcuff me." And he does. With a trembling hand, Ortiz turns back to face me and walks over, placing the cold metal loosely around each wrist. No other words are spoken. None are needed while leading me out of the cell.

At once, the small hum of low conversations ceases to exist as we cross the threshold, and the line against the wall with inmates turns to face the chipped paint behind them. No one meets my stare. No one dares.

Instead, the corridor parts like the sea for Moses as I walk toward my freedom.

They know.

They wait.

I don't forgive. I don't forget.

The streets of Miami will run red by the time I'm through rectifying this costly deed. Those responsible will pay for every tear my Luna shed in my absence.

Chapter 2
LUNA

HOURS BEFORE INCARCERATION...

T HE MUSIC INSIDE the Leon home is loud tonight and so are all the grinding bodies—unfamiliar faces—dancing and drinking in the downstairs area of the house. These strangers are celebrating, imbibing, and they all give me a glassy stare as I make my way through the crowd.

No one stops me or makes small talk, but I can't help but feel as though they're following my every move as I reach the first-floor landing. It's empty, something I am grateful for, but where are the people that live here?

Where's Maritza or Ivan? Thiago?

Something is going on that I'm not privy to.

Something that isn't the norm for me. For us.

It's the opposite.

I'm family. Have been one of them since day one.

And more importantly, it'll be official next year when we say *I do.*

Then why has he been avoiding me for weeks? I shake that thought out of my head and focus on what I do know. What I've seen with my two eyes.

Thiago hasn't proposed yet, but the ring is inside his sock drawer.

He hasn't gotten down on one knee, but he's never shied away from telling me that I'll always be his. His beauty. His queen.

That I'd become the mother to his five children one day, and we'd raise them together. Never apart.

Because I don't care that he's been crowned the head of Miami's largest mob family. That he's killed for profit and does things that are both illegal and immoral. No one is a saint, and anyone who claims to be lives inside of a glass house.

My own family has more than one skeleton in its closet.

My uncle Edgar, Natasha's father, might work for Miami PD now, but everyone in our family knows that in the Dominican Republic he had certain business practices that were lucrative yet dirty. Extortion being one he favored in his youth, forcing Mom and Pop bodegas to pay a monthly stipend in order to avoid violent encounters with him and those under his employ. They paid him to be left alone.

He was never arrested or convicted in D.R. *but* it doesn't negate his past.

Then you have his brother. My father. He takes bribes from both criminals and those with money needing favors from the city council.

Lobbying is real, and it doesn't occur just in our nation's capital. Local government facilitates ordinances and bends the law for those who fund their reelection campaigns.

No one's a saint, and that's a truth I accepted a long time ago.

We all have secrets. A dark side.

Accepting his was never my problem—I embrace *him* as he is, as long as he comes home to me every night. As long as he doesn't let the family business keep him away from the one we'll create some day.

That's what I hold on to when my own home life is in shambles.

My mother hates my father.

My father is unfaithful and proud.

And yet, even as misery drowns them, they stay. They tolerate and pretend because it's convenient for their lifestyle. He has the perfect doting wife for public functions, and she gets to spend his money while pretending to be happy.

I don't want that. Never have.

Material items mean crap when you're unhappy. Alone.

I want more for myself than to conform to an idea that some anti-quated bastard created. Something that I share with the man I love beyond all comprehension. We want a happy life, not something fake or superficial.

"Thiago, stop!" I hear a woman giggle as I reach the second floor of their home, and I pause. In that singular moment—that laughter and *whom* it belongs to stops me cold. My prior thoughts of beautiful days filled with love and memories shrink to the point that my body coils into itself.

A sinking feeling hits my chest and I shake my head.

He wouldn't.

He couldn't.

"Don't overreact, Luna." There has to be an explanation as to why he's with her—someone I despise and who constantly tries to infiltrate our inner circle—of all people in his room. A room that, from where I stand, has a closed door.

"Quit it!"

"Behave, little girl." Thiago and his *guest* say in unison and time ceases to exist; I close my eyes for a brief second. The world disappears. All I hear is that annoying laughter, and I move on autopilot.

I blink and I'm at his door.

I inhale and push it open.

I gasp and the ground beneath my feet feels unstable.

The sight that greets me shatters my heart into a billion and one minuscule pieces. But more than anything, his unapologetic face will forever haunt me.

Those hazel eyes I love watch me standing in the doorway while his arms hold Amberlyn tight, an intimate embrace, with no remorse or care as they lie in his childhood bed. Thiago doesn't let her go. Instead, he pulls her in closer to his naked torso and kisses the crown of her head like he's done with me so many times in the past.

Her head is hidden inside the crook of his neck, but those fire-engine locks and the cheap tattoo of a dragon on her shoulder blade that she got done her senior year of high school are visible. Then there's that ever-present giggle. Obnoxious and loud as if she's being tickled, but the cause isn't his fingers digging into her sides.

No. It's the effect of whispered words that I can't make out.

There isn't an *I can explain,* or *It isn't what you think.*

He doesn't care.

My bottom lip begins to tremble, and a lump lodges itself in my throat. It hurts. Everything in that moment hurts as I watch the man I thought I'd spend the rest of my life with lying in bed with another woman.

Tears gather at the corner of my eyes, but I don't let them fall. I won't give him this too.

No. I've given enough.

I won't stay or accept this. I won't become my mother.

"You broke us." Are my parting words before I rush down the stairs and out the front door without looking back. She can have him.

I'm done.

Chapter 3
THIAGO

"**G**OOD TO SEE you on this side, brother," Ivan says, pulling me in for a hug the moment I'm within reach. It's the first one in five years and I squeeze him just as tight, holding on for a few seconds before pulling back to take him in.

He looks the same, yet older. More mature than the last time we were face to face.

At twenty-six, Ivan looks like a younger version of me: same height, slightly smaller build, and with the kind of tan that comes from spending continuous hours under the sun. In my family, though, that golden tone comes naturally.

It's in our Cuban blood. The Caribbean in us.

"It's good to see you, too."

"Even if I'm not as pretty as Luna?"

"I'm going to ignore that and thank you for the clothes instead." I was arrested while drunk at my parents' home a few hours after Luna ran out with tears in her eyes—taken from my childhood room in nothing but a pair of black boxer briefs and socks because I was in no shape to drive to my penthouse. Those assholes didn't give me a chance to so much as put a shirt on, and my release would've been in that piece-of-shit orange jumpsuit if it were up to the state.

The grey sweatpants and white shirt that Ivan brought, as plain as they are, feel like heaven after so long.

"No worries. Besides, la vieja would have a heart attack if you showed up in whatever hand-me-down crap they gave you." His hazel eyes, a shade or two darker than mine, look toward the back end of the SUV he's driving, and I take account of two other vehicles. They're similar to his and have two men sitting inside of each awaiting orders.

"Speaking of the women in my life...how are they?" I ask as both cars flash their lights in greeting. "Is Luna still home? Is Mom using this as an excuse to throw a party?"

"First..." he holds a finger up "...would it matter if she wasn't?"

"No." Nodding at the cars, I turn my head toward Ivan again. There's no doubt he's talking about my beauty. "I'd find her anywhere."

Ivan smirks, amusement covering his expression. "Nat left about an hour ago, and she looked pissed."

"She'll get her moment." They're upset, and while I understand, moves had to be made to protect those I love. My beauty knows the truth. Moreover, even if it was after and it hurt her, that choice served its purpose. *I'm going to make it up to you, baby. I swear it.* "And Mom? Has anyone reeled her in?"

"That would be a negative. She's Hispanic, bro. There is no reeling her in."

"How many times has she called you in the last hour?"

"At the very least fifteen times."

"Just fifteen?" I chuckle, knowing just how extra the woman could be. "That's nothing when it comes to her."

His phone rings then and Ivan snorts. "Make it sixteen."

"Still a small number." Shaking my head, I focus on his phone and how much they've changed since my arrest. The cheap prepaids I've been using are nothing like the Apple device in his hand. "Did you bring my cell?"

"I did." He pulls open the passenger side door, and sitting atop the seat is a wrapped box with a large bow in all white. I don't have to ask to know that this was Mom's idea, but I shake my head nonetheless. "We should go. The meat has been marinating for two years now."

"That is quite a while." I take him in once again. He's the nicer one of the two, and while the thirst for blood runs in our family, *his* is just a bit tamer than mine. However, that shitty grin and the nervous tick that makes him crack his knuckles, which he's unconsciously done twice now, are still there. I haven't seen him or the family in a while, per my orders, but I've missed them all.

"Too long since you've played," he says low, eyes on something behind me. Following his line of sight, I find a small audience where there shouldn't be one near the rear entrance of the building. "Let's get out of here. It's not—"

I shake my head and he closes his mouth.

I choose to stare at the cameras instead and he steps aside, taking his rightful place behind me and to the right. It's a statement of unity and rebirth with my release.

I'm still sitting at the head of this table.

The De Leons aren't hiding. We don't bow.

Head on and held high, and because I'm an asshole, I wave. Cocky and with a smirk, I give each camera attention while the hijo

de puta at the center of this impromptu news conference glares at me.

Openly. Full of hate.

While the man sputters and gestures wildly with his hand, I hold myself back from snapping his neck like a twig. The reporter closest to him notices the mayor's actions and elbows his cameraman to get the shot. They do, and it takes everything in me not to laugh or shoot him where he stands.

Ivan's car has more than one gun, and I've already seen mine close to my gift.

Ulysses Senot is a close friend of Luna's father, holds office in Miami, and is someone I plan to visit soon. To have a one-on-one. Like men. Him, and that pussy son of his that they tried to set up my beauty with.

Because that's his horse in the race. He'll do favors for his friend as long as my Luna's hand in marriage is on the table. The two old men want to unite the families, and that will never happen. Not in this life or any that follow.

Soon. Holding my palm out, I shift my eyes toward my brother and raise a brow. "Keys."

"In the ignition."

"Get in." He does so without any more prompting, and I follow suit, slamming the door closed before giving a final look at the group watching.

"Do you know where we're going?"

Turning the fob, I close my eyes for a second and bask in the silence that follows his question. Just a miniscule moment where I thank God for Luna and my freedom—this will be my lone instance of empathy and compassion.

I have a job to do and emotions have no place in my decisions, and while family is family, what led to my incarceration was an inside job. A setup. The attempt was made to end the life of Orlando and Maritza Rivera De Leon, and when that didn't go as planned, I was framed with the death of another man. The hired hitman. A man

whose body was found inside my penthouse hung and missing limbs on a night where I'd been elsewhere.

Neither were my doing.

Moreover, whoever is responsible—family or friend—will face the consequences.

My wrath will bathe the earth in their blood.

Opening my eyes, I stare ahead and into my freedom. "I'm in the mood to look at ships."

THE PORT of Miami hasn't changed much since the last time I was here. It's still hot under the mid-morning sun and full of employees covering every single square inch.

They all have a job to do and are paid by either the US Customs administration or independent contractors to do a certain task. They are here to unload, load, and stop people like me from slipping illegal substances in through them and onto the city's streets.

They hope to make a difference. To clean up our country.

Yet, if you pass over a stack of bills to the right employee, all others fall into line.

Now, you become who makes the rules.

Now, they turn a blind eye when your container arrives or when certain meetings need to take place aboard a private ship a few miles offshore that is owned by a diplomat from Panama, a friend of mine that I've personally done favors for—taking the life of the man stalking his daughter and being the provider for his drug of choice.

Cocaine: that lovely white powder that so many covet and pay ridiculous amounts of money to get their hands on.

He owes me, and my collection comes with immunity from searches by US officials while aboard this ship that secretly belongs to me. His name is attached only for legal purposes because the two countries have an agreement, a lobbying interest, and his property is not to be touched while inside the United States.

Money is a dangerous commodity that everyone wants. They crave it. Want the power that comes attached to the said price tag.

A price tag that helps one nation with its debt and the other with exporting goods.

One gives an unwavering alliance, while the other secretly conducts moves to monopolize a market in their backyard. And while this is going on, I use the discretion to my advantage.

Something that at the moment is very useful with the eyes of the city on my back after my release. You can't get inside the port of Miami without searches, identification, and stating your reason for business here. Failure of any of those three, and you will be removed.

No excuse. Unless...you are a De Leon.

Moreover, *if* I conduct business while on international waters, I can't be convicted.

These workers know who I am.

They know why I am here.

And the moment I drive onto the large concrete floor of this port, all work stops and people begin to scatter. Even those that work for our government step back and look the other way as I exit the vehicle and five doors slam closed behind me.

It's almost comical, really. Local authorities—those self-righteous and low on the totem pole—hate me. Yet, you ask the governor of Florida and higher, and I'm just a businessman.

Everything depends on who you have in your pocket. Who owes you. Who you help fund to keep in power.

It's one of the many reasons that Luna's father hates me. I'll never fund the waste of sperm.

Not after he broke her heart by cheating on her mother. Not after the time he tried to smack her during an argument, and I broke his hand before he could ever lay a single finger on her skin.

My men surround me as I walk across, taking my time until we reach the stairs that lead to a lower deck that not many have access to. Taking the few steps down, we reach one of my favorite toys: a boat.

One of the many that I own, but this particular one I've never seen.

I'd left Ivan in charge of buying this powerboat and also with naming her. Little Moon has been sitting here looking pretty, and I let out a whistle of appreciation when I fully take her in.

All black and shiny, she's beautiful and sleek. Meant for racing or fast rides across open water. Perfect for what I need. For transporting myself along with two of my men across open waters where those wishing to put me back behind bars have no jurisdiction.

Climbing aboard, I turn and point at the two men standing to the right of Ivan to follow me. They do, and so does my brother, while the others stay behind to remove the cars and store them nearby for when we return.

"She's beautiful," I tell Ivan while the engine comes to life, purring beneath my feet and into the ocean below as I pull out of the dock. The salty breeze feels good on my face as does the rush of adrenaline that follows when I punch the accelerator and let this boat do what it's meant to. Fast and smooth, we glide over the water, barely touching the surface as we make our way to the ambassador's ship. "Good choice."

"It's my gift to you," Ivan says, the roar of the engine and the sound of crashing waves as we slice through the ocean, forcing him to yell from his seat beside me. "The least I could do." There's a tinge of regret in his tone, and while I know the *why*, I ignore it for now. We'll talk, but this isn't the right time.

There are twelve nautical miles between me and international water, and while those around me hang on to the interior handles or their seats, I relax my stance and let my mind focus on one thing and one thing alone: vengeance.

There's a shift in me the closer we get. A change in energy that brings forth a near demonic rush of rage to my veins. I throb where I stand. I feel the world begin to slow and my breathing with it.

This meeting is a long time coming, and I am due payment.

Ismael Navarro did something he shouldn't, especially since he knows me—my family—and yet he decided to play God for a few extra zeros in his bank account. That betrayal will never be forgiven. More so after I took him under my protection when he was still in high school and his family died in a car accident.

Ismael lived with us. Ate with us. He called my mother *Mima* yet pulled a gun on her from a moving motorcycle the day after her birthday two years ago. His second offense, and for that one, I could no longer wait for retribution.

Unforgivable; the little bitch created his own death certificate that day and the only thing keeping him alive since then is my missing signature.

He's been stewing in his own filth for two years now awaiting trial.

Once near the large vessel, I pull in beside a platform near the back that has one of my men near the controls of a hydraulic lift. I hold a hand up and the movable flat section that resembles a stage begins to descend, slowly, and when it's just within reach to walk across, I hand over the controls to a man who's worked for my family since before I was born.

Miguel is old school, someone I trust, and loyal. He's also who taught me how to drive a boat, and as I move from behind the wheel, he takes over. "Have fun, sir," he calls out as I step onto the steel surface, stopping at the center while the others stand behind me.

It's secure and sturdy and I give the signal to ascend. The rise is slow, but the higher we go, the more I give in to the needs I've kept under lock and key for the last five years.

This is a piece of me. This is who I am.

It's who I'll always be, and as I reach the top, I welcome my demon back.

A killer. Someone without remorse for what must be done.

The somewhat large platform is open and my men, those who stay on this ship for extended periods of time between Miami and pickup locations throughout Latin America, greet me with respect as we board the ship. Heads are bowed and they chant my name lowly as I pass, but I pay no mind for the time being.

Instead, I walk toward the center of the ship and down a long set of stairs that lead to an open ring. Here, I lose the all-white T-shirt and toss it somewhere behind me. I flex my arms and shake out my limbs to expel some of the adrenaline flowing through my system.

This is my playground. My place to let go, and as I step foot into the octagon-shaped area and close my eyes, a feeling of home overtakes my senses and the noise dulls. Here, my other instincts come alive:

I hear the low whimper from nearby.

I breathe in the stench of blood, urine, and chlorine.

I feel the shift in the air as a body is thrown at my feet.

The body tries to crawl away, but my men surround us. The person begs out a broken *please* and a sardonic laugh rumbles through my chest a moment before I settle my eyes on his pathetic form.

Broken. Bleeding. A shell of the man that I grew up with.

"Ismael fucking Navarro." At the sound of his name, another pitiful noise escapes the back of his throat and scared brown eyes look up at me. They're bloodshot and the one on the right has a deep gash over the brow. It looks disgusting: infected and dirty. "How have you been?"

"Thiago, I didn't—"

"Silence."

"Please, I...*fuck*!" he screams out as my foot comes down on a bruised ankle. It snaps—the bone giving way under the force of a single blow—and he learns to listen. Those cracked lips snap closed, and he cries in silence. *Good boy.*

"You messed up, Ismael. There's no coming back from this." I walk around him, taking inventory of the weight loss, the rough scars down his bony back, and the singular open puncture wound on his side. "What you did..."

"It was a mistake. I would've never gone through with it, Thiago." His tears, the way his bottom lip trembles, fail to move me. If anything, it renews my anger. His audacity to ask for any clemency from me burns through my patience like acid on flesh. It bubbles, unleashing its toxicity, and I react. "I swear. Y-you gotta believe me."

"Do I?" Grabbing a fistful of his hair, I yank him up to his knees and bring my face closer to his. Nose to nose. "Give me a reason. Just one."

"I'll tell you who put the hit out. Tell you where he lives."

Chapter 4
THIAGO

LIKE DEAD WEIGHT, I let his body fall back to the ground. The thud and the following whimpers of pain he releases are loud inside the hollow space. "Speak."

"Please. No more."

"Speak," I repeat, moving in closer to his head while Ivan steps to where his broken ankle limply lays. It's rapidly swelling, the previously healed cuts reopening and staining the already filthy floor red. "You have sixty seconds to say your piece."

The men surrounding us create a barrier. They are quiet but

slowly begin to stomp a single foot against the floor. It reverberates throughout the room. It drowns out Ismael's pain.

"Will I walk out of here alive?" I tilt my head at his question, eyes narrowing at a man that I once considered family. He had access to the most important people in my life because of me. Because I saw potential in a kid that needed direction.

"No." No point in lying or giving him false hope.

"Can you make it quick?" A harsh shiver racks his body and his teeth clatter; his lips look to be turning a little blue, too. "Just end it."

"That depends on you." With the toe of my sneaker, I open his mouth and push down on his bottom jaw. Stretch it to the point that the very corner of his mouth tears, becoming red. His life's essence doesn't streak as the cut's isn't big enough, but it has to sting. Feel uncomfortable. "Tell me what I want to know."

He tries to talk around the leather of my Nikes, but instead gags, coughing up what looks to be a large amount of bile and more blood.

A lot of it.

From where I stand above him, I can see he's malnourished. In pain. Spiritless.

And yet it's not enough. Nothing short of his last breath, and that of those involved, will ever be.

I remove my foot, seeing what's in Ivan's hand from the corner of my eye. "You have two choices: merciful or vengeful. Up to you." As the last word slips past my lips, Ivan brings the sledgehammer down on his knee. It's on the opposite leg from the one I broke, but his screams of pain are just as loud.

"FUCK!" Ismael bellows, body writhing, and that brings with it more pain. The change in position forces the shattered pieces of bone to rub and cut flesh, to ruin tendons and ligaments he'll never have use for again.

Kneeling near his head, I block his view while holding one arm back. "Next blow will be to your skull." On my next inhale, I feel the cold against my skin from my weapon of choice and it warms my limbs.

There's nothing like the heavy weight of this metal in my hand as my fingers slip through each hole with ease. The fit is snug and I make a tight fist, savoring this extension of who I am once again. *It's been too long.*

The asshole swallows, grimacing as he fights another bout of gags. "I'll tell you everything."

"Your time is almost up." I bring the custom, solid gold brass knuckles into his line of sight, turning my hand slightly so the lighting in the room glints off each curve. These were a gift from my queen: a solid gold pair of brass knuckles in the shape of a crown with my name in Old English scripture at the center. They're sharp and heavy, and I've broken more than one skull with them. "Five, four, three...two—"

"Alfredo Gaytan." *Is a dead son of a bitch.*

I know the name. Know exactly who he is. But more importantly, I know who he works for.

Gaytan is under the employ of the Senot family—to be more precise, he's the head of Ulysses' wife's security. A man she's been fucking for years without her husband's knowledge because he's too far up the ass of his good friend, Antonio Alejos.

My queen's father.

"Say that again." My voice is gruff, lip curling up at the corner into a snarl. "Say that name again."

"It was Alfredo Gaytan. He hired me to kill the hired hitman and deposit his body in your apartment, and since I've crashed there in the past, no one questioned my coming and going."

"Why kill him? Why not try again?"

"They were losing time." Ismael tries to shrug, but grimaces instead. "He failed to take out his mark, but if they could lock you away, not all was lost." The trembling in his body increases, his entire frame going into shock, but I'm not done yet and signal one of the men near a large industrial hose to bring the extension to me.

"Open it," is all I say once it's in my hands, and within a few short seconds the rumbling of water shooting through a pipe at high speed infiltrates the room. This isn't your average variety garden equipment. No, this is high-pressured and cold—a direct hit hurts like a bitch, and is perfect for rinsing off an enemy's blood from my floor.

The first stream catches the shaking man off guard and he screams, agony riddling the high-in-pitch sound as it reverberates in the once-again quiet room. The jet is heavy and direct; it further opens the wound at his side, splitting the already sensitive skin wide open.

He bleeds onto my floor. He screams my name in a last-ditch plea. "Thiago, por favor. No mas."

I nod and the water is turned off.

I step over his body and his eyes widen.

I fist his hair, yanking him into a half-sitting position, and he closes his eyes.

"Look at me, Ismael." Bloodshot brown eyes shoot open, meeting my hazel ones, and in them I see a mixture of fear and resignation. Understanding and acceptance. "Did you show my mother mercy when you emptied your magazine into her armored vehicle? Did you come to me—show gratitude and loyalty—when Gaytan offered you the job and money?" His mouth opens, his reply sitting on his tongue, but it's not something I need or want. I have the file. I know every detail of the events that lead to the attempt on myself and my family. "The answer is no, old friend. You saw dollar signs and didn't give a single fuck about the people who took you in."

"I'm sorry." It's a broken whisper, a sob catching in his throat.

"No more than I am." With that, I lean over and kiss his forehead before forcing his head back in an uncomfortable-to-swallow position. His jaw and neck are exposed; the last bit of fight left in Ismael comes rushing through as he weakly attempts to fight my hold. Nails dig into my skin, but don't break the surface. Thrashing commences but dies down when my hold is unrelenting. "I'll see you in hell one day."

I bring my brass-knuckled fist down against the lower half of his face, effectively breaking his jaw. There's a crunch from breaking bone, fragments of teeth falling to the ground, and then blood.

Bright and almost glowing, it flows from his now-useless mouth. His screams become muffled because:

He can't fully open his mouth. He can't move it. He can't swallow.

And then I do it again. And again. Each strike consistent in intensity, I don't stop, nor do I wipe away the splatters of red that now paint my skin. Ismael is almost limp in my hold, and yet, his body weight isn't a hindrance for my grip. My fist comes forward again, this time on his cheek and the skin breaks wide open, exposing another piece of broken bone.

Moreover, as his head snaps back and movements still—as his breathing slows—I toss him at Ivan's feet.

I've done my damage. He will die.

Not as fast as a bullet or a knife wound, but the man is slowly choking.

"Do you have anything to add?" I ask my brother, giving him the opportunity for a final act of retribution.

"No, sir." That *sir* serves a purpose as well. It's him officially welcoming me back—not that it's necessary, but more of a show of respect. This motherfucker is someone I trust with my life, and while behind bars, he was my eyes and ears. Following my orders from within, working day in and day out to both keep the family safe and the business running. Because of my father and Ivan, we still hold Miami's drug scene in an iron grip. "But a beer would be nice."

A gurgling noise from below makes me smile. "First round on me after…"

"You go see your girl."

"Pretty much." His phone chimes then and he digs into his back pocket, pulling it out and swiping a finger across the screen. Ivan laughs and shakes his head, tossing me the phone so I can see for myself what has him so amused.

There, in a series of texts from our vieja, is a veiled threat and it's hilarious.

> Tell that boy of mine to make it right and kiss her culo if he has to. No excuse. Tomorrow we party and Luna better be with him. ~Mami

> You show him this, Ivan. ~Mami

> Did you do it? Tell me. Is he still handsome? ~Mami

Christ. I'm cracking up before finishing that last one. It's so like her.

Forceful yet loving. A don't-mess-with-me-or-mine attitude that I learned from her.

My father might've been the leader of the De Leon cartel, feared by many, but my mother was worse. She could forgive any indiscretion except the touching of her family. Blood is sacred.

> Mami, I'm here and I'll see you tomorrow. Love you, but I make no promises on Luna. She's stubborn. ~Thiago (your favorite)

The body on the floor groans, and I shift my eyes to him. He's bleeding and fighting to swallow. The floor beneath his head has a puddle of red saliva.

Another ping comes through, pulling my attention away.

> Mi hijo! I love you so much. Can't wait to hug you. ~Mami

> Me too. ~Thiago

> Okay. Go...but drag her back home if you have to. *kisses* ~Mami

> That, I can do. See you all tomorrow. ~Thiago

Tossing the phone back to my little brother, I call forth a younger man I've never seen before. At no older than twenty, he stands to the side with a tray which holds a bottle of water and a towel. "Thank you..." I say and wait for his name.

"I'm Junior, sir. Miguel's son."

"How long have you been with us, kid?" I knew of his father having a son but was under the impression he lived with his mother in California and was a lot younger.

"Two years, sir." Junior swallows nervously, eyeing the splattering of blood on my hands and chest. "The day I turned eighteen, I left my mom's house and came to live with him. I couldn't deal with her addiction problems anymore."

"Understandable." Taking the bottle, I twist off the cap and pour more than half its contents onto the folded cotton on his tray. "And do you like working for us?"

"Yes, sir."

"Did you learn anything today?"

"I did, sir." While I clean my hands with the towel, I raise a brow and wait for him to elaborate. He's smart and catches on quickly, squaring his shoulders while his eyes focus on the man beneath us. "You don't betray the hand that feeds. You don't go against family. You don't sell yourself for a quick buck, especially when it *will* cost you your life."

"You're going to make your father very proud, kid."

"Thank you—"

"More than one person wants her, Thiago." This comes in the form of a murmur from the floor below—broken and so low that I almost don't make out the words, but I do. It's a warning. The last words before the light leaves his eyes and a vacant look takes over. There's no more breath. No more movement. At 10:08 on the Tuesday morning of my release, Ismael took his last breath, and I feel nothing.

No pity for the twenty-five-year-old.

No moment of reflection.

No forgiveness.

Moreover, while those around me begin to dispose and clean up, I focus on the last words of a dying man that confirm what I already know. There's more than one player in this game, and the prizes differ. However, the one unifying factor is my queen, and it hurts to accept that someone within my own familial tree did this. That they covet what is mine, but they do, and I'll uncover their tracks if it's the last thing I do on this earth.

No one will ever take me away from her again.

Not even God himself, if it came down to it.

Chapter 5
LUNA

"**I**'M COMING FOR YOU."

Those words run through my mind on a constant loop. Four simple words that once put together in the minuscule span of a few minutes have flipped my world on its axis. I'm left standing, unable to move, lost within my head, but the somewhat closed wounds of a few years ago reopen and it knocks the very breath from my lungs.

It shows me how, after all this time, what he did—his lack of faith in us— still hurts.

Moreover, these tumultuous emotions always lead me back to him. Thiago Rivera De Leon.

My soul's other half. My lion.

A man whom I've loved since our adolescence, and I've never learned how to stop doing so. He's my truth that will never change, and a response that I can't duplicate with anyone else. Even at our worst moments, I've always been his.

Something I know deep in my soul will always be a fact even if a part of me hates him just as much. No man measures up, and the very thought of trying to move on has been unacceptable. My own body rebels against me and cries out for his warmth, those strong hands that knew how to touch me, how to drive me crazy with just the faintest hint of a caress.

How to bring me to the highest peak of pleasure with filthy words and a telling grunt that would build in his chest and rumble past parted lips when he found his own release.

Then, after leaving me a boneless mess on his sheets, Thiago would wrap his arms around me—pulling me in close and tipping my face up to his. His eyes would hold warmth and love. His lips would kiss mine with a softness that always made my chest ache.

Because for all the ways he could be an asshole to the outside world, with me he's always been a giant teddy bear. My everything.

Which brings me to the following truths. Two things that I can't deny and are just as hard to swallow.

I miss him.

I'm not ready for him.

My hand vibrates then and I look down, taking in the phone and flashing lights of the screen. I know the name, know that I need to pick up, but can't seem to hit the answer button.

I'm here, but not.

My entire being is assaulted from all angles with flashes of memories; a movie reel that starts at the very beginning and high-lights our best moments. It's fast and hard to keep up, but I do and a small sob catches in my throat as I follow his transformation from handsome teenager to a devastating god of a man.

But then that same movie reel of wonderful images reaches its end and a single tear rolls down my cheek. I'm living it all over again. That day. The very moment he broke my heart.

I see it.

Take in every last detail as if I were inside his bedroom and not my living room.

However, the difference between *then* and *now* is the truth. He betrayed me in a way that I don't know if I'll ever forgive.

Thiago didn't trust me. He chose to lie instead of letting me stand by his side as the queen he always claimed me to be. *He* forgot every promise ever made and chose to steal my choice in the matter.

He didn't cheat. I know that.

I knew it deep within my soul after I cooled off, but by then it was too late. Thiago made me believe so by playing on my deepest fears; that I wasn't enough. That the cursed circle made by my parents would follow me like a crucifix into every relationship.

It hurt. Cut deep.

It took Amberlyn and Ivan months to make me realize that I'm not *them*. It took her opening up, and my noticing that the brother she was in love with is Ivan, to let her in.

Thiago broke us to protect me, and it seems I'll get the explanation I deserve today.

Bang.

Bang.

Bang.

The sudden loud noise within the space causes me to jump and I drop my cell, taking with it the half-empty coffee cup on the table as my hands flail in an attempt to catch the device. I fail, and once more curse the man I love for the mess on my hands. Piping hot liquid spreads quickly in an uneven shape on the soft carpet beneath my high-heeled feet. It's bathed my phone and ruined the leg of my high-waisted white dress pants.

"Dammit!" I hiss as the heat seeps through, burning my skin, and I pull the fabric away as best I can. They're ruined. There's no way to salvage this large of a stain, and I kick off my shoes to begin disrobing when there's another series of hard knocks.

"Lulu, open up!" Nat yells through the door, her voice full of concern. "Are you..." I rush across the room and yank it open before she finishes "...*fuck*."

"Yup."

"Thiago's already out?" Amberlyn asks, peeking in from behind her, worry written across Nat's soft features. "Did any of them contact you?"

"What're you guys doing here?" I ask them, then pause. My brows furrow in confusion. "How do you know?"

"First, good morning-ish." Natasha ticks off with her fingers. "It's already almost ten, and Thompson sent me to check on you." She's dressed for the office; her signature black trousers and blazer look on point. So is Amberlyn. She doesn't work with us in the forensics department but at a bail bonds office nearby.

"Almost ten?" *How long have I been stuck inside my own head?* "What the—"

"And second? Everyone's talking about it. Have you not seen the news this morning?" When I shake my head, Nat huffs, fully walking into the room and straight for the remote on the coffee table. Amberlyn follows her, my mess plain to see, but neither mentions my more-than-likely ruined phone or the spilled disaster, which I'm grateful for. Instead, they focus on the TV screen after Nat turns it on, flipping the channel until we reach the largest Spanish-speaking network and I see his picture. It's one I know very well as it came from my camera and I own the only other copy.

Back in the days when owning a photography studio was my dream. When it was my passion and not just my opening to keep track of Thiago. I became a crime scene photographer to get those charges dropped because while I'm angry at him, the evidence taken from his penthouse wasn't conclusive.

Someone wanted him gone.

"Wasn't that at Maritza's fiftieth?" Amberlyn asks then and I nod, once again living through a memory.

"Mijo, don't be so difficult," his mother whines while I use the power of my pout to persuade him. "Just one. It won't kill you and Ivan already took his."

"Ivan's an ass kisser, Vieja. We both know this."

Her eyes, an almost identical shade of golden honey, narrow. "So are you when you want something from my Luna."

His stare shifts to me and I fidget, the telltale blush sweeping across my skin. There's hunger in those beautiful orbs, but just as powerful is his love for me. It's there. Wide open and never hidden. "I'll never deny kissing her as—"

"So," I interrupt, mock glaring at him because the man has no shame, and this is his mom. Though, by the low giggle she emits, I'll say she's amused by us. "A picture? Just one?"

"This will cost you." Thiago bites down on his bottom lip, eyes roaming my smaller frame. His heated gaze lingers at the strap of my expensive camera that falls over the swell of my breast. "Are you willing to pay?"

"Name your price," I say, but my tone comes out a bit breathy and not one bit the unaffected woman I am trying to portray.

Something he notices, and his smirk deepens. "You know what I want."

"To give me grandchildren?" Maritza interjects, and I am so thankful for that. Because I know what the jerk wants.

His price is my ass; literally.

"Among other things." Thiago raises a brow at me. A challenge. The man knows I'll never deny him anything. "It's a simple yes or no, baby girl."

"Are you serious right now?" I laugh, but it's a nervous one. Embarrassed. Wanting to both strangle and kiss that stupid grin off his face.

"Yes." No hesitation.

"Thiago!" I throw a hand up in exasperation. "That's cheating and you—"

"Nothing's fair in love and war, Luna. Remember that."

When all was said and done, Maritza got her picture of him dressed in the standard Cuban Guayabera with a Corona in his hand, the waves behind him crashing upon the shore. Handsome and a bit arrogant, he smirked at me while a continuous blush bloomed across my cheeks as I fought my need to taste his lips.

Or bite him until the jerk bled a tiny bit.

But then again, Thiago enjoys putting me on the spot. He enjoyed my tendencies to be a little violent—to leave the perfect indentation of my teeth all over his upper body when angry or aroused.

Christ, I need help.

"What are you going to do, Luna?" Nat bumps her shoulder with mine, bringing me back to the present.

"This is my favorite picture of him, you know."

"I do. The fact you still keep it on your nightstand is proof of that."

"Guilty." My eyes shift to my cousin and I give her a sad smile. "When developing the film, I made a copy. The original is his mother's, my gift to her."

"That still doesn't answer my question, Lulu. Help me help you."

"Back then we had it all. We were inseparable." However, a few months after his mother's birthday it all came crashing down at my feet. Natasha opens her mouth then, and I can literally see the questions in her worried gaze, but I shake my head. "Nothing's changed. I expect he'll swing by at one point today."

Because I'm not an idiot; he's kept tabs on me through his younger brother, Ivan. Through guards. Through my uncle. *He just never bothered to call me.*

Crossing her arms over her chest, she puffs out her cheeks. "You're not going into work, are you?"

"No."

"How long?"

"A few days. Tell them I have food poisoning."

"Are you sure? Want me to stay?" Nat moves to stand in front of me, effectively blocking my view of the TV, and places a hand on each shoulder, giving them a squeeze. "Thiago has a date with my foot up his butt. Let me have my moment."

Shaking my head, I let out a chuckle. "Another time."

"One punch and I leave?" I get her need—her anger at someone she once considered a brother. Natasha has seen me at my best and worst, stood by my side when my mother made snide comments and my father shouted his disdain. She's my person through thick and thin. "Pretty please?"

"The first blow is mine."

"Rock, paper, scissors?"

"Mine, babes. You can have a go after...I promise."

"Fine, but I'll be holding you to this."

"You have my word..." looking behind her, I notice how late it already is "...you guys should go. Let's not make it any worse. Thompson's already going to be pissed with my not coming in and..." I turn my head toward a quiet Amberlyn "...how are you here without issue?"

"Day off." That's all she says, but I have a feeling it's more than that. While she isn't the most vocal person when it comes to feelings, actions prove her loyalty. It's written on her face. In the way her brows pinch and lips thin into a line. "Just thought I'd hang out with you...you know? Girls' day."

"Thank you, but I'll take a raincheck."

"Are you sure?" Her eyes plead with me to accept, but this situation is best faced alone. Just me and him. "I know how to hide a body, get us bailed out, and then not get caught while skipping it."

At that, I laugh deeply, loudly, bending over and placing my hands on my knees. This day just keeps getting more ridiculous by the second. "I love you guys so hard."

"I'm serious!"

"I know," I manage through my laughter; it takes me a minute or two, but I manage to get myself upright and wipe my damp eyes. They're both looking at me like I'm crazy, and maybe I am, but I see the amusement in the twitch of their lips. "God, I needed that."

"Glad we could amuse you." Nat gives me a final puppy-dog look, her last-ditch effort at convincing me to let them stay, but I shake my head no. Her shoulders slump and lips purse. "You suck, and fine. I'll cover whatever comes up."

"Thanks, prima. I'll owe you." Pulling her in for a quick hug, I then turn to Amberlyn and give her one as well. "Both of you mean so much to me. Love you." With that, I rush them out the door before they can pitch another attempt, promising to call them later. Much later. Maybe *after a warm bath and a few shots of rum* later.

Agreeing with myself that it's the best strategy I can come up with on short notice, I undo the button on my pants and shimmy out of the ruined garment. Leaving them where they land, I make my way toward my room at the back of my apartment and straight for my shower.

The coffee is still sticky on my skin and I could use a long soak beneath the hot waterfall showerhead. Which is what I do. Taking my time, I strip the remaining garments and fully step inside.

I let the near-boiling water hit my golden skin, relaxing the muscles of my back the longer I stand there. I let the sweet scent of coconut and lime calm my racing heart and then take with it my worries as I rinse off. Time ceases to exist, and I forget the world for that period of time. Twenty minutes or an hour, I have no clue how much time has passed as I close my eyes and breathe in deep through my nose.

Then out through my mouth.

Slowly. Without rush. For that small reprieve, I stop wondering about *him* until there's a sudden knock on the door. The person on the other end is impatient and I turn the water off, grabbing my towel from the rod. I wrap it around myself and step fully onto the mat but have to pause.

Reality is a fickle bitch, and she smacks me with the full force of a freight train and I begin to shake.

Another knock and I walk out of the room on unstable legs.

Three quick raps and I almost stumble, catching myself on a small accent table in the hall.

"Luna, are you in there, sweetie? I have something for you." My neighbor Cicely, an old and cranky lady that's taken a liking to me for some reason, calls through the door, and the sudden bout of nerves evaporates. Just disappears.

"Sweet baby Jesus," I breathe out low, softly banging my forehead against the wall. "I'll be right there!"

"No need to rush." *Then why the hard banging on my door?* "I'll leave the zucchini bread here...drop by later if you get a chance. My Netflix logged off again."

"Give me thirty!"

"No rush but before five, please." With that, she walks away and I turn back to my bedroom on steadier legs. It's the second largest room in the apartment and comes with a balcony attached that wraps around the side of the building, connecting with the living room. Open space and soft colors; it's all pink and white with a touch of gold—a large four-poster bed and armoire.

A small sitting area within and deep walk-in closet. Large windows that overlook Brickell Ave. near downtown Miami.

It's my sanctuary, and as I open the top drawer of my dresser to get a clean pair of panties, I change my mind. A nap sounds like heaven right now, and with Cicely not being in a rush, I slip on the pair of hipsters and walk back to bed.

The moment I crawl under the sheets, the pure exhaustion brought on by his release has me drifting into the state of sleep called limbo. I'm not fully under or awake. I'm not analyzing my life or playing out reunion-like scenarios.

For the moment, I'm just being. And when my stomach rumbles sometime later, I ignore that too for another few minutes until there's a sudden knock at the door.

"I thought she said no rush?" Throwing my legs over the edge, I stand and grab the silk robe laying at the edge of the bed, wrapping it around myself. The belt is barely secured—not even a full bow in place—when I rush out and down the hall, pulling the door open before she begins another series of knocks.

However, in my stupidity, I'm half-naked and regretting it immediately.

Because the person on the other side is not my neighbor or Natasha or Amberlyn. No. This person causes my entire world to stop. Everything around me disappears and my chest grows tight because there, in all his handsome glory, is the man I've vowed to forget and failed.

The man I don't want to love but do.

"I've missed you, baby girl," Thiago says, his voice deeper, richer than I remember, and a shiver runs through me. He's bigger too. All muscles and tattoos and a sinful smirk that causes a rush of wetness to seep through the lace of my panties and coat my inner thighs.

He doesn't say anything, but the way his nostrils flare and hands clench at his sides give away his intentions. *I'm in trouble.*

Damn him for being just as delicious as always.

And God help me too, because while my body cries out for his touch, while my heart nearly beats out of my chest, another emotion pushes all the others back.

I'm angry. Full of ire with my next intake of breath and I can't stop myself. Won't.

I smack him.

Chapter 6
THIAGO

THE DAY WE MET...

I'VE BEEN FOLLOWING her all day. Since the very moment she walked through the large double doors of this pretentious high school where I am a king. Almost worshipped out of a raw fear that comes from knowing who my family is.

What we're capable of. We don't hide it.

We are criminal. Miami royalty.

In a city like this one, nothing stays hidden and I learned from an early age to be proud of each life I've taken. At almost eighteen, I'm far deadlier than my old man, and those around me know this. Fear my temper.

It's why so many try befriending me; they believe doing so will give them a free pass. It's also why the basic females at this private school nearly stampede over each other to be seen with me. For a chance to be with me.

Have I fucked a few? Yes, but they meant nothing.

Not one has stood out among the sea of nobodies like *her*.

No one has ever stopped me in my tracks with just one look.

Like now. The beauty turns her head back in my direction and her brown doe eyes meet mine, causing the world around me to stop. All noise ceases. It's just us inside of this hallway while my heart, that cold bastard, almost beats out of my chest. While my palms sweat and mouth goes dry as I take her in once again.

She's short but curvy, beautiful in a way that's near angelic while the glint in her eyes threatens mischief. She looks soft and her skin holds this golden touch that creates a hunger—the need to taste the exposed skin of her neck where the uniform shirt is unbuttoned is near maddening.

I want her.

I'm also fucked.

I know this, so when she turns back to face the door just a few steps away from her, I pull out my phone and type out a quick message to my father.

> Viejo, I need info on a new student. Everything.
> Her name is Luna Alejos. ~Thiago

His response is quick and just what I expect.

> Important? ~Dad

> Yes. ~Thiago

Because this is. My gut tells me it's unbelievably so.

Done. It'll be delivered within the hour. ~Dad

Pocketing my cell, I do what I've done all day and follow her into class. The seat behind her in biology is empty and I slip into it, leaning forward so I can take a lungful of the sweet scent of coconuts. Her long black hair is down with loose ringlets bouncing gently while she shifts, fighting the more-than-likely urge to tell me to fuck off.

She doesn't, though.

Instead, she emits a low huff and faces forward. Ignoring me. Making this so much sweeter without trying.

I will make this beauty mine.

PRESENT...

THE FEEL of her palm connecting with my cheek brings me back to the present and creates two instant problems:

I'm hard.

I'm amused.

She hasn't changed, and her proclivity for just the right amount of violence forces me to react. To take a step forward and then another, giving my beauty no other choice but to retreat into the apartment, and giving me the perfect opening to follow.

She's trying to evade what's already set in stone. Us. This. The uncontrollable hunger—the almost crippling need we have for each other.

I am hers and she is mine.

Always will be.

"Stop right there, Thiago," she says, expression hard and lips in a thin line. It's cute. Adorable how she follows the demand by holding a delicate hand up between us as the front door closes behind me. *Nothing could stop me from coming for you, beautiful.* "I didn't invite you in, and this..." she points at herself, then me "...isn't happening."

"I've missed you." It comes out gruff, full of every bit of the hunger I've kept buried deep—a need so palpable that she shivers, and her expression softens. Because no matter how angry she is, and justifiably so, she needs this too. Me. Us.

"Liar." The tinge of venom in her tone causes my chest to ache, but I don't outwardly show the effect. "All these years and not so much as a damn phone call, Thiago? Not a letter or note or smoke signal. Nothing."

"I saved those to give you in person." Taking another step into her home, I take off the collared pullover I'm wearing and toss it somewhere behind me. Her eyes wander my chest and lower, cataloging the newest additions to my artwork, something she's trying to avoid but can't control.

It doesn't take long for her to find the feminine crown over my left pec and her name above the five points in her penmanship, a little favor that Ivan managed to pull off when he helped her find the apartment she lives in.

This building is mine and was purchased when her intent to move out of her parents' home became known two months after my sentencing. Plans that she confided to Amberlyn after a big fight with her parents, who continued to celebrate my demise. Little did she know that her new best friend, after I sent her to expose the truth, let it slip to Ivan by mistake.

He likes Amberlyn even if he hasn't admitted it to himself, while she's been in love with him since high school. A fact that's beneficial to me, and I'm not the least bit ashamed of playing dirty when it comes to my queen.

The contract she signed was nothing more than a bullshit pretense necessary at the time, and each month when she pays rent, it goes into a savings account with only her name on it.

However, I think she knew. It's the reason she went along with everything and never put up a fight.

"I don't want them." *Liar.*

This pull between us is palpable. Growing. Fucking torture as I try not to lose the last shred of control I have when it comes to her.

Luna's always been my kryptonite.

We're a lost cause. An unavoidable explosion.

A game we both know will end up one way; with her bent over or riding my cock.

Either way, I'll have her.

"That's a nasty habit you've picked up in my absence."

"Amuse me." Hackles raised, she places a hand on her hip and the robe shifts, giving me a peek at her upper thigh. "What *nasty habit?*"

"Becoming a fraud."

"What did you just say?" There's that fire again. That spark that always made my cock throb, swell to the point of pain. "I'll need a repeat."

I hurt for her. Can feel each bead of pre-come as it rolls down the head and then length, disappearing into the fabric of my boxer briefs.

Luna licks her lips, and I follow the movement with unrestrained hunger. "You'll never be over me, baby girl." This leaves me on a groan, a sound that causes her breath to hitch. "Quit lying to yourself."

It also serves to prove how affected Luna is by my mere presence, and when the two little tight nips appear through the thin material of her robe, I take in the rest of her.

Fuck. Just fuck.

Because the good Lord doesn't have mercy on me, and words will never suffice to describe the perfection before me.

Sinful and every bit of the temptress she is, my beauty stands in the middle of her living room in nothing but a satin robe and a pair of hipsters the color of lust. Red. Thin. Lace. Almost see-through, she's all curves and tan skin on display. All warmth and that ever-present scent of coconut swirling around her.

She's toner than I remember, too, but still thick where I love.

Where I love to grab onto as I maneuver her hips over mine.

Slow to the point of madness.

Fast to the point of delirium.

Her belt slowly starts to come undone, the soft fabric parting and exposing her midsection. However, my eyes settle on her right hip bone and the small tattoo visible just over the waistband of her panties. It's my initial, in my penmanship, with the intricate and bold face of a lion beside it.

Leon is the Spanish translation for lion, and Luna always said my last name couldn't fit me any better. That I remind her of a vicious predator, and I take that as a compliment. As a challenge.

I remember the day she got it, too. It was her eighteenth birthday and against her parents' wishes. They wanted more for her than me, the son of a mob boss and next in line to take over the family's dealings.

Hypocrisy at its finest since her dad is a chauvinistic and corrupt member of the city council. Then you have her mother, Yvette; religious and stuck somewhere between duty to her beliefs and hating the male species.

Both stuck in a loveless marriage where appearances are all that matter.

My eyes travel lower, just a tiny bit, and stop at the juncture of her thighs. Christ. From where I stand, I see the wetness coating her upper thighs and can just make out the pink flesh through the soft lace.

My mouth waters. My muscles coil to the point of pain and I tremble as a deep rumble vibrates through my chest. This moment is five years in the making.

Days and nights of denying myself her taste to protect my family. To keep Ivan out of jail.

She's my reward.

My treasure.

Mine.

"Leave," she says, breathing a bit choppy.

"I can't do that." My own chest expands, hands clenching and unclenching at my sides—fingernails digging into my palms. "I'm not leaving you again. Never. Fucking. Again."

"Please." She's trembling, goose bumps breaking out across her skin. For as much as she's angry, she's missed me too. Needs me. "We'll talk later. After I—"

Whatever bullshit excuse my beauty tries to use dies when my eyes snap to hers. "No."

"Thiago, please..." she swallows hard, squeezing her thighs "...this isn't the right time. Be reasonable."

"I love you." Those three words are my truth and her breaking point.

"No. No!" Luna's head shakes from side to side, the flip in her mood instant. This is the effect of a yo-yoing rollercoaster of emotions, and I see her intent before she reacts. With her next intake of breath, she reaches over and grabs a heavy glass vase, hurling it at my head. "You don't get to do this after what you did. What you tried to make me believe."

It misses the mark as I duck, and it smashes into the wall behind me. "I had no choice."

"There's always a choice!"

"And I took the one that mattered. I pushed you away to mother-fucking save you."

"So you keep saying!" This time it's a picture that barely misses me. "From who?" She's exasperated, and in her annoyance makes another mistake. Her movement, that explosive rage rushing through her Latina blood, exposes her left breast, and I lick my lips. Mouth-watering is the best way to describe her.

She's always been perky: a heavy handful with the most tanta-lizing shade of dusky pink nipples. They're perfect, a bit fuller than the last time I had the privilege of licking—biting—each tight little tip.

I swallow hard, eyes closing for a second. Needing the moment. "I'll tell you everything, but not now."

"Yes, now. You owe me—"

Holding a hand up, I cut her off. Then, desperate hazel meets sacred brown and I hold her stare. I let her see me. Open myself up to the only woman I will ever call mine.

"I owe you more than I will ever be able to repay in fifty lifetimes, Luna." The anger she tries desperately to hold on to begins to melt; it's still there and fighting to resurface, but her own feelings for me won't let them. "I love you and always will, baby girl, and that won't change. Not today or tomorrow."

"Don't do this to me."

"I'm never leaving you again."

"I deserve more than that, Thiago. Need more than words after—"

"And you'll get it all. My life if you so much as ask, but right now..." I trail off. The sight of her soft skin on display, the way her chest rises with every sharp intake of breath, is killing me. Destroying my very will. She's claiming me—tattooing herself into my very DNA without a single touch.

"What?" Without conscious thought, Luna raises a hand out toward me. It hangs in the air between us, her beautiful eyes on my face. "What about right now?"

"Right now..." I lick my lips, almost tasting her in the air around me. Luna's sweet and perfect and the hint of coconut lingering around me is driving me insane, especially when I know that she's decadent everywhere. "I'm going to start by righting the five years' worth of orgasms I owe you."

Her lips part but no words come out. She's stunned into silence, eyes wide, and the small object in her hand—another projectile—slips from her tiny fingers.

The muted thud is loud inside the room.

So is her whimper as I close the distance.

There's no running or escaping. No more denying.

We need this.

We'll talk later. Much later.

Chapter 7
THIAGO

A SINGLE TOUCH.

That's all it takes.

The world dissolves into a low hum the second my fingers wrap around the back of her neck, gripping her just the way she likes: hard. Because for as much as I love her violent tendencies —that passion that only I can bring forth—Luna loves my domination over her much smaller frame.

The way I can bend her to my will.

Maneuver her like my precious little dirty rag doll.

"So beautiful," I croon low, welcoming the electric current that bounces between us; this warmth travels throughout my limbs and then settles on the tip of my engorged cock as I yank her against my hard body.

Chest to chest. Breathing in her every exhale.

Savoring each shiver.

Loving the gasp and then whimper she fights to hold back.

"It's been too long since I've had you like this, beauty."

"Thiago." It's sweet and full of fear; she doesn't want to give in but can't fight the yearning. She doesn't want to need me but can't deny her hunger. "This...*oh God!*"

"I love you." My lips skim from her temple to cheek, pausing at the corner of her mouth. There, I breathe in her intoxicating scent. Coconuts and lime. My demise. "I missed you."

"We shouldn't." It has no conviction behind it. Luna isn't pushing me away but gripping the waistband of my pants. She isn't yelling but giving in. She isn't fighting my hold but inching her way closer.

Each inhale is a silent *more*.

Each exhale is a needy *plea*.

"Look at me." At my command, her head shifts slightly and those sweet lips hover over mine. Right there. I can feel the warmth of her breath on my face, the memory of her naturally sweet mouth causing the last cord of sanity to snap.

I force her back, not stopping until her body meets the wall, pinning her in place with my own hips while my lips descend on hers. My eyes close of their own accord, groaning as her decadent taste brings me back to a different point in time. Back to the first time I kissed her.

The effect is the same after all these years. I become manic. Desperate. Insatiable.

I massage her tongue with my own, reacquainting myself with an addiction that I've been deprived of. Feening for five motherfucking years.

They stole that from me. Us.

Lord, forgive me now because I won't ask for repentance later.

"Please, Thiago. We—"

"Need this." I finish for her because it's the truth. Our love is a gift and a burden. Our weakness and anchor. "Are you going to continue denying it?"

Her response comes in the form of a harsh bite to my bottom lip. It stings, and the lick that follows only makes me harder. Thicker inside my jeans.

My fingers dig into her neck, limiting her eager mouth from moving over mine. "Answer me, Luna. Say it."

"No."

"Is that so?" My eyes leave hers and traverse lower as I take a step back. She's tiny. Small compared to my over six-foot-four frame, and as those beautiful brown eyes darken to almost black, I release my hold on her neck. For now. Only so I can skim a single finger down to her right shoulder and then the left, savoring the way her delicate skin breaks out in goose bumps.

Pushing the soft material off and down her arms, I wait for a protest that never comes. There isn't a single sound of complaint, and I let the material catch at her elbows before undoing the belt at her waist that is holding on by an almost nonexistent bow.

It loosens and I watch as her arms shake before they fall, giving the garment the give it needs to fall at her feet. It pools there, and then she's naked except for the small scrap of indecency she calls underwear.

Her legs squeeze together.

Her abdomen clenches.

I haven't touched her yet.

But then I do.

With the very tip of two fingers, I slowly make my way down the center of her chest while ignoring the two tight tips begging for attention. I'm not ignorant to the way they throb for my touch, but I have a point to prove and don't pause until I reach the edge of her panties. Right at the waistband where I slip those same two fingers beneath the elastic with my eyes on hers.

Watching her. Daring her to deny me.

Instead, Luna parts her legs in offering and moans deep in the back of her throat when I cup her wet cunt. She's soft and swollen and ready for me. She's arching into my touch while her hips gyrate, and I'm a weak man for her.

Another swivel of her hips and I fall to my knees, yanking that offending piece of lace with me. It tears, the sound loud inside the quiet room until...

"Jesus, Thiago...*fuck!*" It's her first scream for me after so long. Nirvana.

I bury my face between her legs. No waiting. No teasing. Fuck, no. I'm a man possessed with years' worth of hunger to make up for.

"My queen," I hiss against her tender flesh, licking a path from her entrance to clit and back again while I undo the button of my jeans. My cock is hard and throbbing, pulsing, and while I enjoy her sweetness, I lower the zipper and pull my length out, fisting it tightly. For every swipe of my tongue, it's a stroke. For every moan, it's a swipe across the swollen-to-the-point-of-pain head with my thumb, spreading the beads of pre-come down my shaft before pumping again.

I fuck her with my tongue slowly. Maddeningly. Punishing us both.

"Please."

Her hips buck and I turn my face, biting the inside of her left thigh. "Patience, baby girl. I'm in no rush."

A hiss escapes the back of her throat then, her fingers fisting my hair and tugging on the dark ends. "Can't wait. I need—"

"Me," I snarl, lip curling over my teeth, and I refocus my attention on what's mine. What she gave me and I'll be the last to ever taste. To fuck. To love. "You need me, and I need you. No one else, Luna. We begin and end with each other."

"You left me," she hisses, pulling my face closer by the hold on my hair. It stings, her fingernails scratching my scalp, but I could give two royal fucks if she makes me bleed. I love her like this: wanton and desperate. Riding my tongue as I slip the tip inside her tiny hole. "How could you do that to me?"

"I'll make it up to you."

"How?" Luna's close, the way her breath catches and thighs tighten around my head tell me as much. "How do you make us right?"

"Like this." I sit back just as the first rush of wetness coats my tongue. The first few drops slide down my chin, and before my girl can protest, I release my cock and smack her clit with the same fingers that just a second ago were jerking my dick.

Her reaction is instant. She comes hard; head thrown back and eyes closed—with those lips I adore open in a silent scream.

"Beautiful," I croon, standing to my full height. My pants fall, pooling at my feet as I take her in—drink in the pure look of rapture on her exotic features. "But now it's my turn, Luna." With one of my hands, I pin both of hers before she can react. As she shivers, I press my hard body against hers. As another moan meets my ears, a shuddering breath leaves my chest. "Does that turn you on, baby girl? How much I want you?"

I'm on fire. Hurting. Unable to comprehend anything past the burning in my veins and the pulsing of my cock.

Her face turns, lips once again hovering, but I don't kiss them. Instead, I rock my hips, pushing my cock deeper into her stomach, leaving a trail of my essence over her skin.

"Thiago." My name tumbles from her lips like a mantra. A sacred prayer.

"Answer me, Miss Alejos. Admit that you'll always be my dirty little whore."

"Yes." But it's too low and I need more. Her admission needs to be loud enough that every neighbor on this floor can hear. Fuck that. Let the world know.

She's mine.

"Not enough."

Those brown orbs snap open and meet mine; in them, I see my future. Our life together. "I hate that I love you."

My lips crash to hers, and I release her hands so I can cradle the back of her neck, positioning her to my liking. We're passion and fire. We're licking and biting and drowning in everything that we've missed.

But then the other hand explores, caressing the tender skin of her breast before pinching a nipple. Her tiny gasp into my mouth is delicious, and I need more of that sound. How she whines after for more of my touch. Always so greedy.

On her next intake of air, I hoist her up and wrap those thighs around my waist. She's hot and right there, but I refocus on her breast, licking a path down her chin and neck, nipping my way down to her cleavage.

Her back arches in an offering and I accept, taking a tip between my teeth while twisting the other between two fingers. Wetness coats the trail leading to my cock, and I bite down hard. Her hips undulate, and I flick my tongue against the pebbled flesh.

"Just fuck me, Thiago. I need it." *Motherfucking finally.*

Her admission makes me feel one hundred feet tall.

"I've always loved that mouth of yours," I say against her supple flesh, giving the pebbled tip a final nip before releasing both. She trembles. Watches me. And I love it, that near crazed look in her eyes as I sweep the expanse of her midsection, fingers spread wide over each rib and lower. I'm reacquainting myself with her curves, paying homage to a body I've missed every night. Because since the age of eighteen, she slept in my bed up until a week before my arrest. When shit went down, I removed her from my life. Made sure that she couldn't be implicated or attached to me.

"I'm not going to beg."

"Just tell me what you need." I hold her above me, tip at her opening. "Say it again."

Luna is a siren, a beautiful demon sent to destroy me, and when she cups my jaw forcibly, the words *fuck me* slipping past her lips...

In one deep stroke, I bury myself to the hilt, ripping a scream full of pleasurable pain from her. *Christ,* she feels amazing. More than. This is my home and heart and everything good in my life. She's perfection. My queen.

The picture on the wall near her head falls and the glass shatters, a piece or two slicing my shin, but I don't stop. Instead, I pull out and drive back in with the same angry intensity. There's the sound of her wetness each time I enter; the slickness runs down my shaft and balls, soaking us both. There's the way her fingernails dig into my shoulder blades, breaking the skin as she holds on to me while I snap my hips into hers.

I can feel the few beads of blood as they roll down my skin.

I love how she tightens, swiveling to meet each of my punishing thrusts.

But more than anything, I love how she brings her mouth to my chin and bites down.

It's what I've been missing all these years. The feel of her slick cunt bouncing on my dick while her mouth is on my skin.

In and out, I ride her without mercy, getting lost in her body. Positioning my hips in a rough rhythm that causes her eyes to roll back and walls to tighten around my dick. And while I fuck her, I don't stop looking at her.

Memorizing every feature. Counting the small smattering of freckles over the bridge of her nose that she hates and I find adorable.

I've missed you. "Open your eyes, Luna."

She does as I ask, her chocolate orbs heavy-lidded. "I'm so close, baby."

That word. The term of endearment. Four letters.

It shatters and puts me back together again.

Releasing her hip, I bring a hand to cup the back of her neck. "I love you, Luna." Her walls squeeze me at that, tightening to almost the point of pain while I peck those kiss-swollen lips. Once, twice, I sweep across them—back and forth before nipping the top one. "I'll be yours in this life and every reincarnation that follows."

Lips parting, I see the unspoken reply. Her desire to say the words back, but the sweetness of her breath grazes my mouth and I tighten my hold, angling her to my liking. Her own tongue peaks out, swiping her bottom lip and the very edge of mine.

"Kiss me." It leaves her on a throaty moan, and I give in without a second thought because I know my girl. Know that Luna's fighting a war within herself—heart over mind—on how to accept my presence back into her life, and this is her giving an inch. It's her olive branch, and I take it. I'll give her the world if she so much as asks, and on her next intake of breath, my mouth slants over hers while my hips pick up the pace. While our tongues battle for domination, I bring my hand on her hip between us and circle her clit. *"Please."*

"That's it, baby girl. Fuck, you feel so good." Tight little circles, three of them, and her walls tighten. They pulse—massaging my cock while my eyes roll back. Luna's milking me, placing me a hair's breadth from the edge, and then she tips me over with a tiny little mewl. It's her tell. My favorite sound in the world. "Son of a bitch," I hiss out from between clenching teeth, slamming in a final time to the hilt as I spill inside of her.

"I can feel you, Thiago. *Oh, God.*"

Rope after rope fills her pussy and I press my palm down against her clit, rubbing her in time with every pulse of my release. "Come for me, Luna. Give me what's mine." Slick with her juices and my come, I pull out just enough that I can bring two fingers down on her clit and tap the sensitive bundle of nerves. Her thighs around my waist tremble, and I do it again. Harder. Enough that the stings cause her mouth to slacken and a soundless scream to escape as her release coats my cock.

We're a mess and panting and I bury my face in the crook of her neck, scraping my teeth over her collarbone as the pulsing—tightening around my length—pulls forth another violent wave of pleasure from me. My fingers hold her hips in place, riding out the second wave in agonizingly slow strokes while her moans turn to whimpers.

It takes a few minutes for her breathing and mine to slow, for the shudders to cease and the deep-seated euphoric feeling of exhaustion to take hold, but when it does, I'm also reminded of another part of us that I've been without for too long:

The after.

That time between coming down from the natural high and the nap she always takes after. And when her body slumps in my hold, I know exactly where I'm heading next.

Luna's room is at the very end of the hall. Even from my jail cell, I took care of what's mine, and her apartment is the best.

Largest bathroom.

Largest bedroom.

The latter is where I'm heading, and it's the right choice because a second or two later there's a low snore from her. It's tiny and cute and it fills my chest with another emotion altogether.

I'm finally home.

Chapter 8
LUNA

I'M ROUSED FROM sleep by kisses on my shoulder and the warmth of a hard body behind me. I'm disoriented and stay still; I have no clue what time it is, and it's something that, along with the soreness between my thighs, scares me. Freaks me out.

But then I hear him.

That low, raspy voice that brings back the memories.

It brings back his near desperate touch after so long. His reverence the second our eyes met.

And now, there's the way he curses me in English and then prays to me in Spanish.

I'm his *weakness* and *Tesoro*.

"You're my motherfucking world, beauty." There's so much emotion in those words, and tears spring to my eyes. More so when Thiago's lips kiss an addition to my tattoo collection that he hasn't seen. Or at least, I don't think he's paid attention to.

It's another mark that represents him. It exposes my weakness.

A pair of MMA gloves like the ones he uses in fights; the difference is the heart at the center where the real pair has his name.

Christ, I want to contradict him. Deny and rage and let go of five years' worth of loneliness, but I don't. I can't.

Not when his arm around my waist tightens and I'm once again drowning in us. In memories that are both painful and a blessing. Not when that same mouth sweeps across my shoulder blade while whispering my name like a blessed mantra.

Thiago's words become a faint whisper then and I can't make out what he's saying, and stupidly, my heart tells me to revel in the moment and forget what brought us here.

And more importantly, I listen.

Against better judgment, I melt into the broad chest pressed against my back and let nostalgia kidnap my senses.

This has always been my favorite place to be and Thiago knows this. It's been our ritual after an encounter like the one we had a while ago. Because after sex, after claiming my body as his, the ruthless killer likes to cuddle. He loves my body against him, fingertips caressing my skin while whispering filthy nothings in my ear.

It's a weakness and need, and I've yearned for another moment like this one. It's why I stay quiet. Why I swallow back my emotions while closing my eyes.

I'm not ready to hash it out.

I'm not ready to send him away.

So, I let his warmth and masculine scent take me under. Let his touch relax me while I pretend it's another place and time. When we were happier. Heading toward a long and happy future together.

I've missed you so much.

It doesn't take long for his rhythmic caresses to become faint—soft. They lull me into a state of complete relaxation, and just before sleep takes me under, I hear his low chuckle. "I've missed you too, beauty. Stubbornness and all."

THE NEXT TIME I open my eyes the room is dark and the bed's empty.

My sheets are cold and the apartment quiet.

And yet, the scent of his cologne embraces every square inch inside the room.

I feel him and don't; it's a limbo I recognize. One that stole months of my life after his arrest and then sentencing. Those days blended into each other, where nothing made sense and I couldn't process my new life.

A *me* without him.

"Damn you, Thiago," I hiss under my breath, ignoring the discomfort and my nakedness while scrambling into a sitting position. My mounting ire doesn't care if I should be reaching for the Tylenol bottle instead of a robe; all I know is that he isn't here.

That he left me again without explanation.

Throwing my legs over the edge of the bed, I stand without looking at the clock or grabbing my phone. Instead, I put on a silk wrap and rush out of the room like a demon out of hell and straight into almost complete darkness. The only source of light is coming from the moonlit sky through the sliding glass door.

An open sliding glass door.

The further I walk, a soothing, salty breeze follows, sweeping through the living room. I follow its path, one foot in front of the other until I'm standing in a doorway with a vast view of the open water off Brickell.

It's beautiful but missing someone, and once again a pang of loneliness hits me in the chest. My balcony is empty, crushing my hope, and I step out onto the veranda while staring ahead.

Is that all he came for?

Is that all I've become?

I'm trying to put my emotions into perspective. I'm trying to understand why I let this happen.

Insecurity is a heinous bitch and I hate her with the passion of a million keyboard warriors.

"I'm an idiot." Leaning with my elbows on the railing, I breathe in and out slowly. Once, twice...six times, I don't stop until the lump in my throat recedes, and mentally repeating *this is not my fault* helps.

"I'm here."

"Fuck!" I yelp, clutching my chest as I whirl around to find him in the doorway, a bottle of beer in his hand. At once, the reproach on my tongue dies and I'm swept away by his handsome features. Even fully dressed, the man is dangerous for me.

Thiago Rivera De Leon is tall, dark, and wickedly handsome. He's all muscles and tattoos. He's the promise of nirvana and heartbreak all rolled into one.

The best of everything. What you shouldn't want but can't walk away from.

His face is partially hidden by the shadows of the night, while his jaw and lips curl up at the corner into a sinful smirk. His eyes have this glowing effect in the moonlight, and they shine with mirth and appreciation.

They roam my body from head to toe, the near-nakedness that is silhouetted by the same moon his focal point. He sees me. The want is in his stare.

And if I don't stop this—us—I'll find myself on my knees worshipping at his throne.

"Stay." It leaves me in a shaky voice.

"Why?" Thiago takes a single step forward and once again, I'm a tumultuous rainbow of emotions—wants and needs and truths that make me weak and at the same time stronger because he's here.

I can stand without him, I've proven as much, but just having him close brings forth a part of me I'd shut down years ago.

"Because you owe me this."

All amusement falls from his face and those hazel eyes pierce mine. "There's so much I need to make amends for."

"Then you can start by giving me a minute while waiting in the living room."

"Is that what you need?"

"It's part of what I deserve."

"Okay, beautiful. No argument from me, but..." he trails off and my lips part, the *but what* sitting on the tip of my tongue as he bends at the waist to place his bottle down on the floor. Then, I blink, and he's sauntering across the space dividing us. His swagger is sexy, and so is the way he doesn't ask for permission when stealing a kiss. One second I'm cursing his handsome face, and the next I'm melting into him as his warm lips meet mine and a hand cups the back of my neck.

It's soft and sweet and torture all at once. It's small nibbles and a caressing tongue against my own. The cold beer only enhances his natural decadence—a unique taste that I've missed.

Dreamed of.

Passion ignites in my veins and I tremble, hands fisting his shirt while he holds me just as tight. Chest to chest. His breathing and mine in sync.

"Thiago," I say. It's breathless and I can't take back the neediness that seeps through each letter. Loving—belonging to this beautiful sinner will only continue destroying me, and it's inevitable.

"*Fuck*, baby girl." It rumbles through his chest; the vibration causes my thighs to press together. He notices this and slows the kiss against my protest, nibbling on my bottom lip while his hand—the one on my neck—keeps me in place. I'm being denied and the pout that follows is almost embarrassing. "If we don't stop, Luna, I'm going to strip you. I'm going to put you on your knees, and I'll let this pouty *mouth*..." he accentuates the word with a swipe of his tongue across the abused flesh "... kiss my cock before I slip inside and let you reacquaint yourself with my weight on your tongue." A shiver rushes through me, and my nipples, the stiff little satin-covered peaks, rub against his chest. "I'm seconds away from mounting you, my queen. From fucking you on all fours with the night's sky and the open water as our backdrop. Is that what you really want?"

"You know what my answer would be."

"Just a second ago you were telling me to give you a minute."

"You knew what kissing me would do."

Thiago nods and the hand on my neck skims from cheek to jaw, his thumb rubbing across my mouth. "But how angry would you be afterward if I didn't step away now?"

"Very."

"That's why that kiss was just to tide us over." His smile is sad but understanding. He's giving me what I need even if my body rebels against the very notion. "I'll be inside waiting. Take your time."

"Okay." That's all I can say, and with one last look, he leaves me to my thoughts. Thoughts that are chaotic and ever changing. One second I'm that girl—the one head over heels in love, but then just as fast I'm angry and bitter. Two sides of a coin with no place to land because either way it falls will hurt. "I need to be honest with him," I mutter low, rubbing my cheek where his hand had been. "It's all I can be."

A moment, a deep breath in, and I turn to face that open glass door. Standing there, I square my shoulders and fight back my desires to forgive and forget. To start over without any more delays.

My heart wants him, but my mind can't stop torturing me with a singular word: distrust.

Thiago's distrust didn't allow me to stand by his side during a challenging time.

Thiago's distrust didn't allow us to face this bump in the road together.

He didn't trust *me* enough to stay.

Chapter 9
LUNA

A TRUTH I can't ignore, and it hurts.

Internally, I crumble where I stand, but on the outside my posture stiffens. In the blink of an eye I go from aroused to exhausted. From happy to near angry tears.

My chest expands and the scent of him surrounds me—even the small breeze coming off the water can't dilute its effect, something that further incenses me.

In the time that he went inside and I turned around, I've become a lit fuse and I stomp inside, hellbent on getting answers. "Why?"

"Take a seat, Luna."

"Don't tell me what to do, Leon."

"Been a while since you've called me by my last name. I've missed it." Alluding to my use of Leon when angry doesn't help his case. Neither does his small smirk.

I watch him through narrowed eyes. "Why?"

"Sit." Thiago isn't moved by my annoyance and pats the cushion of the chair across from his, right beside a table where an ice-cold Corona waits. "Take a sip, breathe, and I'll truthfully answer anything you want."

"I'm not playing—"

"I know. Just humor me, bebe."

With a huff, I walk over, sit, and then cross my legs. I make sure the material of my robe exposes my upper thighs and covers where his eyes wander to continuously. "Talk."

He licks his lips. "Where do you want me to start?"

Pausing with the bottle at my lips, I raise a brow. "At the beginning."

"That night?"

"Make me understand, Thiago," I say after swallowing, my tone a bit biting. "Why would you try to make me believe you cheated?"

"It started three weeks before the night you walked in on me with Amberlyn." I give him a blank stare. There's no reaction from me; I already know that nothing happened. "Do you remember the commotion downstairs and my having to leave?"

I'm nodding before he finishes. It was an ordinary Saturday evening and we were getting ready to go to our favorite club for a night out when screams rent the air. His mother was angry, crying, and Thiago left without so much as an explanation. No one talked about or explained what was happening; his parting words were spoken through gritted teeth and over his shoulder. *Don't leave the premises, Luna. Code Black.*

That meant a loved one was hurt. It meant total lockdown.

Thiago was going to take over soon, but his father still held the position as head. And as such, Ivan and Orlando were on their way home from a fishing trip with an associate. There was a car accident and a few injuries, but things changed after that night. He changed.

The next day, I went home to my parents' house with an empty promise to talk later. That "later" turned into three days without a word, a few excuses over being busy, and then total silence.

"I do."

"And you remember how Dad stepped down right after."

"Yes. The exchange of power happened within seventy-two hours."

Thiago rubs a hand down his face, the muscles in his forearm taut with tension. "There was never a car accident, Luna. He was shot." A gasp escapes me, but he stops me from asking questions with a shake of his head. "There was a hit carried out. They tried to kill him and failed."

"Who would do that?"

"I'm working my way through the list as we speak."

"I need more than that, dammit. Who?"

"You do, but I'm asking for time."

"Give me a good reason as to why I should do give you anything."

"Because there was another attempt made while I was in jail and this one was—"

"Maritza." He gives me a quizzical look, but I take a moment to gather my thoughts. Beer in hand, I take a deep pull while wishing it was something stronger, something to numb me before the pain of what lies ahead hits me in the chest. Those few seconds also help me piece together what I've always found odd. "Your mom called me two years ago and told me to be careful, that she had this bad feeling nagging at her right before her birthday. And you know how she is?"

"I do."

"Once something is off, it's time to be on alert. The woman is rarely wrong, and I listened." Closing my eyes for a second, I take in a deep breath and let it out slowly. "We talked every day, you know. We even met up for lunch on her birthday, but the next thing I know,

Ivan's calling to inform me she fell and couldn't see me. We never made plans after that, and this explains so much."

"I told her to stay away."

"Why would you do that?" That stings—cuts deep, and I press my free hand down over my chest. "Do you know how much I've missed her? Needed her when—"

"Keeping you out of the picture wasn't easy, baby girl. Not on them. Not on me. Not on you…" Leaning toward me, Thiago takes the bottle from me, places it on the table, and then takes my hands in each of his. I don't fight him. I don't so much as move while he gives each a squeeze because I'm almost afraid that if I pull away, he'll stop talking and I need the truth more than my own dignity. "I know this is hard, but I had no other choice. Not when I wasn't here to protect you, and keeping you safe is all that's ever mattered to me. Not when it was one of mine, someone I considered family, that pulled the trigger on Mom."

That confession stuns me. Takes away every single recrimination and leaves me shaken. My mind is racing and my heart aches.

"Who?" is all I manage through the sudden lump in my throat. *Who stole you from me?*

"Ismael *was* the sicario."

"Ismael?" I ask, and I also don't miss the emphasis on the word was. Past tense. Not that he deserves anything less after the Leon family took him in. After Thiago treated him like another little brother. "Why the hell would he do that? Who would dare—"

"Money." There's a slight tick of his jaw and I still in my seat, waiting for the next invisible blow. "They dangled a diamond-studded carrot and he bit. It was one of Senot's men that made the call on both accounts."

"Senot? You…that…Thiago, he's my dad's best friend!"

"Does the name Alfredo Gaytan ring any bells, Luna?" he spits out, dropping my hands and rising to his full height. It's intimidating, but I don't shrink back. And if there's one thing I still trust about the man, it's that he would never lay a hand on me. So I watch him, never taking my eyes off him as he walks away and over to the open glass door, his hands clenching at his sides. "Does it?"

"Yes." Because it does. I've seen the man a few times here and there over the years, especially when Jasmine Senot is present at functions. He's her guard, a job that never made much sense to me when no one really cares about the mayor's wife. They dislike him at times, but she's left alone to be clueless and pretentious. "How is he involved? He's Jasmine's shadow."

"He hired both men."

"Both men?" Christ, nothing makes sense. How much has been kept from me?

"The night Dad was shot and we covered with a car crash, the hitman failed because Ivan reacted at the right moment. He pushed the old man down, covered him the best he could, and then unloaded a magazine in the direction the asshole was shooting from." There's a tinge of shame and anger in his tone. His posture is tense, muscles bulging underneath the fabric of his shirt. Even the tattoo sleeve seems to portray his ire; all black with soft shadowing to contrast the features of this ominous painting representing death. "This happened after the fishing trip, late at night as they were leaving Versailles. Video of the parking lot shows them parting ways with our visitors, walking toward their car after theirs exited the lot, and then three gunshots. The first two missed and the last shattered Dad's knee."

"Christ," I breathe out, feeling more than a little overwhelmed. My mind is going in so many directions that I just don't know what to think. "Why would Gaytan do that? Do you think it's a setup?"

He senses my distress and looks over, the shadow on his face making his eyes almost seem glowing in the moonlight. "Not at first. Unfortunately, and I know you don't want to accept this, but I wouldn't make an accusation like that without solid proof."

"At first?"

"When the guy failed to execute Dad, he was disposed of by Ismael and the body placed inside my home. He was dismembered, with bullet holes that came from Ivan's gun—recovered at the scene

—but pinned on me. That's why I served time. Not for any of the shit I've done, but because someone wanted me out of the picture."

"Who?"

"The list is long, but Senot is at the top."

"I'm not saying he wouldn't, but—"

"Luna..." The way he says my name, the sadness in his voice, makes my heart clench. "Baby girl, I've had the video of this trans-action taking place outside of The Acere Bar, *my* fucking bar on 36th street, for years. Since the night before Ivan picked up the traitor and took him offshore on holiday. They, Gaytan and Ismael, were caught discussing payment and their target: my mother. Their faces are clear to see, and ironically enough, all of this on the side of the building where everyone believes there are no cameras."

"I'm sorry, Thiago. So sorry this is where we stand."

He turns to fully face me. "It's not your fault."

"No. It's not." Standing from my seat, I slowly make my way across the room to him. Because while I am still mad at the way he pushed me aside—made me doubt us—what's been done is more than a disrespect. It's personal. I can see it in his eyes how Ismael's betrayal cut deep, and while the world might not see his heart, it's always been open to me. Reaching him, I wrap my arms around his midsection and bury my face in his chest. "You have every right to feel as you do and handle their punishment as you see fit, Thiago. I'll never begrudge you that."

"But can you—"

"I wasn't done." Inhaling deep, I take his masculine scent deep into my lungs and tears spring to my eyes when I feel his lips at the crown of my head, he too breathing me in. It's sad and telling. Right now there's too much for me to process, and forgiveness isn't some-thing I can promise. *I need time.* "I'll give you that things were hectic. That you were busy keeping everyone safe, but that still doesn't explain—why shut me out? Why abandon me?"

Two fingers appear in my line of sight a second before he's tipping my face up to his. He doesn't kiss me, but for a moment just stares. Eyes locked and my heart racing, I gift myself the luxury of getting lost in his hazel orbs. The world around us moves, time continues to tick, but when we are like this, nothing registers.

"...kill you."

"What?" I missed everything he said except for those two words and I step back, disentangling myself from his arms. "Repeat that?"

"You were the original second hit." That realization is my breaking point. My body begins to shake, and my knees feel weak. "I broke us to protect you."

"Leave."

"Bebe, we should—"

"No, Thiago. I need you to leave." Turning from him, I walk toward the front door and open it, holding on to the knob to avoid grabbing him. He's behind me; the sound of his heavy footsteps and dominating presence gives me goose bumps.

His hand grips my forearm, but he doesn't turn me around. Just holds on. "Luna."

Just my name. A raspy reverence.

"Time," I say, voice low yet firm. There's no anger, but more of an overwhelming need to breathe without his presence choking me. Distracting me. "Give me time to think and make sense of everything on my own, because right now I'm lost. In less than twenty-four hours you've come back and brought with you a truth I've both longed for and at the same time, feared. Please, just leave and wait for me to be ready."

"Okay." Then his body is right behind mine; heat sears my near-naked form as his broad chest presses into my back, his lips skimming my temple. "I'll leave, but this isn't the end, nor will it be for long. I love you, Luna. Please remember that if nothing else."

A kiss to my cheek.

Another whisper of my name.

And then he's gone, leaving me an overwhelmed ball of emotions that leads me on shaky legs to my kitchen. There's only one thing I need and without pause, I open my fridge and pull out the bottle of

Mamajuana I keep inside. The Brugal rum and spice mixture has to help—make me forget for a little while the chaotic mess my life is.

Twisting the top off, I bring the bottle to my lips and take a large sip. It doesn't do more than burn a tiny bit going down, and before the mellow warmth can spread, I take three more pulls the size of a shot to speed the process along.

The alcohol rushes through me and on an empty stomach, the effects start after another minute. Once the buzz kicks in, I walk back to the living room and while taking a smaller sip, I park my butt on an oversized chair and make a silent toast.

For the Leons.

For my broken heart.

For my own list.

Because Thiago is right about one thing; revenge will be sweet.

Chapter 10
THIAGO

IT'S BITTERSWEET PULLING into the driveway of my childhood home thirty minutes later. I've missed the place and the people inside, but my mind is elsewhere. With her.

Always Luna.

Anger and hurt are a deadly combination, and my queen is drowning in both. They're feelings I expect, know she'll hide behind until ready, but I won't let her wallow in.

Hate me now, but our love will never die.

When I left, the betrayal—the fear I played upon that day more than five years ago—had reopened like a wound, and she's dealing with the aftermath. Confronting what she's buried deep inside all these years while accepting the reality she was ignorant to.

Her words cut, but I'll proudly wear the scars. It's a necessary evil in order to heal and let go of the past. She'll have her moment, a chance to clear her head, but then I'm coming back.

Turning off the ignition, I undo my seatbelt and open the door, placing a single foot on the pavers below when the front door is thrown open. At the entrance is a short Latina in her early fifties with a megawatt grin on her face. Her chin quivers, and she rushes down the three steps, almost tripping in her haste.

"Mi hijo!" she yells out, tears running down her cheeks. Her light hazel eyes with a touch of green in them are taking me in—from head to toe—and cataloging the subtle differences. I was never a small guy, my stature and love for mixed martial arts kept me in shape, but with not a lot to do in jail I picked up another hobby. Lifting weights kept me focused. Kept me from snapping the neck of every cocky cop who quickly learned to lower their heads and keep walking. "Orlando, hurry up. My baby is here."

Those words have barely left her lips when she crashes into me. Her arms go around my midsection and a sob shakes her much smaller frame.

I hug her back just as tight. "Mom, I'm okay. I'm here."

She slaps my arm and then goes back to hugging me. "Let me have my moment."

A chuckle escapes. "Please, take your time."

"Always my smart ass child," my vieja says, and I can hear the pain in her voice. Feel the tears soak my shirt. "But these five years were hard, Thiago. What those assholes did—"

"No more of that tonight." At my interruption, she looks up with a raised brow. Because no matter how old you are or how feared you are, Cuban mothers demand respect. However, when you're her oldest and favorite, you get away with certain things. No flip flops will be thrown at my head nor will a flying hand go to the back of my head. Instead, there's the tremble at the corner of her lips and then the full-on smile when I kiss her forehead. "I love you, Mom. Missed you and your cooking."

"Oh my God! I'm sorry, kid." And just like that she's flustered and moving back, heading back inside while my father stands at the top of the landing with a smile. Maritza De Leon is on a mission now and doesn't stop until she reaches the door; there, she turns to look back from over her shoulder. "Your favorite on the menu; white rice with black beans, picadillo, and sweet plantains. I'll be in the kitchen getting you a plate…give me ten."

"Sounds perfect." Not that she heard me. The flash that nearly tackled me is gone and the door slamming behind her is all the proof I have that she was ever here.

"That woman is something else." The admiration in my father's tone makes me look over and I catch the smirk on his face. Orlando De Leon has always been larger than life in my eyes. A man of his word and loyal to those he loves. A man that will end a life without a second thought and then go home and kiss his wife goodnight.

I lean back against the side of the car. "Quit being a creeper, Viejo."

"Kid, it was cute when you were younger, but quit calling us old." The hold he has on his cane is firm and there is very little hobble in his step. He begins to walk toward me, and I don't argue. He's a proud man, and this is his way of showing me he's okay. "Because this old bastard can still kick your ass."

Smirking, I raise a brow. "I'd like to see you try."

"Punk."

"So testy."

"Come here, asshole." Dad stops in front of me, pulling me into a bone-crushing hug. "Good to have you home, son. We've missed you."

"Miss you, too. All of you." My arms wrap around him and hold him just as tight for a minute before stepping back. "How has she really been? Anything I should know about?"

"Your mother is a warrior, Thiago. A rock." He looks behind him toward the house and smiles. "She's angry because of what's been done and expects answers soon. This is your warning. The questions will come."

"I know." As soon as the last word leaves my mouth, both demeanors change. His and mine. The seriousness of the situation and what's to come isn't a game. Someone tried to hurt us—kill and dismantle us—and it's not something I will ever let go of. "Ismael is dead."

"We kept him alive for you. Trust me, I'll share the video with you at another time of his stay with us." In his brown eyes there is no warmth; the instincts of a killer are very much present. "That hijo de puta fucked with the wrong man's wife. He was lucky I left him for you—my wrath would've dismembered him an inch of flesh at a time while feeding the bite-sized pieces to the local predators."

"Have Georgie and Kline gotten bigger?" Those two gators behind the house do come in handy from time to time. "When I left, they were about five feet give or take."

"About eight now."

"Good." Rubbing my chin, I consider my options when it comes to the next name on my list. His connection to a certain family. His loyalty to the whore he fucks behind her husband's back. "Stop feeding them for a few days."

"Yes, sir." There's a bit of a chuckle in his tone, but I can also see the pride on his face. And while they kept a firm hold in my absence —Ivan and Dad—I'm now here to right this wrong. To send a message to anyone opposing our control over the city of Miami. "Anything else for your first night back? Which we didn't expect you for, by the way. We thought you and Luna would—"

"She needs time, Viejo." Throwing an arm over his shoulder, I turn us toward the stairs and begin to ascend. "A lot was hidden and now thrown at her. Luna just needs to cope and wrap her head around the truth."

"You make sure Luna's here on Saturday?"

"I'm picking her up before five."

"Good." he says, voice firm. "She belongs here with us. She's one of us."

I rub my other hand over my chest, where her name is etched into my skin. "Something else I'll be making official soon enough."

Mom appears at the doorway and waves us on before the man can comment. "Food's getting cold. Hurry and wash up."

"You heard your wife. Move it or I'll carry you."

"Try it and I'll shoot you." Raising his cane, he tries to hit me with the solid teak end, but I duck out of the way. "Now go and eat. We can continue our talk after dinner. There's something I want to show you."

"Should I be concerned?"

"It's about your cousin Jadiel and his sister's boyfriend."

"Talk business later and let's get him fed, Orlando. That mierda he's been forced to eat the last few years is unacceptable." At Mom's reproach, I give the old man a nod to let him know I heard and agree. We'll talk. I'll assess.

And God help that singao and whatever crap he's caught up in now.

"THAT WAS AMAZING, VIEJA. THANK YOU," I say, sitting back and patting my stomach after my second plate of home cooking. It's one of my favorite meals and a hot seller in two of our restaurants. "That hit the spot, and it'll probably put me to sleep in a little bit."

My phone atop the table vibrates then and I pick it up, the name Malcolm Asher flashing across the screen. It's his second call in the span of thirty minutes and I pick up while holding a finger up to my mother. Her nose and mouth scrunch up and her chin juts out in the *who is it* expression. I mouth *Malcolm* and she goes back to the counter near the stove where a large flan sits and coffee is percolating.

"News travels fast, Asher?" I say in greeting before taking a sip of my drink and placing it back atop the table.

"When dangerous men are released? Faster than you think." He chuckles, what sounds like a chainsaw in the background. There are birds in the distance; it doesn't sound one bit like he's in the city. "I'll be heading your way tomorrow. Are you available?"

I scratch my jaw, contemplating my plans. "After midday and not for long."

"I won't hold you up, then, but we do need to talk." There's something in his tone, an almost urgent quality—as if he needs to do this but rather be elsewhere—that catches my attention.

"Then I'll see you tomorrow."

"Thank you."

The tone of the call isn't a social one and I hang up, placing the device on the table before looking toward my father who's standing at the fridge, beer in hand. "Asher will be here tomorrow."

"For the reunion?" he asks, taking a sip. "Didn't your mother tell you it's been pushed back to Saturday?"

Before he's done, I'm shaking my head. "Business, and I have a feeling this has everything to do with the Fosters."

"Why don't you invite him to stay a few days." This time it's Mom who speaks. "You know I'd love to have everyone over." There are a few associates that I welcome into our homes, those that have been in business with us for years, and Malcolm is one of those. A crazy fucker, but honest and dependable.

"I'll extend the request."

"It's been so long since I've seen him and Mariah. Since you've been able to relax, Thiago…have a drink and a decent meal with the family. The bullshit they put you through and…" Mom trails off as her bottom lip trembles, a small sob causing her body to shake, and at once, I stand from my chair. The legs of the chair scrape against the travertine tiles before tipping over in my haste to reach her. She's across the large kitchen and standing by the sink, gripping the dishrag tightly in one fist as she stares at me. "Everything was a mess and I worried—prayed every single night that Papa Dios would keep you safe."

"He did. I'm home, and everything will be okay."

"Ivan hasn't stopped beating himself up over everything and I couldn't help him. Or you." Dad tries to grab her before I do, but the shake of my head stops him. He slips out of the room after giving me a pointed look, but I ignore him and focus on Mom. Those watery hazel eyes and the sadness in them cement my resolve to bury every motherfucker involved with my incarceration. "I'm sorry."

Two words. Two simple motherfucking words, and they are the wrong ones.

They stop me in my tracks just a few steps from her. Close enough that I grab the rag in her hand and toss it before taking both her hands in mine and closing my eyes. Then, I breathe in and out.

I keep in mind where I am and why.

God, not today.

I'm not asking for patience nor understanding. I'm not asking for anything but the will to calm myself while I reign in my sudden bout of ire. Because I'll be damned if this woman ever apologizes to me without just cause, especially for shit she has nothing to do with.

A couple of seconds and my eyes snap open, nostrils flaring as I say the next words slowly. As calmly as I can muster. "I never want to hear you say that again, Maritza De Leon." What I just did is a cardinal sin for Hispanics everywhere. We don't use our parents' Christian names. Never. They are Mom and Dad until *they* die and even then, there is no pass go and collect fifty. "Understood."

However, her reaction is worthy of whatever reproach I receive next, especially as her shoulders square and chin tips up. "I'm going to pretend I didn't hear that."

"And I'm going to pretend you forgot who you are."

"I know damn well who I am, Thiago." Her hands slip from mine and she reaches up to cup my chin. "Don't confuse my tears for anything other than anger for my family."

"Good." I kiss her forehead and then pull away, standing to my full height. Her eyes narrow for a second as I watch, impatience starting to color her features. "Because I need you strong for what's to come."

"This family stands behind you."

"I know."

"Are you prepared to make those decisions when the time comes? No matter who it is?" She's alluding to the Senots and maybe even Luna's family, but my suspicions run deeper. Much deeper, and maybe even closer than they think.

"I am."

Her head tilts to the side, studying me. "Something else is on your mind, Thiago." Not a question, but more of a perception.

"There is, but I need you calm and collected first."

Without a word, she walks over to the sink and opens the faucet, letting a bit of water pool in her palms before bringing both wet hands to her face. She does this a few times while I watch, and the old man sneaks a look in the room while her back is turned.

He mouths the words *dead motherfuckers* as I wave him off with two fingers. She's his wife, and I get his need to step in, but I have the perfect way of distracting her.

"Whatever you need, I can handle."

"Luna."

From the corner of my eye I see my father throw his hands up as if saying *hallelujah* while she begins to smile. A devious one at that. "Whatever it is, consider it done."

"Good, because that's one woman we can't show any signs of weakness to." At that, Mom throws her head back and laughs. Her entire body shakes and when she looks at me again, her red-rimmed eyes shine with amusement now. "She's as stubborn as you are and is angry. I get that. I accept my part in the mess I didn't originally create but made worse by pushing her away instead of explaining.

However, and this is where I need you; there are things that you can explain woman to woman that will come off as condescending from me. She doesn't need for me to explain her role or the difficulty of war, but you can listen and give her guidance as someone who knows this life."

"Her forgiveness won't come easily."

"I know, and that's another battle I'm prepared to bleed for."

Chapter 11
THIAGO

IT'S A LITTLE after ten a.m. and I'm standing outside her door, breakfast in hand. I know what she likes, what she'll need, and can motherfucking guarantee that her hangover will thank me for the gesture. Because I know my queen, and the Mamajuana she likes to keep in her fridge was pulled out last night. Just like I know she drank more than she first intended.

Her drink of choice, Brugal, is a traitorous bastard. The Dominican rum on its own is strong, but when steeped with this special blend of spices, it can knock you on your ass. There's no longer a harsh burn or taste and there in itself lies the problem; you don't feel it until it's too late.

"Rise and shine, baby girl," I say while making my presence known; three quick raps against the door and I hear movement from the inside. Nothing loud, but more like a distant grumbling, and I smile. Another hard knock and the word *motherfucker* follows shortly after.

"I'm coming!" Luna calls out, then there's a crash and the sound of glass meeting the floor seconds before the door is thrown wide open. My queen stands there with her eyes closed and a hand rubbing her right temple, face a little wet from washing. She's wearing an oversized shirt—*my* shirt from my time on our high school baseball team—and a grumpy expression.

No makeup and hair a mess, Luna is a vision and my cock swells, pressing against the inseam of my dark grey slacks since I'm not wearing any underwear. *Motherfuck* is right, and my need for another taste almost drops me to my knees.

So close to what's mine.

So close to my version of heaven.

It's also the second time she opens the door without looking, and her gun is nowhere in sight.

"Nat, I told you to please back—"

"Open your eyes, beautiful."

"Lord," she says while tipping her face up, "this is not the time for jokes."

"Never thought that a personal delivery of pastries from Vicky Bakery and a Starbucks coffee would be considered anything other than glorious. From what I remember—"

Luna holds her hand out, looking at me through narrowed slits. "Gimme and go."

"I want a kiss for my troubles."

"Thiago, I swear to God now isn't the time to mess with me." That small hand smacks my chest, and my cock gives another harsh jerk. I can feel the bead of pre-come at the very tip and bite back a groan when it rolls down the underside. "Hand them over."

"Which ones?" Lifting them out of her reach, I take a step forward. "Guava and cream cheese or just the quesito? Maybe you're in the mood for something a little more indulgent?"

Luna doesn't back away and that sweet, sleep-rumbled scent of her skin assaults my senses. "I'm not a toy, and you need to learn some patience."

"Love you too."

"I forgot how much of a morning person you are. *Stubborn too.*" The last part is mumbled under her breath, but I heard her loud and clear. Her sass is adorable. "Thank you for breakfast…yada yada…goodbye."

"I would believe the put-off act if there wasn't a smile curling at the edge of your lips."

There's a sound that leaves the back of her throat, this wild mixture of a scream and curse word, before she stomps back inside. I'm watching her sweet ass—following the naturally exaggerated sway of her hips—when she steps right over the small broken glass figurine that somehow managed to break a few steps from the doorway.

"Shit!" She hops on one foot, bringing her injured one up. Blood is already seeping from the cut, and before she can fully assess the damage, I'm dropping her breakfast on the accent table near us and then picking her up in two strides.

At first, she tries to fight my hold, but one kiss to her bare shoulder where my shirt has slipped off and a low *shhh* has her settling down.

Her kitchen isn't far from where we are and I walk over, placing her atop the cold granite counter. Luna sucks in a breath at the contact, but I don't acknowledge the sexy sound. Instead, I take her foot in my hand and place a kiss over the large hibiscus flower tattoo at the top. It's bright and large and holds a special meaning for the two of us.

In the large garden at the back of her parents' house a week after I met her, surrounded by this very flower, I stole my first taste of her lips. While Luna's father was at work and mother out shopping, I kissed her for almost an hour, hand on her perky tit, until we were both out of breath and smiling.

"Perv."

"For you, without an ounce of shame." The cut looks to be a little deep, but nothing that will require stitches. "Hold on and don't complain."

"What are you going to do?"

"Take care of my girl." Picking her up, I bring us to her large farmhouse sink and place her sideways atop the countertop with her foot inside the basin. She hisses when I turn the water on right over the cut, but it's a necessary evil in order to make sure there isn't any fragment of glass left inside. With the very tip of my pointer finger, I feel over the cut while washing away the small rivulets falling down her heel. "No glass inside and it isn't deep, baby girl, but you will need a Band-Aid."

"Thank you." Her voice is small and holds a tinge of fear, and I know it has everything to do with her lack of clothes and my proximity. She's not ready, and that's okay. I'm here to make my presence known and show that I'm not going anywhere. "My first-aid kit is in—"

"Drawer on the left side of the fridge." At my response, she gives me a quizzical expression. "You've always put one in that drawer, Luna."

"That's not true."

"Bebe…" I raise a brow and begin to tick off each place by wiggling one of her cute toes "…at my old penthouse, my parents' house, and yours. If you opened that drawer in particular after you've been around, there's a good chance you've moved it there or brought one with you."

"I—"

"Quit arguing and be a good patient." Turning the water off, I lean over and place a chaste kiss at the corner of her lips. "Stay put."

A nod is her response, but she doesn't question me when I walk out of the kitchen and toward the front door. There, I grab her breakfast, make sure the door is locked, and go straight for the magic drawer. Her eyes are on me the entire time, or more specifically, the bag in my hand, but I'm already grabbing the kit and turning back to her.

Then, there's a bit of trepidation as I place all of the items down beside her. "I should probably do this myself."

The "myself" has more to do with her dislike of pain and the one time I disinfected a cut by pouring alcohol straight into an open wound.

"Relax, Luna. This won't hurt."

"That's what you said last time when—" I silence her with a quick, harsh kiss as my mouth slants over hers, swallowing the gasp that escapes. This isn't slow or sweet; it's a claiming of those petal-soft lips, and a deep rumble builds in my chest when a soft mewl escapes from the back of her throat.

She gives in to my possessive need. To how my fingers wrap around the long strands of her hair, tipping her head back to my liking. The angle puts her at my mercy with her pretty little throat exposed, an expanse of skin that calls to me and I run my teeth down her chin and over the base.

"Fuck, Luna. Just fuck," I groan, licking her fragrant neck where her mouthwatering scent is the strongest. It's her and coconuts and this faint hint of lime that makes me throb against her cabinets. "You'll always be my biggest weakness and treasure. I love you more than my own life."

"This isn't taking care of my foot," she moans, the fingers of her left hand gripping my long-sleeved shirt right above where it's rolled at the elbow. It's pulling me closer. Holding me against her. "Maybe you should stop."

"I will." My teeth scrape across her collarbones. "I am."

"Please do."

"As you wish." Yet I don't move. Not yet. Instead, my hand caresses her leg from shin to thigh, gripping the firm flesh just shy of painful. "Right now."

Another nip and she lets out a sigh.

Another inch higher and the heat from her pussy sears me.

Another needy sound and I pull back, removing her grip on my shirt before grabbing the first-aid kit and opening it. Inside she has the basics and an addition that makes me chuckle.

"Not that funny, jerk." There's no real annoyance in her tone, though. The mirth is there and so is the bit of sparkle in her brown eyes that are looking at me with warmth. "You know I hate the alcohol wipes. They sting."

"So you decided to trade it for the smallest bottle of hydrogen peroxide I've ever seen?"

"Yes. No shame either." Luna's perfectly sculpted right brow rises; the look she's giving me would make a weaker man step back or fumble. Me, I like the challenge. The daring attitude. "It's painless and bubbles up to let me know I won't lose a limb. Win-win if you ask me."

Unscrewing the top of the bottle, I hold it over her injured foot before she can pull away. "I didn't, but I'll take your word for it."

"Jerk."

"More like Dr. Leon." Then I pour. She flinches a tiny bit and I raise my own brow, silently calling her out on the bullshit she spewed earlier. "Thought it didn't hurt?"

"Not as much," she spits through clenched teeth. "This time it did, though."

"Of course. It's a one-time thing." A little more of the hydrogen goes on the faintly bleeding wound. "Now, sit still and let me finish."

"Finish what?"

I don't answer her. Instead, I grab one of the cotton rounds inside of a small Ziplock bag and wipe the bit of blood still flowing. It's not a huge amount and the cut is as clean as can be. No glass or dirt and after drying it off, I open her antibiotic ointment, smearing a bit across the gash. It seals and no more drops of blood flow, letting me place a Band-Aid on.

The ones she has are...*entertaining*, to say the least.

SpongeBob. A lot of them. An obscene amount, and I grab one with the yellow sponge giving a cheesy grin to the wearer.

"There. All better." Lifting her foot out of the large farmhouse sink, I kiss the small bandaged cut before turning her to face me. Her legs go over the edge of the counter and I step between them. Then, we're face to face and I place a chaste peck to her lips. "How're you feeling, beautiful?"

"The truth?"

"Always."

"At peace for the first time in years."

Placing my forehead against hers, I close my eyes. "I've missed you too."

"Thiago, I'm not ready—"

"I know." Sliding my fingers from her calves to thighs, I grab one in each hand and easily lift her up. She wraps them around my waist, legs crossed at the ankles while I grab her breakfast with the hand not supporting her weight.

Her face burrows into my neck as I walk us out and I don't miss the tiny kiss she gives my neck. Pleasure rocks me at the simple gesture and my cock flexes against her heat, but neither of us comments on it.

We just enjoy the moment and then I hold her for a minute or two longer once I'm at the foot of her bed. Just standing with her in my arms is enough to get me by for the few days I'll be away.

Forty-fucking-eight hours of agonizing hell.

Bending at the waist, I place her on the mattress with the bag beside us. Once she's on, I point to the headboard. "Get situated while I take things out for you."

"I can do..." Luna trails off at the look I give her. Turning onto her hands and knees, the vixen crawls across the bed and it takes every bit of the near nonexistent strength I possess to keep me from following.

I grit my teeth.

I press down hard on my throbbing length to alleviate the pain.

Nothing works, and by the look on her face, the little brat knows exactly what she's doing to me.

"Shut it."

"I wasn't going to say anything."

"You just did."

"Can you feed me now?"

"One day soon you'll pay for that, beauty." Walking around the bed, I take my time and I also don't hide just how hard for her I am. Her eyes immediately drop and then widen before her small pink tongue makes an appearance. Right to left, my queen licks her bottom lip before taking the lush flesh between her teeth. "Eyes up here."

"Not apologizing." A hint of pink sweeps across her cheeks.

"Didn't ask you to." Opening the large plastic bag, I pull out a drink tray and the small box with her pastries. There are even a few toasted pieces of Cuban bread with butter and a pinch of salt still slightly warm inside of their aluminum foil wrapping. Everything is sealed and while the piping hot coffee kept everything warm, it's cooled enough to be drinkable. "Want me to grab you a plate?"

"Gimme."

"You'll get crumbs—"

"Clean later, eat now." As she says this, I pass over her salted caramel mocha latte. Her small hands wrap around the cup while I pull the comforter over her exposed legs. For my safety—sanity— not hers. "How is this the perfect temp?"

"Bought it hotter than hades so it'd be kid's temp by the time I got here. I remember your tricks."

She takes a sip, a small smile on her lips. "Good, because I really needed this."

"Glad I could offer you some comfort after a night of drinking."

"It was needed."

"That bad?"

"Memories, videotapes, and a visit from an ex will do that to a woman."

"I'm your always, not an ex." My phone vibrates inside my pocket and I pull it out, giving it a quick glance.

> Sir, just a reminder that Mr. Asher's plane is due to land soon. ~Miguel

"Everything okay?"

At her question, I pocket the device and nod. "Just have a meeting to attend." *Or several.*

"So soon?'

"Malcolm is flying in," I say, opening the box of pastries and placing them beside her on the bed. Her TV remote is also on the bed, but not within reach and I rectify that. "He needs to talk and said it was urgent."

"Be careful."

"Is that concern I detect in your tone?"

"Get out."

"You're adorable." Bending over, I tip her face up to mine with a finger and kiss her lips. A soft peck, and then I pull back. "Eat, relax, and then catch a nap. Be lazy, and I'll have dinner delivered tonight."

"That's not necessary—"

"I take care of mine. End of."

"But I'm..." she trails off, and we both know it's because she can't say the words.

"Not going to deny me." I can see the urge to do just that, to lie to me, but my queen remains silent instead. *Good girl.* "By the way, beautiful, Mom's expecting you this weekend. It's my welcome home and she wants the entire family there."

A flash of hurt crosses her features; I know being kept away hurt them both, but we need to start mending fences. She loves my mother and my mother adores her.

"I'm not sure that's a good idea. Not yet."

It's hard, but I hold back my amusement. I knew she'd say that. "She also sent a warning attached to that invite, babe, and if you're not ready by five on Saturday, she'll come pick you up herself."

Luna huffs, but there's no real anger there. "Maritza is more stubborn than you are."

"She is." Not going to refute that.

"What if you tell her I have plans with my parents?" At my incredulous look, her shoulders slump. "Never mind. That's a shit excuse and she'll never buy it."

"Exactly." It's hard, but I hold back a smirk. "I'll be here at four-thirty. Be ready."

"I'll drive myself and Natasha will be coming with me."

"I'll pick you up and Natasha can drive herself."

"Be reasonable!"

"Be happy that I'm not kidnapping you now and dragging you everywhere with me. I'm more than impatient to have you back where you belong. With me. With our family." Another kiss, I steal a quesito pastry, and then I'm walking out of the room. Her offended yell follows me out of her sanctuary and then apartment door. My beauty is still as stingy with her sweets now as I remembered, and I adore her all the more for it.

My Luna is hurt, but there. She's still the same girl I fell in love with.

Chapter 12
THIAGO

"**H**E'LL BE LANDING soon, sir," Miguel says as I slip into the all-black SUV waiting for me outside of Luna's building. Leaving her again this soon isn't something I want, but I understand her need for space. To wrap her head around the truth, and while the choices I made cut deep, I always knew that I'd be back for her.

Nothing could keep me from taking care of her, and now that I'm free, I'll make her my wife.

"How soon?"

"ETA is thirty."

"Then I want to be walking inside in fifteen." Looking outside my window, I take in the blue waters glistening between two buildings as he pulls away from the curb. How the waves crash upon the rock formation that serves as a wall, leaving behind a fine sea mist in the area that infiltrates the senses and gives you a sense of calm that's fraudulent. The ocean isn't to be trusted.

It's volatile and unpredictable and a silent killer.

Moreover, it reminds me of the beautiful woman I left stewing in her emotions; peaceful yet dangerous. Luna is my perfect storm.

Her soft face this morning after a drunken trip down memory lane made me remember nights out partying in the past.

The warm smile she naturally gifted me as I cleaned the small cut made my heart thump.

The way she burrowed her face into my neck, admitting in her own way that she missed me—made my cock throb.

"And will we be entering from the back entrance or...?" His question pulls me from my thoughts, and I meet his eyes in the rearview mirror. He knows where my mind is. He knows *her*.

I smirk, brow raised. "The front. I'm not hiding."

"I'll make the necessary arrangements." We're at a red light near the entrance to I-95 and he pulls out his phone, sending out a quick message before placing the device inside the vehicle's cup holder. A ping comes through a second later and he spares the screen no more than a glance before nodding. "No traffic and an announcement has been made. Just walk through."

"Thank you, old man." A car pulls up alongside us and the driver's completely unaware of my being. Maybe it's idiocy. Carelessness. Or maybe it's the conversation he's having with a woman, Mrs. Senot herself, and it seems heated. His hand slams down on the steering wheel while she frowns, eyes flicking around to make sure no one's taken notice of Antonio's hostile, emotional state.

However, my father-in-law is unmistakable in his pompous suit, now waving a hand in the air as the light turns green and Miguel places his foot on the accelerator. And that's when his face turns, and he notices my driver. He knows Miguel and at once turns a bit further in his driver side seat to look into the back windows that will never show my identity. The tints won't allow it, and even though I'm tempted to lower my window and extend a greeting, I just watch his minor freak-out. *Guilty is a very ugly color, old man.*

"My pleasure, kid." At Miguel's response, I turn my attention back to him. He's the only one outside of my parents that can call me that, and it's because I see him as family. Not that he would in front of anyone; he lives by a code of respect. The man's worked for us long enough and has been more than loyal; I owe him. It's because of him that my mother is alive and without a single scratch. Miguel maneuvered them away, broke through an abandoned building with the front of her armored vehicle before taking a swift right that knocked Ismael off his bike while knocking him unconscious. "It's good to have you home. We've all missed you and Luna."

"Miguel, what you've done for—"

"I'd die for the Leons." I give him a nod because words aren't needed. I know where he stands. I trust him. Miguel focuses on the drive while I dissect the reason for the visitor touching down in my city within the half hour.

The world and its inhabitants revolve around one sole purpose: making money. It's the reason why people get out of bed, go to work, kill a few people, and then lay their heads down at night with a few extra zeros in their accounts. It's why men like me exist.

Illegal business practices aren't abnormal. They are the *norm* so many fail to see.

Greed.

Sex.

Drugs.

They go hand in hand and play inside the most out-in-the-open playgrounds. Criminals don't hide. Not anymore.

Instead, we move in social circles where excess is common and discretion is key. We own legitimate ventures and filter our *dirty* funds through them. It's a simple concept, one that my visitor is all too familiar with.

Malcolm Asher takes, launders, and repeats without failure to produce perfectly accounted-for wealth. Through a few well-played moves, he turned our side ventures into multiple avenues to clean our illegal gains. Any business qualifies as long as you move cash, high quantities, and through a few family-style Cuban restaurants, three bars, real-estate in lower income areas, and a laundromat; we have more than enough.

He's a friend, dangerous, and someone I treat like family.

Someone who watches my interest with a certain piece-of-shit asshole that tried to steal from me while I was in jail—that I plan to dispose of after I deal with more immediate issues.

I think he's planning on doing that himself, and I wouldn't complain if the price is right.

"Thiago, we're here."

"I'm going in alone." Inside the gift box Ivan had for me were extra magazines for my Ruger SR9, my new iPhone, and a pack of gum. I appreciated all three, and before opening the door, I tuck my gun into the waistband of my pants and pocket an extra clip. "Stay close. I'll call."

"Of course." The SUV pulls away a few seconds after I exit, blending in with the light-for-a-weekday traffic.

Then, I walk through the main doors without pause.

No one stops me or asks questions, but they all look. Those who live here know me, fear my last name, and they should. So when they move to step out of my way, I smirk. When they rush to tell tourists to move, I give a nod.

Respect is something earned, and I appreciate those with enough common sense to not piss off a killer.

"Welcome back, Mr. De Leon." Ninette says as I approach the TSA checkpoint. She's a friend of my mother's, and one hard-ass old lady. They went to school together in Cuba, and both families fled with the Mariel. "We missed you."

I'm smiling at her, and once close, I give her a hug. The woman is like my aunt and I've missed her too. "You okay? Treatment going as planned?"

"Not leaving this earth yet, Thiago." She pulls back and cups my chin, her eyes watery. "The devil isn't ready for me yet. Thinks I'm too mouthy."

At her response, a chuckle escapes. "Is that why Miguel hasn't put a ring on it? You whine too much?"

She smacks my arm. "Brat."

"And yet you still love me?"

All amusement drops from her face then, and before I can ask what's wrong, she's hugging me again. Tightly. Ninette burrows her face into my chest, but I can still make out her muffled words loud and clear. "Those responsible don't deserve to live, Thiago."

Giving her a final squeeze, I put my mouth close to her temple. "They'll get no mercy from me."

"Good." Righting herself, she discreetly wipes her cheeks before signaling for me to pass. "Go through. There's a table waiting for you at The Clover.

Bending a bit, I kiss her forehead and walk through the TSA employees only entrance. Those in line murmur and other agents look at me, but I make it to an empty monorail cart without further delay.

Malcolm hasn't landed but will do so shortly, and a few minutes after I reach the terminal bar, I spot him. He's not alone, but Carmelo and two others stay a few steps behind, the former carrying something in his hand.

His eyes meet mine and he enters the establishment, bypassing the hostess who's all too eager to assist.

"I'm not surprised by your call," I say with a smirk, amused by the look of disappointment on the girl's face. That, and I have an inkling as to why the sudden visit, because men in our position are only motivated by two very powerful reasons:

Money.

A woman.

Not that I call him out on this. Instead, I raise a brow and wait.

"Good. Then you know why I'm here." Malcolm extends a hand, and when I grab it, he pulls me out of my chair and into a man hug. "Happy to see you out, Rivera. That was a shit case and setup."

"I know." Nodding, I give him a tight squeeze and let go, taking my seat once again. There's no point in correcting my full last name: my father is De Leon, I'm Rivera, and Ivan is Junior to them. "It's cost me something far more valuable than time."

A waiter stops by then with two pints of stout and menus, but I wave him off. I won't be here for long. He bumps into Carmelo as he scurries off, and I'm not surprised by Malcolm's man slipping him a few bills to stay away.

"Then I won't take any more of it." Malcolm holds a hand up and Carmelo gives him a folder. It's a quick transaction, and then he's gone. Back to his post as security with the other two who stayed outside.

"I want to liquidate their debt. The Fosters will owe me." His tone is one of finality, and I'm half tempted to knock him down a peg. The only thing that stops me is our friendship.

I've known him for years, and he's not a man to react without reason. Whatever this is about has to be important.

"Why?"

At my question, he slides the folder over. "Open it."

And I do, ire overtaking my senses. My eyes harden. "That poor girl is innocent," I hiss out. "She's nothing like them."

"She's mine." At his words, my eyes snap to his and I see so much of myself in him at that moment. Malcolm might be older, but that's the reaction of a man protecting what's his. "Their lives will end by my hands. Agree or don't, Thiago, it makes no difference. This is a courtesy visit because of our friendship, but my compliance with our agreement died the very minute they touched her."

I'd kill anyone that touched my Luna. And it's that thought that keeps me from having a reaction of my own. This isn't Chicago where he is feared. Malcolm is in my playground, but the motives behind the words are the bruises on London's face in these photos.

I accept that without a single hesitation.

I understand him because if it were me, I'd have killed them already and just delivered the heads.

"Fuck the money." I sit back, my large frame causing the back of the chair to protest. My hands are clenching and jaw ticking. "Keep it, burn it...donate it for all I care."

"Then what do you want in exchange?" he asks, mimicking my position. For a moment I watch him. Unwavering. Calculating. "If not money...?"

"I'll be there to witness." Not up for negotiation.

"Done."

"Good." I stand then and Malcolm follows, walking out after tossing a few more bills to cover the untouched drinks and their discretion. "Are you heading back home or staying in Miami for a few days?"

"My flight leaves in half an hour."

"Mom will be sad she missed you." I chuckle, scratching my jaw. "She's on party-planning crazy mode."

"Wish I could, but London needs me." He does look a bit contrite; the man loves my mom's pernil and congri with yuca. She makes the dishes for him every visit without fail.

"Say no more. Next time." I give him a slap on the back, but my eyes narrow on the next breath. London doesn't need more bullshit thrown at her. "Be good to her, Asher. Or I'll shoot you myself."

He pulls back, matching my smirk. "Are you going after Luna?"

"I am." *I already have.* My phone beeps then and I pull it out, reading a text from Ivan.

Senot Junior just arrived at Luna's with flowers.
Red roses at that. ~Little Bro

A dark cloud overtakes my senses and the plastic in my hand groans under the pressure of my hold. "Call me when you're ready to proceed." It's a barely contained snarl, tinged with the storm brewing within.

Malcolm's smile drops, concern overtaking his features. "You okay?"

"Just have a girl to reclaim and a motherfucker to kill."

Chapter 13
LUNA

AND THEN HE'S gone again, leaving me a confused, hungover ball of a mess.

When I opened the door earlier, I thought it was Nat or my mother, both of which pestered me all day yesterday for similar reasons. One, demanding to know how our tumultuous reunion went —to know if I cursed him out or kicked him in the balls—while the other all but warned me to not see him again.

Little do they know I did neither.

I gave in to Thiago's touch like a whore who hasn't seen a man in a decade. Like an addict feigning for his next hit.

Hungry.

Desperate.

Almost begging.

It's why I've avoided them. It's also why I mistook Thiago for them.

I'm still struggling with the reality that he's back.

The front door slams shut behind him and I close my eyes, taking in the emotions that having him close again evokes. There's love and butterflies and worst of all…fear.

Not of him per se, but the hurt being an *us* could bring.

I hate him for putting me in this position to begin with, because had he spoken to me—explained the situation—we wouldn't be caught up in this mess. Waiting for him would've never been an issue; my trust in him before that day had been unbreakable.

Now, though, I'm not sure how to feel.

Why was it so easy for me to believe the worst? Why did I fall for that bull crap so easily?

"This is such a mess," I whisper to the empty room and do something that's both equally stupid and heartwarming. Grabbing the remote from beside me, I press the play button like I did last night and scoot down a bit to get comfortable.

A few seconds later the TV flickers and we appear on the screen. We're younger, a year or two at the most after meeting, and laughing at something Natasha is saying on the other side of the camera. His arm is thrown over my shoulder while holding me close; he's chuckling into the side of my head after one of his baseball games.

One where the winning home run was his.

Where the city's dark prince dedicated the moment to his beauty.

On the screen I'm wearing one of his shirts while he looks handsome in the team uniform; the name De Leon and the number twenty-four on both our torsos in a large and bold font. Moreover, it's the sight of us happy and carefree that pushed me toward drink number six or ten late last night.

I lost track after a while.

Going through family videos and watching us grow up together —cheer for the other during important milestones—hit me hard in the chest. I ached. I cried. I cursed.

More so when we were so close to having it all before it was snatched away.

The phone beside me vibrates and I look over, grimacing when my father's name flashes across the screen. He wants the same as my mother, more so, and I have no desire to speak with either of them and fight. It's just not worth it.

> Answer your phone, Luna. ~Dad

> Quit avoiding me. I will show up at your apartment. ~Dad

My reply is quick and the same one I've given every time he tries to communicate. He's not the same man that raised me, his position here in Miami has gone to his head, and I'm only his daughter when he wants something.

> Can't. I'm washing my hair. ~Luna

> Call me back, child. We need to talk. ~Dad

> Sure... ~Luna

Maybe next year? Instead, I exit that video and go back to the file with the name Mrs. De Leon on it. There, I click on the last video which was from our trip to the Dominican Republic five months before his initial arrest. It starts before takeoff, just the two of us, and he's getting situated in his seat while I'm smiling into my new video camera, the one he'd given me the night before for my birthday.

People continue to pass by us in our first-class seats. Some look, but most avoid eye contact while the twenty-five-year-old heir of the De Leon dynasty looks at me with equal parts hunger and adoration.

With his unfiltered love, my heart pitter patters now like it did then, and more so when he turns my face to meet his lips.

Bringing a hand to my mouth, I touch the same abused flesh that still tingles from his earlier kisses. His taste lingers. His masculine scent surrounds me.

"How do I let him go?" The answer to that is that I don't think I ever can.

A deep and tired sigh escapes me at that large tidbit of truth, and I fast forward the movie. Now, we're at the hotel that same evening, walking down the privately owned beach belonging to the resort so I can catch the moonlit sky and the waves crashing upon the shore.

That trip had been my heaven, a much-needed recharge after an exhausting semester of college, and immediately I'm transported back to that night.

My excited ramblings make him laugh as we make our way to the shore. There's minimal lighting, the moon and stars guiding us down the private path, and only once we cross onto the sand do I stop. Miles of gorgeous beach stretch out on either side of us while I take it all in: the salty breeze, the soothing sound of waves crashing, and the warmth of the muscled body that steps behind me, his mouth at my ear.

A shiver rushes down my spine and a small gasp leaves my throat; I almost drop my camera.

Thiago's quick hand snatches it mid-air while chuckling. We're not in the shot, and I'm not going to stop it from recording the conversation. "Careful, baby girl." He hands it back, bringing it over my right eye. "I want to explore the functions later tonight and can't do that if it's full of sand."

"What do you have in mind?" My hands shake from his proximity as I take the small device, the picture on the screen jerky and out of focus. There's the water and dark endless sky, but you can't quite make out the details, and yet at that moment, I'm standing there with him and nothing else matters.

The palpable need is burning bright, our love stronger than ever.

"I want you to ride my cock out on the balcony with the tropical view as a backdrop." It leaves him on a groan, a rough exhale against my neck. He nips at the skin there between words, licking the tender flesh afterward. *"I want to capture you falling helplessly—see my little cock slut give in to my demands and then cry out with a need so desperate to come that you give in to the delirium. Crazy beautiful and accepting of every touch and kiss, I want to record your fall as I pull each orgasm from your body."*

"Thiago," I whimper, the camera shaking from the trembling in my body. *"Can we go back now?"*

A deep laugh rumbles through his chest. *"Patience, beautiful. Let's get your footage first."*

"You always put me first." My voice is low, and I'm nearly languid in his hold. How he does this to me I'll never understand. One minute I'm desperate to feel him between my thighs, taking me, and the next I'm a lovesick, swooning mess. He's my devil. My weakness. The best thing that's ever happened to me. *"Thank you so much for bringing me here."*

"I'd do anything to see a smile grace your lips, my queen. Anything to make you happy." His lips skim down my temple and toward my cheek, and when he pauses to breathe me in, goose bumps rise. I feel his grin against my skin. *"Besides, I have a payment plan already set up for you. I even have the perfect outfit for you to wear while servicing my needs."*

"Jerk!" I'm not mad, and he knows it. There's no hiding my own smile as I smack his arm.

"Your jerk."

"And that's all I'll ever need." It's breathy and a bit whiny as he lavishes my throat with open-mouthed kisses. *"Just you."*

"Keep talking like that and we'll get married before leaving the island." The seriousness in his tone causes my head to tilt in order to give him better access and a rush of wetness to ruin my panties. *"The part of your family I like is already here, bebe, and we can turn the reunion into a wedding without much difficulty."*

"Don't tempt me."

"I'm not waiting forever to make it official." More kisses before he runs the tip of his tongue back to my ear and exhales. It's a rough one. One that tells me he's already planning. In his head, our nuptials are a done deal.

Turning in his arms, I stand on the tips of my toes so I can reach his lips. A mouth that's smirking down at me while those hazel eyes, the brightest shade of honey, show his true emotions.

He's happy. In love. Hungry for me.

"I love you, Thiago."

"You mean everything to me, Luna."

"And someday soon, I'll wear a pretty white dress and walk down the aisle toward you. I want to be tied to you, Mr. De Leon, in every way humanly possible. To be your wife."

"I approve of this plan. You have until the end of the year to be my wife." His mouth lowers to mine under the Dominican sky before I can give him a smart-ass retort about putting a ring on it.

Then everything changed. Drastically. Without warning.

One minute we were the perfect couple, and then...*nothing*.

But as I watch this video—take in every single second and revisit with my love—one of the many holes left behind by his absence begins to heal. The pain is less. The hollowness doesn't feel as suffocating.

There's no rush or worry as we embrace, we're taking our time and while all you see on the large screen is the sand or the occasional tan flesh of his arms and our feet, the love between us is palpable. We're not in most of the shots, and it's so out of focus most people would say it's crap, but to me it's a prized possession.

Knock. Knock. Knock.

The sudden banging on my door pulls me from my thoughts and I pause the video. The person at the door is a bit impatient and I look over at the clock on my nightstand, which reads a little past noon.

I'm not expecting anyone at the moment and once again leave the sanctity of my bed, stumbling over a small gift that I know for a fact wasn't there before.

"He's killing me," I mutter under my breath, annoyed and excited all in the same breath. Fingering the small bow around the palm-sized box, I pull on one end when there's another set of hard knocks. "The hell?"

Determined to not make the same mistake again, I hobble over to my armoire, careful not to reopen my cut, and open the third drawer where I keep my workout clothes. At the very top sits a pair of purple yoga pants and a black tank top with a built-in-bra that I recently purchased, and I whip off *his* old shirt before shimmying into my clothes and making sure everything is in its rightful place.

I'm not wearing underwear, and whoever is on the other side of my door impatiently knocking doesn't need a show.

"I'm coming," I yell out, and the insistent thumping stops. "At least they have common sense." Rolling my eyes, I stand against the solid wooden door and look through the peephole. There's a shadow there, definitely male by the size of its silhouette, but I can't make out just who it is. I also know it's not Thiago since our agreement stood for this Saturday.

An entrance table near me has a small drawer that's just the right size to conceal my Glock, and I step over to it slowly without making much noise. Slowly, I pull it open and take out my piece, check the safety, and then do what most women wouldn't do in my position.

On the count of ten, I unlock my door and then step back, pointing my firearm straight at the entrance. "Come in."

Within the span of four heartbeats, the knob begins to turn and the door is pushed open, revealing a very confused man holding a large bouquet of red roses. "Luna, what the?"

"Claudio, what are you doing here?" I lower my gun and without taking my eyes off his, put the safety back in place. I'm not putting it away—showing—anyone where I hide my weapons—but I do take precautions, especially when I see how nervous it makes him.

I'm not a fan of the man, but I hold no ill will toward him as of yet. He's just creepy. An ass kisser. Someone that, unfortunately, I've had to be courteous to over the years when at a family function and his family is present. Or while attending some bull-crap reception for the city as a favor to my father when we're on speaking terms.

His brown eyes watch my hand where the Glock is firmly in my grip. "I just thought you'd need some cheering up with *you know who's* recent release."

"That's very thoughtful of you, but I'm more than okay."

For the first time since opening the door to a weapon being aimed at him, his eyes snap to mine. "Are you sure? My father and yours said that—"

"Our fathers needs to learn how to mind his business." *And watch his back, because if I find out he's behind Thiago's arrest, I'll kill him myself. Him, and anyone else involved.* There's a tick of his jaw at my words; he doesn't like my unapologetic response, and I shrug. "Are those for me?"

"Yes." Another tick as he hands them over, his fingers lingering a bit longer than necessary against the one not holding my gun. "Can I come in?"

"Sure." My smile is politely forced, and had he not been a man so full of himself, Claudio would see this. But then again, what can you expect from an over-privileged kid whose father's political career has given him a veil to hide behind, and that alone makes his common South Florida good looks unattractive. "Please take a seat while I put these in water."

"Thank you. Some coffee would be nice as well."

The urge to roll my eyes is strong, but I keep a game face like a true champ. "Sorry. I'm all out." I even add an apologetic shrug. "Need to go grocery shopping. My maid refuses to do so for me."

"Good help is hard to find," he says, his expression one of complete understanding, and I bristle internally. My sarcasm has gone completely over his head, and that response is generic at best. It's what people who undervalue their employees or the working force of the country like to say in order to disguise their greed and asshole mentality. "I have a girl that could probably help you once a week if you're interested. She picks up my laundry, groceries, and details my car."

Silently, I ask the Lord to give me strength. I'm tired, moody, and Thiago leaving me a bit horny doesn't help. Because while I might not like my papi at the moment, whoever set him up has to pay, and I will gladly help us get the retribution we deserve.

Moreover, my first opportunity to do so is now. Claudio likes to talk an awful lot and could share something useful. Something to help put the timeline or direction of these puzzle pieces in order.

If they're involved, he's too cocky not to gloat if I goad him just right. I've avoided all talk of Thiago for years, and today that ends. I'm not wasting any more time, especially since it's his mother's guard who ordered the hit.

Why, and under whose direction?

"Give me a moment," I say instead while holding out the flowers. "Let me fix this."

"A glass of water is fine, too."

"Sure. Coming right up." Turning toward the kitchen, I head for the sink and place my gun atop the counter. There, I make a show of opening the faucet and letting the water run to just the right temperature while thinking of ways to bring up the topic of my ex without being too obvious. That, and come up with a list of viable reasons as to why he needs to go immediately after.

So far, I have a stomach virus or contagious rash of some kind at the top of my list.

The latter of the two will need some name made up for it, but it shouldn't be too hard. I'm more than positive that keeping up with medical terms for diagnosis isn't something he does.

"Where to put these?" I remember there's a small vase inside the cabinet below and to the left of me, and I bend to grab it while muttering a low curse under my breath. This visit could've happened at any other time and I would've been appreciative. Prepared. Entertaining anyone is the last thing I want to do, especially when I think about the video on pause inside my room.

Thiago did make good on his promise on the beach that night. He made me cry out in a prayer to his name over and over again. *Get it together, woman. Now is not the time.*

"Easier said than done." Opening the wrappings, I find some old leaves, dying stems, and a few rubber bands holding the bouquet together. I'm wondering where he bought these. They don't seem all that fresh, and I'll have to cut a good chunk off the bottom to keep up the pretenses before putting them in water. *So much work for something that'll just go in the garbage once he leaves.* Turning to grab my garbage bin from under the opposite counter, I'm stopped in my tracks when I find Claudio at the entrance watching me. "Is there something you need?"

He shakes his head, smirking at me. "Just enjoying the view."

Standing back up, I narrow my eyes. "Don't start."

For years my father has tried to push me toward him, talking him up at every opportunity and as a dig at the De Leons. Not that it ever fazed Thiago. He knows where I've always stood—that I don't find this man-child the least bit attractive—and following my father's wishes to gain approval isn't something I care for.

Claudio's mouth goes from lazy smirk to a thin line. Exasperation marring his features. "When are you going to give me a chance, Luna? I've been patient and—"

"I wouldn't finish that if I were you."

"Why not? We could be so good together."

"Leave."

Men suffer from one particular issue that becomes a downfall in most cases. Their egos are fragile. Unable to handle rejection without spewing vitriol back to appease their own wounds. This will be one of those cases.

I can see it.

The change in his demeanor. The harsh breathing and hateful retort brewing.

"Stop being stubborn and proud for one second. Thiago isn't coming back for you." The way he spits out his name, the venom coating each letter, makes me angry—furious that the idiot considers himself above him, but I merely raise a brow. This is what I'll need; a careless moment from him. "What you had is done and soon enough, he'll find himself a new plaything. That's what all men like him do. They use and then discard."

"Is that so?" My tone is mocking as I drop the bouquet, not caring where it falls, my arms crossing over my chest. "Do fill me in on how men like him work. This is riveting stuff."

"He'll do it again." It's a barely contained snarl, lips curling over his teeth. "You should be thanking his enemies for their prayers."

"Prayers? What prayers?" *Keep talking, idiot. Confirm what Thiago said.* "What does that even mean?"

"It means God listened, and those with the means to do so helped expedite that excrement of a family's downfall."

"Get out," I hiss out through clenched teeth, my fury rising to the surface in a volcanic rush, and I take the few steps between us to jam my finger in his chest. He staggers a bit, his face contorting, but the pain registers on my next intake of breath and I'm the one jumping back. "*Fuck.*"

It's a mistake. Because in my tumultuous ire, I didn't pay attention to the small box there.

Another box with a bow. Another box with a bow and sharp corners that has dug itself into my cut and at once, it reopens. Blood rushes to the surface, saturating the bandages Thiago put in place for me, dripping onto the floor below. I'm now hobbling, with my foot raised high as I curse my luck and watch the jerk before me grin.

Not a normal smile. This one is creepy, and I move back when his hand reaches out for me. "Let me help you with that."

"No."

"Luna, you need—"

"I'll give you exactly thirty seconds to walk out this door before I shoot."

Chapter 14
LUNA

OUR EYES SNAP toward the magnificent force standing a few feet from Claudio's back. His Ruger's raised and pointing straight at the now paling man, cocked and ready to shoot without a single shred of remorse in his eyes. "Ten, eleven...fourteen."

"Luna, are you just going to let him—"

"Seventeen, eighteen," I count for Thiago and Claudio's eyes narrow, the hate in them clear as day to see. "Go, and don't come back. Spare yourself the embarrassment."

"This isn't over," he spits out and turns, running into a hard wall the size of a man who is breathing harshly and glaring. "Excuse me."

"Of course." Claudio fixes his tie and then makes to walk around a motionless Thiago. He makes it a step past, just a single one, when Leon speaks again, causing Claudio to look back. "But before you go, I have a message for your father."

"My father doesn't have time for...fuck!" Without warning, Thiago brings the butt of the gun across Claudio's face, breaking his nose and more than likely his cheekbone. A deep gash opens across his face and he screams, a pitiful sound that hurts my ears. His skin becomes saturated by the crimson gushing from the cut; his clothes are also ruined. Not that it deters the mob boss. Instead, he gets close to the whimpering fool and whispers a parting threat that sends a chill through my bones. "This is just a hello from me, Jr. Just a friendly reminder to stay in your lane and keep those putrid eyes off what's mine. Do that, and you'll avoid a lengthier conversation. Understood?"

"Yes." It's low and meek.

"Now, as for your father..." Thiago lifts his gun once more, this time placing the barrel right under his chin while turning them sideways. So I can see. So that a large open wall is their background, and I cock my head to the side. *What is he doing?* He pulls the trigger, and nothing comes out. Does it again, and I think Claudio is close to pissing himself.

"Leon, let him go. Please don't—" The heated stare he sends me shuts me up. It's not anger in his eyes, but more of an animalistic hunger that almost pulls a low moan from me.

There's a smirk on his lips when he turns to look at the man he's holding. He's aware of how much of a turn-on seeing his devilish side is, and even after all these years, it still has the same effect. My skin erupts in goose bumps and my thighs clench—heart races. "Let him know I'll be dropping by his office this upcoming week and will come bearing gifts. The largest one in particular will leave him speechless."

Claudio hasn't realized that Thiago moved the gun just enough out of the way, that when he pulls the trigger, the bullet lodges itself into a wall instead of his head. Nothing registers, and the look of pure terror on his face will forever be etched into my mind. Eyes wide and with a scream caught in his throat, I don't think he's breathing, and it isn't until Thiago taps his chin with the hot metal that he reacts.

Without looking my way, he rushes out the door without closing it.

Something that Thiago remedies quickly after. I count to ten, and the entrance slams shut and the lock is engaged.

Another few seconds pass, and he's back inside the room. It's just the two of us.

The tension is palpable. Our hunger near demonic.

I breathe in and it's his scent that surrounds me once again. That unique scent of man and woods with just the right hint of citrus that makes me react. On my next inhale, my body moves without permission and I launch myself into his arms.

I kiss him.

There's no pause or remembering what brought us here or even asking every single *why* question that floats through my mind. Instead, I give in to my needs without a single care as to the repercussions.

He catches me easily, devouring my mouth as I give in to my need. Forget the bloody cut on my foot or the reason why I shouldn't —right now none of that matters.

Not a damn thing.

All I can focus on is his taste and the feel of him pressing against me. How he came into my home like an angry beast and showed Claudio out.

How he told him that no matter what…

I. Am. His.

And I'm almost ashamed to admit how much that affected me. I needed to hear that even if I'm not ready to get back to the us we once were.

"Motherfuck, beauty," he growls, hands splayed across each asscheek and squeezing when I nibble on his bottom lip. "I need you. Let me feel you."

He's hard against me. Throbbing.

And I gyrate, giving myself a taste of what I can't deny wanting.

My eyes roll back, that small thrust of my hips adding pressure against my clit, and a rush of wetness soaks my yoga pants, the thin material doing a poor job of separating us.

I feel him. His thickness. His heat.

It helps to remind me of something I've missed all these years and my mouth waters.

Thiago is delicious from head to toe and the silkiness of his cock on my tongue is orgasmic in itself.

He grunts as I run myself over his cloth-covered length, fingertips digging into my skin. "Behave. I'm trying to give you the time you asked for."

"I'm going to need you to break that promise..." my mouth trails open-mouthed kisses across his chin and then lower over to his Adam's apple "...just for a little while. Just a quick. Hard. Ride." I punctuate each word with a flick of my tongue over his skin, a reminder of what I've done to his swollen, reddish-purple head before taking him down my throat.

No gag reflexes. Something we discovered the first time I gave him a blow job.

"*Fuck*, you're dangerous." Not a complaint, and a second or two later we're moving toward my living room where he lowers me to the ground. He takes a step back. Just one, and I hate it. "Are you sure, Luna? I'm going to need you to say you want this."

I don't answer. Instead, I give him my back and find the large sectional a few feet from me, the armrest being what's closest. His heated stare follows me as I walk to it and pause. The heat of his hunger licks at my flesh.

My skin prickles with excitement. My heart flutters with emotions I'm not ready to visit.

So I give in to my need without pause or thought.

Bending at the waist, I bite my lip to hold back a grin when he groans. My hips shimmy and I dip a finger beneath the waistline of my pants, lowering them slowly, revealing the curves he's worshipped since we were teens.

His low *son of a bitch* sends a thrill of excitement through my small frame and goose bumps rise. A shiver rocks me, his name tumbles past my lips, and then his hands find their home as he grips my hips.

His hold is strong. Fingers digging in to the point of pain, and I welcome the sting because it proves he's really here. With me.

"Finish lowering them, beauty. All the way to your ankles." One hand releases its hold, while the other bends me forward. All the way until my cheek rests against the leather and my pants fall to the floor.

Without panties, I'm easy access. Open for him.

Lifting my face a bit, I look back and take in his reaction. Take in the way his eyes roam down my body and he licks his lips.

"Like what you see?"

"You've always been my definition of perfection." His other hand is behind me, palming a cheek before coming down on a single hard smack. It stings, but I welcome the bite. Welcome the heat that follows and the wetness that pools at my entrance as he undoes his belt and lets it fall to the floor.

That clang makes me bite my lip, eyes on his. I follow his every movement, count the seconds that it takes for Thiago to pop the button of his slacks and then lower his zipper.

He's taking his time. Savoring my need.

And I'm soaked for him.

I'm desperate to feel him inside.

My eyes close as I shake. I'm trying to calm down—to breathe through this manic yearning burning my veins.

Another smack. Then another.

"Please," I whimper, eyes snapping open.

"Keep them on me, bebe." He alternates between the two cheeks and then skims his finger lower where he encounters my wetness. His hum of approval makes me clench. The lone finger he dips inside makes me moan.

But nothing excites me more than the feel of his blunt head parting my folds, spreading my wetness, before snapping his hips forward. One swift thrust and he's buried to the hilt, my walls gripping him tight.

"Can't go slow, Luna. Forgive me."

"Thiago, I want...*fuck*!" It's a scream as pleasure and pain crash into each other, leaving me gasping for breath. I feel every ridge of his cock—every throb as he pulls out and slams back in without pause. His rhythm is near punishing, fast and hard and *oh so good* that my toes curl.

Long fingers grip around my dark hair, wrapping the strands around his fist. One harsh tug and my back arches, head tipping back to an almost uncomfortable angle.

"Thank you." I know why he says that. I can feel it in his touch. The reverent way his lips press against the tattoo in his honor at the back of my neck. Up until now he hasn't seen it, but now it's staring at him in the face.

Thiago doesn't pause his strokes—the fast pace in which he rides me—while mouthing the words *I love you* against my skin. Each syllable, his tight hold, marking me as his.

Those deep strokes cement my truth; I'm his girl, his future, and his willing whore.

My lips part but no sounds come out as he bends his knee a bit, changing the angle. He's right there, pressing against the one spot that causes my eyes to roll back and hips to buck in desperation. I'm tightening around him. I can feel my walls try and to pull him in deeper.

"You feel so good, mami. So tight and wet...like heaven." The hand at my hip slips between my body and the couch, his fingers rubbing tight circles where I'm most sensitive. Two more strokes and I'm standing at that precipice, teetering on an orgasm so strong my eyes tear up.

"Please." It leaves me on a shaky whimper, my hips pushing back against his. The *slap slap slap* of our skin is loud, and beads of sweat roll down my back. "Need more."

"Give it to me. Let me feel...*fuck*, yes...again." His hips push harder, pistoning at a pace that leaves me on the tip of my toes and fingers digging into the armrest. "Come on my cock, Luna. Mark me."

That's it.

Two words and I'm thrown over the edge. My moans are loud and yet, even at my highest peak, I hear his accompanying grunt a few seconds later. The sounds of his pleasure break me all over again, and I clench around him as another wave of bliss rocks through me.

I'm left gasping and sweaty and completely sated. I'm left accepting that no matter where life leads us, I'll always end up right here. Beneath him. Reveling in his touch.

It takes a while for my heart to stop racing and for the shaking of my limbs to cease, but when they do, reality sets in and I can't stop the words from escaping. "How do I forget, Thiago. How do I let the anger go?"

He doesn't answer right away. Instead he pulls up his pants, leaving them open at the waist and then pulls me to stand with my back against his chest. His warmth seeps into my skin, and it's a balm to my soul. His lips press against his tattoo on my neck and I sigh.

"I know this isn't easy, Luna." Thiago's voice is softer now than I've ever heard it. It's a mixture of apologetic and full of regret while keeping that raspy quality I find sexy. "I'm not expecting you to forgive me or let this go overnight, but I will tell you that I'm not willing to back down or let us end. We will never have an expiration date nor go our separate ways, beautiful. Not now. Not ever."

"So then you are *expecting* me to just forgive and forget," I accuse, turning in his arms and jamming my finger into his chest. "Be honest. Admit it."

There's a tsk that comes from the back of his throat and my eyes meet his. "Nothing in life is easy, and what's worth fighting for is always hard." Strong hands cup my face, and Thiago's thumbs caresses my cheeks. His face is so close, and yet, he doesn't move to kiss me. I'm both thankful and full of denial that it's exactly what I need. "All I need from you is to believe that I'll fight for you. For us."

"I know you will." My indignation evaporates at those words and I melt into his touch. "You're more stubborn than I am."

A ghost of a smile crosses his features before they harden once more. Not in anger, but in determination. "If you asked me to, Luna, I'd burn the world to ashes if it meant I have your heart again." My eyes close at the heaviness—truth—in his words. They fill my heart with joy and on the same breath, I hate that we're here to begin with. That life threw us into this messed-up loop. "I'm sorry I hurt you. Sorrier than you'll ever begin to comprehend, but I'll make this up to you. As God is my witness, I will earn your forgiveness through actions, and in the meantime, I'll just have to wait for you to catch up."

Chapter 15
THIAGO

THE SOUND OF voices rumbling meets my ears as I come to a stop a few feet from a large room on the top floor of our transport vessel. We're off the coast of Miami, back out on international water, and the people on the other side of this metal door are awaiting my entrance.

They're loud, some throwing out a curse or two in Spanish while they argue over the Caribbean Series that Cuba lost back in February to Panama. Ironic since this large ship belongs to a diplomat from there. At least, that's what the United States government chooses to believe.

From beside me, I catch Ivan shake his head at the ridiculousness and I roll my eyes in silent response before pocketing my phone after texting Luna. I haven't seen my queen in two days, forty-eight hours where I've given her a break from my presence without being too far away.

I'm in the flowers that arrive each morning along with breakfast, and then at night, on the note scribbled over her favorite wine's label. Just a simple *I Love You, Beauty* that I know she enjoys. Her response every time a delivery shows up gives that much away.

The text messages with emojis.

The one picture of her in my shirt while sipping from a glass.

The smile in her voice during our five-minute conversations whenever I get a chance, is proof that I'm wearing her down.

"Cabron, you still owe me money from the series before that. Get out of here with that mierda," comes from inside the room, and I know the voice. I almost laugh because my father takes this too seriously as do most in Latin American countries.

These are grown men, some even family—the kind of assholes that will take a life if necessary without blinking twice, but when it comes to baseball, they lose composure faster than a bullet dislodges from my gun.

"Go ahead and give me two," I say to my brother and Miguel, who follow my instructions without a backward glance. The large metal doors open, and the room grows quiet; they know I'm here—what I expect—and my men don't disappoint.

My father was the same in his time as king of the 305.

Respect. Silence. Loyalty.

No excuse. Either you are with the De Leons or you're viewed as an enemy.

As they slip inside and the doors close, no one asks where I am. Instead, the constant thud of fists meeting solid wood reverberates throughout the floor and I smile.

It's their greeting. A welcoming.

It's one I embrace as I pull open the doors, walking inside and straight for the head of a large, teak table that's currently full. Men gather all around it, standing while those fists never stop pounding. They're smiling as I take my seat: a large chair that resembles a throne in all black that's carved out of imported ebony wood.

And it's only once I've taken my place that the noise stops, and my men sit.

"Gentlemen," I say, looking each one in the eye. The men here are a group I trust. That I've personally vetted with Ivan's help. "Before we begin, I want to thank both my brother and father for stepping in when I couldn't personally attend. For following my instructions and keeping this family strong, proud, and feared."

"Leon Pride," they chant in unison.

"Over the last five years, I've set in motion a change to our structure that will take effect immediately. If you aren't within these walls, sitting inside this room, then you're not one of us." Grabbing my glass with four fingers' worth of rum inside, I lift, and the others follow. "It's time to grow, and so will the profits. It's time to burn our names into the history books as the largest cartel operating within the US."

"Leon Pride."

"There will be changes," I say, meeting my father's eyes. He nods at me, raising his glass a little bit higher. Total trust in his eyes. "Blood will be shed. There will be motherfucking anarchy in this city by the time I remove all the filth, and then, it'll be our family that cleans up the mess. To the victors of war go the spoils, and ours will be cleaning out every dirty city official's office."

"Leon Pride."

"Leon Pride." With a smirk on my face, I bring the glass to my lips and take a sip before holding a hand up. It's a signal for Miguel, who leaves the room and comes right back with the help of his son, dragging with him the kind of scum we will begin disposing of.

He's my gift to the group. Where this mess began.

The man kicking and screaming—the one being pushed toward me—works as an office assistant for the judge that convicted me, a man with ideas of grandeur and rising to a higher rank by winning favors not by merit. He falls to his knees at my feet, scrambling to move back, but Miguel's presence keeps him right where he is, crying and praying to a man that will not show mercy.

He's also the one who recommended his deceased cousin to Senot as a hitman, and in return, he'd get a job with him as the Director of Public Affairs. A job that's way above his skill set and knowledge, and while I'll never knock someone's hustle, he stepped outside his lane and bit off more than he could ever hope to chew.

His cousin was the same man found dead inside my penthouse.

He's the man that will die tonight.

"Where did you find him?" Dad asks, his hand at his waist where he pulls out a 9mm and points it at Roger's head. "This son of a bitch owes me one."

"Where do all little boys go when they're scared?" Pushing my chair back, I turn enough so that I'm facing the whimpering bitch.

"His mother's house in—"

"Texas," I finish for my viejo, taking another sip from my glass before cutting my eyes to the guilty guest at my feet. "Isn't that right, Roger?"

"Please don't hurt me." Without prompting, he's crawling toward me and once at my Ferragamo loafers, he kisses each one. "I made a mistake...I'll work it off. I'll do anything you want me to."

"Is that right?"

"Yes. Anything." I'll give the asshole a few points for being smart enough to not look me in the eye.

"Tell me who approached you."

"W-what do you mean? I-I—"

"Someone told you to entice Ulysses because we both know you aren't smart enough to concoct this yourself." If he's offended by my slight, Roger hides it well behind a quivering lip and the snot rolling over it. *Disgusting.* His mouth opens to reply, but before he does I hold a finger up, silencing him. "The truth, Mr. Charles. Just confirm what I know, and we can all move forward with our day."

"It was Jasmine Senot." The information given to me in jail regarding his involvement was missing one tiny detail that I now see plain as day. His motives are obvious. Simple. Somehow, he fell for her, too, and this was the idiot's way to win some brownie points. It's written all over his face—this hurts him to give her up. "She wants her husband dead and used his dislike of you in her favor."

Infatuation is a dangerous thing and often overlooked as nothing more than a crush or basic attraction. To me, though, it goes deeper. Much deeper. A person believing themselves in love will do just about anything for the object of their desires:

Lie.

Cheat.

Steal.

Kill.

All apply and none are off-limits.

"I appreciate the honesty, Roger. So much so that here's what I'll do for you."

"Thank you. I'm so sorry and I'll—"

"Close your eyes when speaking to me." He does as I ask, and ten seconds later, I give the nod of approval.

Roger Charles doesn't see the first bullet coming nor the next. They hit him so fast as every gun inside the room empties a magazine, producing life-ending holes throughout his tall and lanky frame; by the fourth gunshot, and with eyes wide open, he's dead.

Blood stains the floor, rivulets that wet the soles of my dress shoes, and as the last shot rings out, I take a final sip of my drink.

Let them come for us now; I'm prepared and will kill anyone who stands in my way.

Even if that means I put a bullet between my father-in-law's eyes. Because that motherfucker isn't innocent in all this, and when the time comes for retribution, they'll all fall.

My Luna will know how dirty his, Ulysses, and Jasmine's hands are compared to mine.

"Did you make it to the safe house okay?" I ask Ivan, placing my cell with the secured line between my right shoulder and ear. It's a little past eleven a.m. the next morning, and I'm overlooking a medium-sized shipment of illegal firearms being brought aboard by a group of Dominicans via a yacht. This delivery is a gift for a favor. For the protection of an underground manufacturer's family from the Philippines that uses the D.R. as a hub —his wife and young daughter—while they were on vacation in Miami three months ago. I gave the okay from my cell, and this is his token of appreciation. "Were they right?"

"Yeah, that son of a bitch is here. Mauricio Hernandez was drunk off his ass and partying it up near the Malecon when I arrived." He's in Cuba now, having left immediately after the execution of Roger. It's how we planned it after word came in yesterday morning from my men on the island of what this piece of shit had done. What he proudly told anyone who would listen.

Casper Jameson is a good man. An asshole. The British motherfucker is part of my family, honest, and someone I do business with on a regular basis.

What's been taken from him isn't something that any of us in this unified circle can ignore, nor will we want to. You don't harm the women in this lifestyle. They are respected, if nothing else.

Mother or wife; they are never to be touched.

What Mauricio has done deserves nothing short of a painful death, and that's something he knows.

It's why he's hiding from the Jamesons. Why he's living his life up zero to a hundred without pause because you can only go undetected for so long.

His biggest mistake was going to Cuba.

He signed his death certificate the very moment he stepped foot onto its soil.

"You grabbed him?" I say before clearing my throat and taking a sip from the ice-cold glass of water I'm nursing. It's one of Luna's rules: a night out drinking equals two bottles of water and ibuprofen before bed.

"Within the hour." There's the sound of someone yelling in the background, a male voice on the verge of panic and a thump on metal shortly after. "I'm delivering him to the compound now and then awaiting Casper's arrival...." there's a pause on his end and then the firing of a gun "*...not so mouthy now, asshole?*"

"Difficult guest?"

"The crying is getting on my last nerve. I would've shot him by now, but Casper deserves that honor."

"Agreed."

"Can you text me his ETA once you get it, bro?" he asks before saying something to our personal driver over there.

"Done." The last of the crates is brought below and the large metal ramp used just above sea level is closed. "Expect my call within the next half an hour."

"Thanks. See you tomorrow."

"Cuidate."

"Always." The line goes dead then and I turn, leaning back against the railing. The waves below are a bit choppy, slightly rocking us, and I crack my neck. It's been a long night and I haven't slept as of yet, celebrating with those following me into this next stage of our growth. We toasted to our future. We disposed of a body.

I set my plan into motion.

Pressing the number eight on my screen, I wait for the phone to ring. It does so three times before there's a click on the line.

"About time you called, you arse. How's life treating you on the outside?"

The smile in his tone, even as he mourns his mother, makes me chuckle. "It's getting there. I'm adjusting."

"That's good to hear. Are you free, or...?" In other words, can you work or are you playing the role of a good boy?

"Probation for two years." The few men cleaning the other side of this top floor don't see me and their discussion on some unimportant bullshit becomes loud. As the volume rises, there are a few curse words thrown about—a threat or two—and I leave my place by the railing. All it takes for them to become silent is a mere five steps: the sight of my hulking frame makes them mute.

"Everything okay, mate?" he asks, more than likely having heard the small commotion.

"Is the pigeon in its cage?" I say instead, glaring at the young bunch. They're new, that much is obvious. They're nothing more than hired help to do the grunt work.

They need better training. A hands-on approach.

"Ezra keeps it clean and maintained." His tone isn't as jovial anymore. He's all business now.

"Good." The sound of my ice clinking inside of the glass becomes loud as I move this conversation inside. Opening the door, I give the soldiers a final glare and let the door slam shut behind me. I'll deal with them later. "You in the States?"

"In Chicago. Why?" Casper sounds as if he's moving around a room, almost agitated, and I wonder what has him in this state. He doesn't know that my brother flew out once we got word of the unwanted visitor on the island and the crimes he's committed.

"Pack a bag and head to the airport because you're needed in Cuba tonight, my friend. Ivan will be there to pick you up."

"Tonight?" There is the opening and closing of a few doors and then what sounds like his cousin talking. "What's going on? Why is your little brother in Cuba?"

"Because Ivan has your mother's killer in a holding cell in Havana."

Chapter 16
LUNA

CHRIST. IT'S AS if nothing's changed.

As if the years haven't passed us by.

As if Thiago didn't leave for five years and this is just another weekend.

The long entrance winds as we drive toward the De Leon house Saturday mid-afternoon: an ostentatious home sitting at the center of a seven-acre lot with nothing surrounding it.

No neighbors close enough to hear or see.

No trespassing by those wanting to make friends with the notorious family.

The car stops and the man beside me squeezes one of my hands —the same one he's held on to since we left my apartment—and then turns off the ignition. He's watching me. Looking for any sign of distress.

There isn't any. Not a single twitch.

To be honest, this reminds me of every other dinner I've attended since meeting Thiago. The same expensive cars fill the roundabout driveway. The same crazy bunch of characters milling about on the front wrap-around porch with his parental figures at the center. Always at the center.

Orlando and Maritza look the same, just a smidge older. Same smiles. Same soft eyes. Same welcoming expression.

They're watching us inside of a vehicle I didn't know Thiago still owned. From my understanding, after Ivan let it slip in conversation, his brother sold everything he owned before his sentencing. His penthouse, multiple large SUVs, and a boat named My Beauty.

All gone. All our memories forgotten.

A small pang hits me at the center of my chest, that sadness that I can't escape, but I push it back. Instead, I focus on what still remains. What I'm sitting inside of.

This car is special; a fully loaded all-white Audi that was given to him as a gift his senior year of high school. This car was witness to many kisses, his expert hands fondling out front of my parents' house. Our school. All over the city of Miami.

It's where I gave him my first blow job overlooking a high-end restaurant on Collins Ave.

"And you say I'm the perv?"

"This is new," I say instead, fighting to control the soft heat sweeping my cheeks. "Did you have it tricked out à la *Pimp My Ride*?"

It's been kept pristine in his absence. Customized with everything the latest model has.

I should know, I own one.

"Quit stalling." His tone is playful, and so is the smirk on his lips. He's so handsome.

My attraction to him is just as strong. It makes me weak. But I don't show this and instead roll my eyes. "I'm not."

"Then what are you doing?" Lifting our joined hands, he turns our wrists and lays a kiss to my knuckles. "Because it looks like you're avoiding."

"Feeling lucky, Thiago?"

That makes him pause and his right brow lifts. "What do you have in mind?"

"Five hundred dollars says your Mom rushes over within the next sixty seconds."

"I'll take that bet, but I don't want your money."

"What do you want, then?" I ask with more excitement than I should show. My curiosity is piqued and thighs clench at the heated look that follows. Thiago's eyes sweep from the very top of my head to my exposed legs in the small sundress I'm wearing. Nothing fancy; a soft cotton coral number that drapes over my curves in a flattering way. With a sweetheart neckline, a tight bodice, and flowing skirt, it's comfortable while still being sexy. It's accompanied by tan wedge sandals, a pair of hoop earrings, my signature winged liner and lip gloss combo, and the man is struggling to keep his eyes off.

The desired effect I am after.

He licks his bottom lip, head tilted to the side as he lingers at my knees. "A date."

"A what?" Because I need to hear that again. Just to make sure. I'm also ignoring the small thrill of excitement that flows through me at that. "We're playing for money, not—"

"A date, Luna. I want to take you out on a date." The last word hasn't fully passed through his kissable lips when my door is wrenched open and I'm being pulled from the car by a walking floral scent that I'm familiar with.

Maritza doesn't say anything once our eyes meet, but her smile matches the one breaking free across my face. It's sweet and warm and everything I've been missing for the past few years. A maternal love that you can't duplicate or falsify.

Hazel eyes that look so much like her son's become watery and her bottom lip trembles. "Mi Niña." *Her girl.*

That's all she says. Two words.

In an instant everything rushes to the forefront.

The feeling of abandonment.

The resentment at his idiotic betrayal.

The love that will always be there for his family.

Tears fall from my eyes without permission; I feel vulnerable. My emotions are running rampant—fluctuating between hurt and love. Between pulling her in for a hug and running away.

Not that it matters as a second later Maritza takes the decision from me, wrapping her small arms tightly around me as a small sob escapes.

"None of that, beautiful. We don't deserve them." At her response I open my eyes, not realizing that I'd closed them. There's no one. Not even Thiago. From one end to the other, I look for his family members but come up empty. "Thiago signaled for them to scram. His pissed-off face actually sent them running. It was hilarious to see."

Pulling back, I settle my stare on her as my lips twitch. I'm sure I look a mess, crazy with tear tracks, blotchy skin, and smile. "Why?"

"Why do you think," she counters, her perfectly sculpted brow raised. *She's where he gets it from.*

"Mari, at the moment, I have no idea what to think or which way is up. Struggling is more like it. Confused definitely. But understanding him? Yeah, that's something I lost five years ago."

"Is it something you want to reconnect with?"

"I still love him, but—"

"Then follow me. It's time you hear something."

"Where are we...*okay.*" She takes my hand in hers and all but drags me behind her, around the side of the first floor and to a door not many have access to. If your name isn't Maritza or Orlando, you don't dare enter. This is their office, and like all the main rooms, it has a door to be used in case of an emergency.

Without pause, she keys in the code and walks in after a series of beeps. Once inside, she signals for me to take a seat. "A drink?"

"Rum, please."

"Brugal or Havana?"

"Hostess choice." Maritza nods and brings out a special edition Havana Club they keep for important occasions. The Maximo Extra version is worth a few grand and this household from what I remember always keeps a minimum of three bottles at all times.

Pouring three fingers' worth into a set of snifters, she closes the bottle and walks back over, taking a seat on the large couch. The room is on the larger side for an office with a full sitting area in front of the large windows and a fireplace that's nothing more than a decorative piece.

I take the offered drink. "Salud."

"Salud."

That first sip goes down smooth. The sweet notes of fruits and vanilla are pleasant and mixed with the smokiness of the old wooden barrels it's produced in, becoming a soothing mixture. Not a single flavor overpowers the other and I hum, taking a second and third taste before placing the glass atop the coffee table.

Mari does the same, her body turning to face mine. "I know it's hard, mi Lunita."

"More than hard. I feel lost."

"But this doesn't have to be the end." There's something in her tone that causes me to tilt my head to the side, and I'm left trying to decipher what she means. Because she's talking as if—what it seems like is—she's been in my position. *That can't be right. Orlando adores her.* "All couples go through rough patches, sweetheart, and trust me when I say I've wanted to kill my husband a time or two in the last thirty years. He's messed up. I've messed up. It's life…our life," she says, taking my hands in hers and giving them both a squeeze. "Not a damn thing has been easy for any of us, and if Thiago is guilty of one thing, it's being too overprotective when it comes to you."

"He didn't even give me the chance to choose him." My voice betrays me, and she hears my pain; understands the betrayal.

"And that's what hurts the most, isn't it? You feel as though he didn't trust you to stay." She hits the nail on the proverbial head and tears fill my eyes once again, my chin trembling. The look she gives me is soft and full of understanding. "Let it out, Luna. It's okay to be mad. It's okay to feel how you do, and anyone saying otherwise deserves to be shot."

A small giggle escapes, but just as soon that amusement dies. This rollercoaster is taking its toll on me. Within the span of a few days my world—the normal I fought so hard to build for myself—has shattered into a million and one pieces.

"Why?" At my question Maritza nods, understanding me without further explanation.

"My son is the best person to explain this."

"He claims he didn't have a choice."

"That's not what I meant." A final squeeze and Maritza releases my hand, shifting forward so she can reach a small remote atop the coffee table in front of us. She presses a few buttons, sits back, and I'm met with a voice I know. A younger version of the one that showed up at my door less than a week ago.

One I both love and hate. That I can't live without.

I love him now just as much as I did years ago.

"Mom, this isn't easy for me. Hurting Luna wasn't..." Thiago trails, his voice a bit slurred. There's a tinge of pain and self-recrimination in his tone, and the faint sound of ice clinking inside of a glass fills the silence. *"Everything is fucked up. A complete and utter mess."*

"You could go see her," his mother says on the recording, a bit of a scold there. *"Explain."*

"And say what?" It's a tortured yell and I feel the weight of

emotions crushing my chest. It's palpable and haunting and my heart breaks for him. For us. *"Am I supposed to tell her that some asshole put a hit out on her? Admit that I failed to protect my family...that I can't find the son of a bitch who shot Dad?"*

"Son, this isn't your fault."

He scoffs. *"Right now we have no idea what tomorrow will bring, Vieja. I'm being investigated, Dad is injured, and Ivan blames himself for leaving behind evidence at the scene that brought the MDP to my door. I'm the suspect of a crime I didn't commit but the Major has a hard-on for."* The ice clinks again and then he sighs. *"Pushing her away, no matter how much it hurts, is all I have left. I'm not doing it for shits and giggles or because I'm an untrusting asshole. It's the complete opposite, Mom. With her out of the picture, they'll turn the focus back on us. They'll come for me and not her. She'll be safe and that's all that matters."*

"But you're not giving her a choice."

"That's where you're wrong."

"Son, I don't understand. Help me out—"

"A long time ago, I explained to her that at times things are not what they seem. That I'll need her to trust me blindly." Something rustles and the recording goes quiet for a minute or two. Utter silence that takes me back to that conversation. To my agreement and then his promise. *"My heart is hers to keep safe,"* he says so low, but I hear. I feel the depth of those words now as much as I did when we were kids. *"I trust her to remember that. To know that I'll always come back. That what I've done is to keep her safe."*

"Speaking of...?" His mom's voice wavers with emotion on the recording, and I look over to see the same tears in her eyes as I have in mine. *"Security? Are you leaving her unprotected?"*

"Never." I can almost see his handsome face send her a glare. *"She'll have someone around at all times. Not disclosing who, but Ivan has instructions and he'll explain things eventually. For now, everyone needs to fall the fuck back and not make it any worse."*

"Why are you making it sound as if you're going away? Like you won't be able to fix this in a few weeks?"

"Because I've made sure the target is on my back now."

Maritza hits a button and the recording stops. Her eyes are on me. Waiting for my reaction.

The truth is that right now I'm caught between love and loss. Between confusion and running out of this room in search of Thiago so I can kiss him stupid.

I feel like a jerk.

I feel too much at once.

"Did that help at all?" she asks after a bit, her phone in her hand as she types something out. "Are you ready to see him? Because I can only keep him at bay for so long."

Turning the screen in my direction, she lets me see his texts.

> What's taking so long? ~Thiago

> Is she okay? ~Thiago

> What did you do? ~Thiago

"When did those come in? I didn't hear your phone."

She shrugs, smiling. "A few minutes after you went mute."

I'm embarrassed and nod. "How long was that?"

"Say ten minutes, give or take."

Not horrible. "Tell him to cool it. I'll see him in a bit."

"Okay." And she does just that, hitting send and then tossing the device on the oversized chair across from us. "So, what now? Do you think you'll get past this?"

"Maybe."

"*Maybe* you will after making the man work for it?"

Twisting in my seat, I give her my undivided attention, hands crossed over my chest. "Keep going, Mari. You seem to have a plan."

"Lunita, I want you to forgive my son and move on more than

anything, but…" she leans over, in her eyes I see that devilish glint her boys are known for "…he has some atoning to do. You both do." After hearing his confession and recalling our conversation years ago, I should've demanded the truth and not swallow his idiotic mistake. "He let you down and you forgot that as his queen, you come before everyone…including myself. Two wrongs don't make a right, but that doesn't mean that he should get off completely easy. Make him work for it. Chase you."

"You mean make up for the five years of radio silence." That devious side, that coquettish part of every woman's personality steps to the forefront and my shoulders square. My chin juts forward. One of my fears in seeing Maritza today; the defending her son without considering my feelings.

That his side is all that matters.

And I was wrong. Completely.

"Exactly." Standing up, she holds a hand out, pulling me up when I take it. "The women in this family are fierce, strong, and don't take bull from anyone. Especially their men. We are fifty-fifty partners and it's time you show him as much."

"Making him suffer a bit would make me feel better." *I'll make up for my mistake later. Much later and with my mouth.*

"Good. Because I want grandkids and soon, Luna."

Chapter 17

THIAGO

"**W**ELL, THAT DIDN'T take long at all, primo."

I turn my head slightly, acknowledging the intruder while keeping my focus on the door to my parents' office where I know Luna is. It's the best place for their conversation. For her to calm down without everyone being in her face.

Maybe I should check on them?

"Something on your mind, Jadiel?" My cousin is not alone, and the man beside him takes a step back at my brusque tone. "Speak."

"Just wanted to say hello, boss." The amusement in his voice grates on my nerves. But then again, I've never liked him either. Tolerated is a better descriptor of our relationship. "That, and introduce you to my future brother-in-law. He works for me."

I don't miss the false bravado. I see his cocky expression.

Jadiel Gomez is the spitting image of his father with illusions of grandeur that don't belong to either of them. He's the son of my father's sister and a man who considers himself more than what he will ever be.

It's one of the reasons that neither was present for the meeting held a few days ago.

My aunt, God rest her soul, was a beautiful human being who married Andres out of love while he saw an opportunity. They are her heirs. They are nothing but trouble.

And I have my eyes set on both while they covet my position. Believe that it belongs to them since he is older by three years. A belief that makes no sense as his mother was never interested or in line to take over. That place belonged to Orlando as the oldest and now me as his son.

Ignoring the idiot, I turn my attention to the man standing slightly behind him. "Name."

"Sergio, Mr. De Leon. I'm Celeste's fiancé." Celeste, Jadiel's sister, is nothing like them. She's a sweet girl with the disposition of her mother and terrible taste in men. Men like this asshole who thinks he's special. Someone who will try and manipulate her with the help of the other men in her life.

If I angle my gun just right, I could kill them with one bullet.
"Is that so?"

"Yes." So enthusiastic. A pathetic puppy.

I take two things away from his sorry introduction; he doesn't belong, and my cousin is pulling the strings. Sergio doesn't step forward to extend a hand nor does he look at me in the eye. Instead, he flicks his eyes toward Jadiel for approval.

My cousin gives a minute nod, and he speaks.

My cousin coughs, and he focuses on the wall behind me.

"And you work for Jadiel?"

"I—"

"Before you answer, you do understand I'm his boss? That my word is law?"

"I'm—"

"Cousin, don't be—" they begin in unison, but I hold a hand up, effectively silencing them.

"Teach your pet some respect, cousin." Finally, there's a reaction from Sergio and his hands tighten into fists. His lips thin, and mine stretch into a smirk. "Your job is a simple one and doesn't require a personal staff. You manage transport. Nothing more."

"Thiago, I do a lot more than schedule deliveries," he sneers, stupidly taking a step forward. Close enough, but I want to see how far he'd like to take this.

"You're a glorified errand boy. You do what I say."

Another two steps, his hands clenching. "Fuck—"

He doesn't get to finish his sentence as my hand shoots out, grabbing his neck and squeezing. My hold is tight, his face turning red. "What were you saying? I can't hear you?" I lift him off the floor, his feet dangling a foot or two off the ground. "Fuck me? Was that it?"

"Let him go," Sergio says, and it's the wrong move. Rule number one in this life: pay attention to your surroundings. Ivan cocks his gun right before pressing it to his neck, digging the barrel in deep.

"Kneel at his feet."

"Ivan, we—"

"You have ten seconds before I pull the trigger." My brother removes the gun but keeps it aimed for his head. "Get on your knees."

Sergio does so, his face ashen. His body also begins to shake. "Don't shoot me. Please."

Fucking pussy.

"Shut the fuck up and speak when spoken to," Ivan hisses out, finger twitching on the trigger.

In my hold, Jadiel becomes a bit limp and I let him drop. His head hits the expensive flooring and the sound of the crash is loud, but with the office being soundproofed, they won't hear a thing. No one to protect him. No one to feel bad for him since my aunt is dead and his father is an alcoholic asshole.

Crouching down, I watch him splutter with a hand on his throat as he fights to get enough air into his abused lungs. There's a bluish tint to his lips, his body writhing, and I feel no remorse.

He is my blood, but there is no love in me for the egotistical bitch.

Running the family is his ultimate hard-on, and our business interests don't align. The De Leons move drugs, weapons, and control the port by force and fear. Racketeering. That's how we hold this city hostage. Why everyone bows down.

Without our approval, getting a product in is difficult and bringing it down through the state's interstate leads to other complications. Being caught is one of them.

So they pay. A lot.

We don't traffic in humans. We don't kidnap pretty girls to sell them overseas.

I'll kill him first.

"Let's try this again, shall we?" His answer comes in the shape of a groan, and I take it under consideration. "What is your role in the De Leon Dynasty? Title and explanation."

"Lieutenant in charge of logistics."

"What else?" Pulling my phone out of my pocket, I wave him on before sending a text to Mom. "Give me the specifics."

"I make the schedules, coordinate the movement of merchandise, and send out soldiers to collect payments."

"What else?"

"That is it." Voice low. Meek.

"And who do you work for?"

"You."

"You're a member of this familia, Jadiel, but that doesn't give you leniency or protection against discipline." Condescendingly, I smack his cheek a few times, the force behind the hit just shy of painful. "Blatant disrespect won't be tolerated. Not by you, your father, or the gopher marrying your sister. A sister that wouldn't appreciate this sort of behavior."

"Apologize, asshole." My eyes shift toward Ivan and I stifle a chuckle. The man is near pissing himself. "This is our boss, and you'll lick his boots if asked."

"I'm sorry."

Pathetic at best, and I shake my head at him. "You don't seem to understand the severity of this infraction. Take him out back. We'll discuss his role with Celeste before I head out tonight."

"Understood." Ivan looks down at Sergio, his expression one of disgust. "Get up."

"Please, it's a misunderstanding."

"I said get the fuck up."

"What's going on here?" a voice says and my brother looks toward the opposite entrance where the foyer is. I don't waste my time. I don't owe him an explanation.

"Mind your business, uncle. This doesn't concern you."

"This is my son and—"

"Unless you want to end up on your bad knees, turn around and walk away," I say, standing to my full height and placing my shoe on his son's chest. Jadiel groans, his much lankier frame protesting. That's another difference between us; he's an office guy, while I like to dirty my hands. "You're only making it worse."

"Today is about celebrating, Thiago. No need for violence." His hands are up, eyes on Jadiel. They share a look; a warning from one man to the other. "Apologize to him. Now."

"I'm sorry, boss. I was just trying to be funny and it got out of hand."

I remove my shoe and step back, extending a hand. My cousin takes it and I yank him up with one harsh pull, bringing him close in what looks to be a man-hug, mouth near his ear. "I'm going to pretend this didn't happen, but you ever step out of line again, and you'll be joining me out at sea for a hosted event. Understood?" Even if he tries to hide it, I still feel the shiver that runs down his spine. He's afraid of me. Not even close to being able to handle being inside an octagon with me. "Cousin or not, I will kill you, your father, and the sack of mierda looking to marry Celeste. Watch yourself and don't ever let this happen again."

When I let him go, his father is there but Sergio and Ivan are nowhere to be seen.

"Can we be dismissed, sobrino? I'd like to discuss my son's behavior with him."

"You do that." Walking over to Andres, I kiss his cheek. "Because my patience can only run for so long."

They walk out and I stand my ground. Watching the door. Thinking.

Puzzle pieces start making sense, and that's when the danger begins.

They have no idea of the target on their backs.

"Run, motherfuckers," I say, and there's a click of a lock disengaging not far from me. The door to my mother's office opens and she comes out, smiling at me in a way that says *you're in so much trouble* and then continues on her way toward the back. No words. Nothing.

Not that it matters, because I'm already looking at the doorway awaiting her appearance. And when she does, all smiles and that sassy, defiant look in her eyes, I'm done for.

Luna arches a brow and I bite my lip.

She walks past me, and I'm following close behind.

There's somewhere I should be, but I don't give three flying fucks, and just before exiting through the kitchen and out onto the terrace, I stop to grab us two ice-cold beers. This takes a total of sixty seconds, that's it, and when I step out and people begin to clap —whistling obnoxiously loud—I smile.

Not because of the welcome back.

Not because of the people here.

I'm smiling at the sight of my father embracing his daughter after so long and the warm way her eyes meet mine. They're happy and bright, and I'm to going destroy the lives of so many to keep that lightness there.

Some of those assholes are here. Watching. Muttering under their breaths.

But all in due time.

Ivan now stands near the back and to the right with a woman beside him that I recognize from the file upstairs. He tilts his head in the direction of the far end of the lot where we keep a special housing unit that resembles an old-school jail. Dirty, rank, and with special inhabitants that feast on anything within reach.

He mouths the words, *Miguel* and *Sergio* while holding up two fingers. Cell two and Miguel is handling him.

I'm in no rush. The asshole can wait.

Scratching my chin, I look at the faces of each and every one in attendance. Friends, associates, foot soldiers, and family. All smiling. All waiting on some big speech.

"I want to thank you all for attending the celebration of my release from the state hotel." Silence meets my ears. Not so much as a bird chirp. "My stay was fun. Enlightening. But most of all, it gave me time to think. To prepare." Raising my bottle, I settle my eyes on Luna while those around us mimic my action with their own drinks. "To the future." This time I receive a unanimous chant while she gives me a nod. "To a new era of violence in Miami." A yell in support while her eyes show understanding. She knows I'll never hurt an innocent, but may God have mercy on those responsible because I never will. "To the death of our enemies, because this is my public declaration of war to those that have done us wrong."

I don't miss how two figures shrink back and subtly walk away from the group celebrating. I don't miss Celeste's strange reaction or how she looks for Sergio through the throngs of people. Over a hundred in attendance, and three are missing. Three that are connected. Three with my eyes now on their every move.

For today, I'll play along, but come light tomorrow I'm going on a hunt and the woman standing beside Ivan with a scared expression on her face is the key to my success.

Chapter 18
THIAGO

PEOPLE BEGIN TO disperse when I make my way across the terrace to Luna. She's all I have eyes for at the moment, the only person that deserves a detailed explanation, but it'll have to wait. At least until my personal guest leaves.

"That was some speech, *boss*," she croons, hand on her hip, accentuating her curves. My parents move away, entertaining a few associates and their wives while I ignore the world around us for just a few more seconds. "Invigorating."

"You know, you're the only person in this world whose sarcasm I find amusing. Cute, even."

"That's because I'm adorable in every single way." The way she bites her bottom lip makes me want to fuck that pretty little mouth. Watch her lips stretch around my girth and choke as I hit the back of her throat.

"Is that so."

"It is."

"You are very dangerous, beauty." I move closer, crowding her space. Her heat sears me as I press against her, chest to chest. Lips hovering. "And I love the way you bite."

She places a hand on my chest, right over my beating heart. "This conversation feels very familiar to me. A repeat of every family function right before you say the words..."

"I have a meeting to attend." There's no anger or reproach, but I do see the burning curiosity. "And while this time is no different, I want you to accompany me. It might help keep the person calm."

"Are you serious?"

"I am." I've made mistakes, plenty of them, but knowing that she doubted my commitment to her is the one I regret the most. Before, I kept her from the darker side of the business. Kept her in the know without any gritty details, but that ends now. "Come on. Let's go talk to her."

"Okay. Sure, let me..." Luna trails off, her face scrunching up in confusion. There aren't many women in this industry, and the few we are aware of don't make moves outside of the West Coast. "Her?"

"Gaytan's wife is here."

"Carlotta is here?" I'm not the least bit surprised by her question, or more importantly, that she knows the woman's name. My girl is smart, cunning, and has access in different forms to the MPD database. "Why?"

I don't answer her, but I do extend a hand and wait. This is my asking her to trust me and follow my lead. To stand by my side.

A deep exhale follows, but my girl slips her hand into mine and lets me lead her away. We pass nosy guests, those who want to talk business or kiss ass, as we head toward the back building. The closer we get, the more guards stand at the post.

There are five of them up the cobbled path leading to the door and two more blocking the entrance. They all move aside as we walk straight through and up a small stairway off to the left that leads to a conference room.

It's not fancy or meant to entertain important acquaintances; it's an interrogation room before the horrors below swallow you whole. This is where my family gives you a chance to stop being a singao and take responsibility for your actions.

This is our confessional. Your last rights.

Upon entry, we find her and Ivan sitting at the far end of the long table, one on each side. They're not talking, but he was kind enough to find her a bottle of water and a few napkins to dab her red-rimmed eyes.

"Evening, Mrs. Gaytan." At the sound of my voice she startles, almost knocking the bottle over. "I apologize now for the less-than-stellar accommodations for this impromptu meeting."

"No apologies necessary, Mr. De Leon. I'm used to living in a less-than-safe neighborhood with my two children." Tears well up in her eyes and spill, but Carlotta is quick to dab her eyes. "My husband is never around. Never calls. He abandoned us."

"Have you taken him to court?" Luna asks and Carlotta gasps, noticing her presence. She recognizes Luna. Not that it deters my queen. No, she just walks toward where Ivan sits and takes a chair beside his. His eyes meet mine, but I shake my head. The reason that Luna is here will be more than self-explanatory in a few minutes. Once seated, she meets Gaytan's wife's stare head-on. "Because I can assure you, he makes very good money being the personal guard to Mayor Senot's wife."

"The courts stand with those who work for the city. Technically, he protects an official and as such, they seem to have immunity when it comes to child support cases or divorce."

"You've tried to divorce him?" Luna pushes the box of Kleenex closer to her.

"Twice now, and it was thrown out of court because the man refuses to sign. He actually had the audacity to tell the judge he was trying to win me and the children back." The venom in her tone doesn't surprise me. That piece of shit deserves every bit of my wrath coming his way. He's going to burn alive for his sins.

"How can I help you? Maybe I can talk to someone down at the precinct—my uncle is MDP and can help get the case given to another judge." My queen is beautiful in her anger for this woman, in the way she's helped calm down a fragile victim who up until now had no one in her corner. No one believed her.

But unfortunately, wishful thinking isn't how the world works.

People in power don't help or care unless it has some kind of personal gain attached.

"Where do you live, Mrs.—?" I begin, but the shake of her head cuts me off.

"Please don't attach me to that man's name or crimes. I have babies to take care of and feed."

"Of course..." I offer her a reassuring smile instead of a correction; she's dealt with enough. "But I do need you to answer the question, Ms. Suarez. Where do you live?"

"A low-income housing project at the center of the city." Her answer is succinct and doesn't give away her location. Nor does she ask how I know her maiden name. She's trying to protect her kids in case something goes wrong, and I don't press because after today, it won't matter.

"Okay." Pulling the chair out, I take a seat and lean back, scratching my jaw. "Are your kids somewhere safe for the next few hours?" Luna gives me a strange look at that, almost pleading with me not to scare her.

"Yes, sir." Carlotta isn't, though. If anything, she sits straighter in her seat. Brave woman. "I've done as you asked me to. I dropped them off before coming here."

"Good." Opening the laptop in front of me, I press my thumb to the scanner for access and pull up a tracking app. "When did you last see him? Do you know where your husband is today?"

"I do. It's a workday and *she* loves meeting up with friends for dinner," Carlotta spits out before taking a sip from her water bottle. I'm sure this is all weighing heavily on her head; the first time you help end a life is never easy. However, her husband's betrayal is burning her from within, and it's the dominating emotion she's focusing on. The years of hurt and neglect are cutting deep. "Ivan gave me the small tracker yesterday. I knew he'd show up if I mentioned going to social media to blast him via our text exchange, especially since our oldest has a vitamin deficiency and asthma. Within half an hour he was pounding on my door, smashing my phone and laptop and then pushing me around. My neighbor, a small-time dealer at that, stepped in and threw him out on his ass. While they fought, I slipped the small device onto the Mercedes symbol of his car."

There on the screen of my computer is a bright green light alerting me to his location. It's moving, traveling through Bal Harbour as we speak.

"I'm going to be very blunt with you, Ms. Suarez." She nods and sits back, her expression showing a hint of fear. "Your husband won't make it past the next seventy-two hours. He's done things that are unforgivable; hiring a hitman to kill my father and mother is one of them." Her bottom lip trembles but she keeps her tears at bay. Accepts this with as much grace as she has left. "He will pay with his life and you will disappear. Leave Florida. Start over wherever you want with the two million I've deposited into your account. There's nothing left for you here in Miami."

"Can I bring my mother? She's old and—"

"Yes."

"Thank you."

My eyes shift to Ivan's and I make a circular motion with my hand. "Get her to safety and ready your most trusted. Pick him up, no witnesses, and drop him off at the old stadium."

"I'll message you when I have him, brother." As he stands, Carlotta does the same, but pauses just before reaching for her purse. Her focus is on Luna. Just her.

"I'm sorry, Ms. Alejos. I'm so sorry that your world has been flipped multiple times because of the pure selfishness of others." Carlotta takes a deep breath and lets it out slowly while trying to find the right words to express herself. "I know it's going to hurt, but open your eyes, *please*, because those that hide behind the veil of righteousness are the vilest." Opening her large handbag, she pulls out a slim plastic case and walks over to me, pushing it into my hand. "My plan was to give this to you and ask that you share it with her. There are things on this recording that you both need to see. To hear."

I grip the case, eyes on hers. "Thank you."

"What's been done isn't right, Mr. De Leon. The people they've hurt...it needs to end." Carlotta's voice is just above a whisper toward the end, her eyes growing misty. "You know, when I married Alfredo, I was completely head over heels in love with him." The ghost of a smile appears for mere seconds. It's gone just as fast. "Blind and giving and forgiving, but the version of the man who said, 'I do' and the one on this recording—cheating and snorting coke—are two very different people. Money changes people, and it's made him unrecognizable to us."

"I'll make it look like a car accident. Your children will never know the truth."

"Thank you." Her eyes close then and the tears fall. Her body shakes, the sob escaping, and it's my queen that comes around the table to provide comfort.

Her arms encircle the crying woman and hold her tight, whispering something too low to make out. And that's more than fine with me; her compassion and beautiful heart is one of the things I love most about her. Carlotta pulls back slightly after a few minutes, nodding to Luna. "It'll be okay. I'm going to be okay."

"Yes, you are. Never forget that."

Mrs. Suarez's eyes flick to mine, a clear mixture of gratitude and sadness in the chocolate orbs. "She's a keeper. Don't ever let her go." Without another word, she turns and walks out to meet Ivan on the landing.

My beauty is silent, contemplative, as I take the few remaining steps between us and wrap my arm around her shoulders. "Are you okay?" I ask, laying a kiss to the side of her head. "Need anything?"

"A full hug and a beer would be nice." She shrugs, looking up at me from beneath long lashes. "These last few days have been something else."

Wrapping my arms around her, I tuck her under my chin, lips against her hair. "Not all bad, though? Right?"

"Nightmarish is more like it." My eyes narrow, but she doesn't see this. Instead, she's burrowing deeper and giggling to herself. However, that amusement dies just as fast and she pulls back enough to look me in the eye. "Why do I feel like this is just the tip of the iceberg? Like what's coming might break me?"

"I'll always hold you together, beauty." I lower my head to hers and peck those sweet lips once. Just a quick press. "Even the crazy pieces."

"You jerk!" she spits out, smacking me in the chest. Her mind moves from plaguing thoughts to abusing me, and I'll gladly take that heavy load and make it mine. I never want to see that sad and worried look on her face. "The only insane individual here is you."

"Is that so?"

"Yes, it is."

"Run."

"What?" she half laughs, half splutters.

"Run, little Luna."

"Do you think you'll catch me if I do?" She's already moving toward the exit, a small step at a time.

"Always." As I say this, her hand reaches back for the door. The doorknob twists but I see no rush in her. Instead, I feel like she's tempting. Wanting me to grab her. "You have five seconds."

"I only need two," she yells and then she's gone, rushing down the steps while I wait another beat and follow. Luna is halfway down when I step over the threshold and see her looking back at me with mirth in her eyes.

Wrong move. She stumbles, but rights herself and I find that as my opening. Grabbing onto the metal railing, I go down a few steps and then jump over, landing on the floor below. I hear her gasp without looking up, but I do catch her arm as she tries to zoom past me.

One gentle tug and I have her in my embrace again, looking down at her. "Gotcha."

"That was cheating," she gripes, trying to pinch me. Violent little thing.

"Nothing's fair in love and war." I know I've said those same words to her in the past, and I meant them then as much as I do now. I'll do whatever it takes to keep her. To always call her mine. "Now, let's go. We've been gone long enough."

With my hand on the small of her back, I guide us outside of the building where the faint pulsing beat of salsa hits us. It's slow at first: a bob of my head and the swing of her hips. Next, we hear the laughter coming from the guests back at the main house and the clapping of hands.

She looks up at me.

It's a silent request. A plea to drop everything for a while and enjoy ourselves.

And I do, pursing my lips and then bumping her shoulder with mine. "Five hundred bucks says my father is going to start a rueda before I can take you out myself."

"I'm not taking that bet."

"Why not?" I'm grabbing Luna's hand, twirling her around as we make it to the edge of the now-lit yard. There are twinkling lights all around us and a few couples showing off their dance moves as we reenter. Everyone notices us, they're smiling, all except my old man who looks ready to pull his favorite daughter away from me and out onto the dance floor.

"Because he'll do just that and then I'm—"

"Bebe, the only man you'll be dancing with right now is me," I croon and then turn her again, pulling her against my chest. "Are you ready to show these people how it's done?"

"Do you even remember how?"

"Wrong words." Before she can reply, I'm tipping her back low. Low enough that her hair skims the ground before I bring her back up, body pressed tightly against my own as our feet move.

It's synchronized perfection.

A sensual cadence burns from the inside as I follow her, moving to the island beat while people gather around. Their clapping matches our moves, the noises becoming one as she turns, her back to my front.

Those hips gyrate and her hands are in mine as she drops low and then rises, pushing her ass against my hard-as-steel cock. It's sexy. Motherfucking beautiful.

And more so when she turns a second later with fire in her eyes, teeth embedded in her bottom lip.

It's a look I've seen before a hundred times.

It's want. Hunger. *Trouble.*

"Come a little closer, Thiago." Luna crooks a finger. "I don't bite."

Grabbing her other hand, I turn her once, twice—five times in fast succession. Her giggles ring out, her eyes bright each time she catches sight of my shitty grin. And when she wobbles a bit from the speed in which I turn her, I bring her back to my chest with my lips at her ear. "I proudly wear your marks. Do your worst."

Luna's lips part, her sweet breath fanning across my mouth, but before she can reply...

"May I cut in?" My father stands to the side of us with a proud grin on his face. He's oblivious to our exchange and I just barely hold back my smirk. "I need my dance partner, son. To show these people how it's done."

It's comical how her lips snap shut and eyes widen. I can almost imagine the inappropriateness of whatever retort she has on the tip of her sweet tongue.

"If the lady wants?" At my response, her eyes narrow and she subtly brings her high-wedged foot down over mine. It doesn't hurt like she thinks, but instead sends my receptors into overdrive. Pleasurable pain traverses through my over six-foot frame and settles on the tip of my engorged cock, causing it to give a harsh jerk behind the metal of my zipper. "Well, Luna? Do you?"

"Orlando," her voice is soft, the perfect innocent vixen, "can you have them play *Llororas*?"

Dad's eyes flick to mine and you can see the mirth in them. Asshole. "Of course, mi niña." He extends his hand out and she places hers in his, but then pauses and turns back to face me. Rising on the tip of her toes, she presses her lips to my chin. Just leaves them there, her flesh on mine and my nostrils flare, her scent pulsing through my veins.

"Luna." There's warning in my tone, but she doesn't adhere to it. Instead, she nips the skin there and pulls back enough to once again meet my heated stare.

"Enjoy the show."

Chapter 19
THIAGO

MY EYES FOLLOW her every move across the decent-sized dance area my parents set out for the gathering. It's made from some kind of wood flooring, interconnecting pieces, and designed by a family friend that's an architect in South Florida when he remodeled the home a few years back for my mother's fiftieth.

Hendrix Parker is also the man responsible for designing my new home.

A body sidles next to me and I cock my head to the side. I've been expecting her. "Let me have it, Nat."

"I'm still mad, asshole." Natasha pinches my side and I laugh, swatting her hand away. "You hurt us all by doing that crap and then leaving. She was a wreck, Leon."

"I know." I can feel her eyes on the side of my face, how she's fighting to keep her voice down. Not that I care either way. She's Luna's cousin and I care about her like I do my own family, but right now, what she has to say doesn't matter a single lick to me. My eyes are on my girl. On how she throws her head back and laughs at something my viejo says.

How her hips sway perfectly in time with each beat as the singer declares that the girl who's done him wrong will cry. Suffer like he did.

It's a jab at me.

Her way of flicking me metaphorically off while saying *eat your heart out*.

What she fails to understand is that I would rather eat her instead. Lick. Bite. Devour.

"Are you even listening to me?"

"Not really." Not going to lie to her.

There's a huff and then another pinch. "Can you look at me, dammit?"

"Taking my eyes off Luna is nearly impossible after so long, Nat. Sorry." My beauty accepts the hand of another dancer, my godfather this time, and is turned three quick times before following his quick footwork. They push back and come forth on the count of three, turning to the right as the circle around them does the same. Six couples on the floor and all moving in one unified choreograph.

A quick hand movement—extending her away from her dance partner—and she's back with my dad now.

"Looking at her like that isn't helping me stay mad," Natasha deadpans after a lengthy sigh. "I know you love her, Thiago, but—"

"No buts." For a brief moment, I look over while ignoring some-one's high-pitched whistle. Sounds like it came from my mother, and her loud *dale* a few seconds later confirms it. "I've loved—love her now as much as I did when we met in high school. That will never change, Nat." Her eyes soften and the harsh line her lips were set in quirks up just the tiniest bit at the corner. "And I'd also like to think you know me enough to know that I couldn't give a flying, bloody fuck about who doesn't agree with our relationship. I fucked up, I let her down in one aspect, but she also forgot to trust me. Forgot every single thing I've told her over the years."

"Wait, I think your mis—"

"Am I?" I narrow my eyes. "Isn't this where you tell me to leave her alone?"

"Not at all, jerk." Natasha's eyes grow misty, her expression sad as she punches the same side she's pinched twice. Violent family.

"Hands to yourself, Alejos. I take the abuse from her and no one else."

"Shut up. You owed me that last one."

"Keep it up and I'll tell your father who crashed his '69 Stingray your senior year."

"You wouldn't."

"Try me."

"Fine." She even makes an exaggerated show of putting her hands behind her back. "Better?"

"Much." At her dramatic action, a chuckle escapes me, causing her to giggle. It's stupid and makes no sense why I find it so amusing, but I do. It reminds me of all the idiotic conversations I've had with her over the years. How close our little group has always been. She's been like a little sister to me and always in our corner; someone I trust. My laughter ceases and I clear my throat. "I'm sorry, Nat. Hurting either of you wasn't my plan, but at the time I had no choice but to make things appear a certain way. With everything going on, and the MDPs detectives sniffing around, I needed her away from this. From me. Should I have come to her, yes, but at the same time, we both know she would've fought me tooth and nail to help. I was working on borrowed time and leaving her alone… caught in the middle, was unacceptable to me."

She nods, her body language a bit less stiff. "What about having men put on her for protection? To keep her safe while you were—"

"Who says I didn't?"

"Then why?" she asks, and Natasha doesn't need to elaborate for me to understand.

"Because I needed the hit placed on her head back on me. It's all I had at the moment, Nat, and in order to keep her safe, I made it seem as if she was nothing to me when in fact, she's my world."

"But why go the cheating route?"

"Because it works. Plain and simple." It sucks, but it's the truth. No sugarcoating. "The same night Luna found me with Amberlyn, the hit shifted back to my family. We knew that would happen and took the necessary precautions, like armoring the vehicles."

"Like Maritza's."

"Exactly."

In a move I'm not expecting, Nat hugs me tight once before stepping back and as she does, I catch Luna's eyes. Her smile is bright and cheeks flushed. She's also holding a thumb up at me which makes me roll my eyes.

"Go to her."

"What?" Luna crooks a finger behind my father's back and mouths the words *come get me.*

"...all I want is for you guys to be happy." I catch the end of Natasha's words and pull my eyes away from the woman I love beyond all comprehension. "I also want my cousin to smile every single day like she's been doing since news of your release broke out. And while I might still be a smidge mad at you, Leon..." she holds up two fingers to show just how tiny her anger is "...I'll never stand in the way of her happiness."

"Thank you, Nat."

"Just never break her heart again."

"Never again will we ever be apart," is all I say before making my way toward the coquettish woman daring me to steal her away. And I do just that. Without giving the old man a chance to refuse or block my attempt, I have her in my arms and holding her close as a bachata begins to play. Her body and mine are one as we move. Her mouth, those berry-colored lips parting as I grip her hip and anchor her to me. "You're mine now."

"I've always been yours."

"WAKE UP, ASSHOLE," I sneer early the next day while grabbing a bucket full of dirty mop water and throwing the contents at his head. The wetness spreads all around Sergio, one rivulet coming to a stop just in front of my all-white Pumas.

At once, Sergio sputters as a few drops of water rolling down his face slip between parted lips. His face scrunches up before his taste buds fully decipher the nasty taste; it's the same water used to clean the mess my large hogs leave behind on the premises.

"What the fuck?"

I toss him an old rag. "Sit up and clean your face."

Sergio glares at me, not fully taking me in as I stand in the doorway to one of our detainment cells. The bright Florida sun is harsh on the eyes and he begins to squint soon after. "Who the fuck is there? I demand to be—" His words die as I take two steps forward, my hard stare meeting his now scared one.

"Good. You're learning some manners." The table is an old, scratched up wooden piece of shit in a hideous pine color and the dirty water from the bucket pools at the center. The walls are an off-white that now seems yellow in the daylight, and the only thing dry is a chair against the wall and I grab it, flipping it around so I can sit backwards. "Full name?"

"Where am I, Thiago? Where's Jadiel?" His eyes shift around nervously, taking in his surroundings. "What day is it?"

Miguel, who stands behind him, reaches out and grabs a fistful of his black hair and yanks back on his ponytail, causing Sergio's neck to extend into an uncomfortable position. He stares at my guard, mouth agape, throat bobbing harshly as Miguel's hand comes down across his cheek. "Only answer what is asked. Nothing else."

"Okay." That earns him another strike. Sergio's face is now red, and the fingerprints left behind are becoming more pronounced.

"That's enough." At my mock admonishment, my guard lets him go, pushing him forward and toward the Ruger now atop the table. "Let's give the man a chance to answer." Scared eyes meet mine. He's sweating. "What. Is. Your. Full. Name?"

He swallows hard. "Sergio Martinez."

"And your age?"

"Twenty-nine."

"Where were you born?"

"New Jersey."

"Where in Jersey?" I ask, even though I already know the answer. I also know that's not the last name on his birth certificate. Martinez is his deceased grandmother's maiden name.

Why's he choosing to lie? Don't know, but it won't remain a mystery for long. Today is his only warning because Sergio Martin, not Martinez, is from the same city as my Luna.

He hung out at the same places. He was friends with her male older cousin from her mother's side who passed away from a car crash the night of his twenty-second birthday.

They weren't close—he barely knew my queen—but I do remember her sad eyes when they found out. I remember Yvette dragging her and Natasha back to Westfield for a weekend of mass, a vigil, and then burial.

"Westfield, New Jersey," Sergio coughs a bit, his mouth still tasting like shit from the filthy water. "May I have a drink, please?"

"Only because you said *please* so nicely." I tap the back of the chair and stand, heading toward the far end where I keep a small refrigerator. It isn't plugged in, but there are two water bottles inside that are just a bit over hot. "I apologize for the lack of provisions. This is all I have."

Sergio grimaces when his fingers wrap around the water bottle. "No worries. I understand, sir."

My eyes shift to Miguel, who's holding back a laugh, then back to him. "Go ahead and drink up, Sergio. We need to wrap up this little chat."

I'll give him points for keeping the disgust out of his expression while taking a large gulp of the old water. I have no idea how long that's been there nor do I care; it serves a purpose.

"Now, are we done?"

He drains the entire bottle. *Guess hot beats dirty.* "Yes."

"Good." I don't retake my seat, choosing instead to walk around to him. The closer I get, the more he shrinks back and when I stop just within reach, Sergio almost falls over.

And in that moment of fear.

That singular second of realization...

I strike.

Grabbing his wrist, I slam it against the wooden table with one hand and take my Ruger with the other. The barrel against his skin gets his attention. "Don't fucking move." He doesn't listen and I lift the gun, bringing it down with force against his knuckles. Once. Twice. A total of five times, breaking the bones there.

His scream rents the air. His sob follows. *Pussy.*

"Fuck. Please...*please* stop," he cries out, fighting to pull his hand from my grip. If anything, he further injures himself. Dislocated his wrist. "We're family!"

That one pisses me off and the next strike is to his mouth and then neck, causing him to choke. To shut the fuck up and lose a tooth in the process. There's spluttering and gasping and even blood dribbling from the split lip, but I'm not done.

Before his next intake of breath, I'm jamming my Ruger just under his chin. "We're not family, *Martinez.* Dating my cousin doesn't make you one of us. That shit is earned." My finger twitches on the trigger while his body shakes, the pain radiating from his expression. "Now, answer my next question."

"Anything. I don't want problems."

It's meek and I crack a smile. "Why did you move here?"

"For school, and then I liked—"

"The truth, Sergio," I cut him off. "Don't let me be the reason my cousin doesn't finish planning this wedding."

"I moved here to follow a dream."

"So you're a chaser now?" My phone vibrates inside my pocket and I let him go, taking a few steps back. I pull it out and read the message.

> Pick up is done. Dropping off the sack of potatoes now. ~Little Bro

I type my reply just as fast.

> Thank you. See you soon. ~Thiago

"Yes."

"Okay," I say and let him go, stepping back to accept the small towel my guard has for me. My hands have a little blood on them and so do my new sneakers. *Fucking asshole.* "Let's get him cleaned up and back home within the next twenty-four hours. If anyone asks, he was busy doing a little favor for me and fell on the job. Understood?"

"Of course, boss. We all know the man can be clumsy."

"I didn't hear your response, Sergio. Understood?"

"Yes, I'm clumsy and fell."

I walk out without another word and find one of the two watchmen standing at the ready. He doesn't ask questions, but once I move past him, goes inside to help Miguel.

There are far more important things to focus on today than Sergio, even though my eye is on him. He's full of shit, and his secret isn't as hidden as he thinks.

He's useful at the moment, I'll give him that.

Easy to break.

However, Jadiel is what keeps him alive, but once I discover how deep his betrayal runs, I'll break both their necks personally.

Chapter 20
THIAGO

IT'S THREE O'CLOCK by the time I arrive at an abandoned stadium near Jackson Memorial Hospital on Monday. It's old, unsafe, and dirty. It's full of rats and used needles—random articles of clothing thrown about different areas of the premises.

Sad. This place wasn't always like this.

In its heyday, the stadium was used for spring training by some of the largest baseball associations nationwide; it's also where the home team began as a minor league club.

Now, though, it's a condemned site and only a few brave crackheads come inside to use or fuck. Then there's me and my family. When we occupy, the surrounding population scatters and hides— they pretend the giant eyesore doesn't exist.

I like it that way.

It's why I haven't torn it down.

As of 2001, while being nothing more than a kid, I'm the owner. A gift from my father when the city wanted to blow it up, taking with it memories of Miami's baseball dreams.

Before our team became a major league threat.

Before we won championships.

I'm a baseball fan and the city cashed in on the much-needed relief from the self-made debt that the then mayor at the time was responsible for. The transaction was all in cash. No traces, which served him just fine as he escaped a lengthy prison sentence due to the miraculous funds he "proved" to just be misplaced by the last auditors.

Stepping through the hole in the shitty fencing, I make my way in through the main doors. They're busted, rusted, and useless, but I don't keep the place for its beautiful facade.

This is an untouched territory in the heart of Miami, and right at the center of what used to be the luxurious lobby is an almost naked Gaytan. He's tied up, hands above his head on a large truss that's seen better days.

There's a *drip drip drip* above him. Most of the ceiling is gone and what's left doesn't protect him from nature. That, and somewhere above is a leaking pipe that's unleashing its torment, one drop at a time.

Right over the same spot now for three days.

All day.

Every few seconds.

Softening the skin at the crown of his head.

His eyes widen when he fully takes me in. Recognition takes over; he sees his death in my eyes. "Evening, Alfredo," I say, stopping just a few feet from his filth. There's no one else here besides me. It's unnecessary when the people in Allapattah and surrounding areas mostly work for you in one capacity or another. "How's your day going? Are you hungry or thirsty?"

"Let me go." His fight or flight has kicked in and he struggles against his bonds.

"Why would I do that?"

"This is a mistake. You're making a terrible mistake!" There's fear in his eyes and his body gives a slight shake when I pull a few things out of my pocket: phone, money clip, and my brass knuckles. "The Senots won't take—"

"Quiet." His lips snap shut, eyes shifting away from my glare. "Not another word unless I ask a direct question. Understood?" Gaytan is smart enough to nod his head, the action causing his face to contort in pain; there's a large bruise on his neck. "Good boy."

He doesn't like being addressed like a dog, and I could give two flying fucks.

Giving him my back, I turn and grab a small wooden stool Ivan left for me. I drag it slowly toward him, pushing aside whatever garbage is in my path—the noise loud inside the large, open, and mostly dilapidated structure.

Then I place it a few steps from him. If he'd been loose, it'd be within reach.

Close but not.

A taunt.

One that I bolster by placing my items atop it before adding my loaded gun to that same pile.

No safety. A quick pull of the trigger and one of us would be dead.

"You never answered my questions, by the way," I say and get no reply. "How are you? Hungry?"

"Are you offering me a last meal?" Alfredo's reply—the sarcasm —grates on my nerves, and before his next intake of breath, I back-hand him across the mouth, fully aware that my gold rings will knock out a tooth or two. The two at the front bear the brunt of the force, the metal breaking them in half.

Leaning forward, I smirk. "Want it to be?"

"Fuck you!" It leaves him on a bloody lisp, his lips split where the broken teeth embedded. I don't reply, but I do grab my gun, pointing it straight at his head with a brow arched. "Please don't."

"What happened to *fuck me?*" A pull of the trigger and a bullet dislodges; it barely misses his arm. Just barely.

"Are you insane!" Arching, he fights to pull away—stresses his shoulder and pops the one on the left without me placing a single finger on him. "Son of a bitch." It's a hiss, teeth clenching tight as his position only adds stress to the dislocated area. "You're going back to jail where you belong. Mr. Senot can—"

"Suck my dick." The next bullet exits the chamber and lodges into his thigh, the same side as his dislocated shoulder. His scream of pain is loud, but I'm not moved at all. Instead, I give him a bored look. Dramatics bore me. "Are you done?"

No answer. Not any that I can decipher as he writhes, blood flowing from the wound, complaining in gibberish that only he can understand. Sure, there's a *fuck* here or there thrown about, but the rest is a bunch of nonsensical groans that add up to shit.

So, I fire again.

The third bullet grazes his side over the bluish marks on his right ribs. There's a bit of red that rushes to the surface, the heated burn of the bullet leaving its marks, but no deep cut or puncture. It's a flesh wound, but if you go by his pathetic wails, you'd think I cut off a limb with a rusty saw.

Pussy. Tilting my head, I lower my Ruger to the area just below his belt and wait.

"Please don't." Sweat forms at his brow and upper chest now, the hairs at the latter matting against his tan skin. "Not there."

I almost chuckle. Almost. He acts as if he'll have the chance to use it again.

"Then don't test my patience again." At my words, he nods and I lower my weapon. It takes its place once again on the stool as I remove my shirt, the white Ralph Lauren polo going with the rest of my belongings. "Now, are we ready to play twenty questions? Will you behave?"

"Yes." A low whisper, his body shaking as reality sets in.

"Okay." Walking closer, I take inspection of the damage already inflicted and roll my eyes at my brother's handiwork. There's a ring all the men in my family wear, a thick gold band with our last name branded over the top with a yellow topaz on the left of the large "D" for my mother's birth month. It's gaudy, very Cuban, and mine is retrofitted to carry Luna's stone on the right.

Ivan's, though, is a bit more eccentric.

A bit more brutal.

His letters are in 3D and pointy; they embed the letters onto the skin if he throws a punch and it lands at just the right angle, a perfected bitch-slap that marks Gaytan right over the back of his shaved head.

"First question." There are bruises across his back large enough to come from a shoe sole and the cut over his left eyebrow that's swollen, but his eye is fine. "Why are you here?"

"I don't know." The first sign of a liar is the inability to look you in the eye. His shitty eyes look past my shoulder and focus on the entrance.

"Final warning." My tone is icy, dripping with the ire I have the power to unleash at any moment. "Answer the fucking question."

"I'm telling you the...*Jesus*," he cries out, body fighting to pull away from the hand I've placed over his injured shoulder, digging my fingertips in to the point his body shakes from the pain. His teeth grit together so hard he cuts his own tongue. Tears well up in his eyes as I watch him, and just when his lips part to speak again, I kick his legs further apart so his weight drops, forcing his bonds to stretch the muscle. "It wasn't me."

"What wasn't you? Be specific, Alfredo." The rope cuts into his wrist and he winces when I finger the bound flesh. "What is it that you didn't do?"

"I-I didn't…" Alfredo pauses, swallowing hard. His mouth is bloody; rivulets stain the beard at his chin and then neck. "I didn't hire Ismael."

"Hmm." That's all I say. I'm not here to comfort him.

"It's the truth."

"Are you sure about that? Last chance."

"Yes. It was…" He mumbles the name I need. It's low, almost too low for me to hear, but I do as if Alfredo shouted it.

"Louder." Just because I can. Because we both know there's no feasible way that it'll stay hidden for long.

That *she'll* stay hidden

"I'll pay with my life to save—"

"Your bitch the heartache? A death sentence?" My glower alone forces him to arch away, adding more pressure to the joints of his arms. "Because we both know Jasmine doesn't give a fuck about either of you."

"She loves ME!" Gaytan suddenly yells out, his own anger bursting forth. The idiot still doesn't see how he's been played in all of this. "She approached me before Ulysses asked me to do so—to fucking end your piece-of-shit family—but when I said no, he promised me something I couldn't deny. We were banking on you discovering his plan and ending him. That you would set *us* free."

"And yet here you are, just like Roger." With a quickness Gaytan doesn't expect, I pull out a small knife from my front pocket and flick the blade open. I'm quick with it, my arm slicing through the air and across the ropes tethering him to the truss. A single slice cuts through the rope just below his right wrist, while the second motion breaks what's left around the wooden beam. He falls, his bruised and bloody body meeting the dirty concrete floor below. "But then again, she probably made him feel important. Blew him while professing some poetic shit that made his simpleton mind bow at her feet."

Gaytan's eyes are closed now, his body trembling. "Roger?"

"Was fucking her too," I answer, breaking the last of his spirit. "He thought himself in love until the very end, but then self-preservation kicked in and…"

"He gave us away." So much sadness in his tone. Heartbreak.

"He gave *her* away." Because Alfredo needs to understand that he's of no importance. To me. To her. To Roger. To his kids that'll grow up in a safe and healthy environment after his death. "You're nothing but an overrated gopher who drank the Kool-Aid and bought the bullshit attached. You were a pity fuck. A necessity in order to achieve compliance from a man not worth pig shit."

"Roger was my friend." Tears drop from his eyes, his face contorted in anguish. In mourning, and I smile. I find his emotional pain amusing.

"Is that betrayal I detect in your voice?" With a smirk on my face, I place a foot atop his torso and press down right over the flesh wound. It bleeds, opening just a little bit deeper. "Do you need a hug or pat on the back? Do you need me to supply the fake condolences?"

"I cared about him."

"Roger is dead and on his way to being shark chum off the coast of the Bahamas."

"Just end me." It's a whimper, pathetic and unmoving.

"With pleasure…" he nods, closing his eyes in wait "…but not yet."

Gaytan frowns. "Why are you prolonging—"

"Because I can. Because the family you abandoned also deserves some retribution." Brown orbs snap open and meet my amused ones. His shock is evident. He didn't think me to be so thorough. "Those kids will never know how much of a scum you were. They'll grow up happy, healthy, and Carlotta will find a man worthy of her. She'll never depend on a man again. She'll never put up with scraps in order to maintain those kids. They'll move on while you rot. They'll truly live while you become nothing but an unpleasant memory not to be revisited."

"How much do you know?"

And there's the fifty million dollar question.

How much? How little? Why am I fucking with him?

"You're alive just to confirm what I already know." Bringing the hand with the knife in my grip up, I turn the blade, letting the sunlight filtering through a hole in the roof glint off the metal. "Nothing more."

Gaytan coughs then, his abdomen constricting, and he grimaces. Tries to fold into himself.

He's in pain without reprieve.

He's facing his reality without an ounce of hope.

It takes him a moment to compose himself, to stop squirming beneath my foot on his torso. "Jasmine never hid her lovers, you know. I accepted them."

"Why?"

"Because she promised me that I'd always be her number one."

"And Ulysses? Does he know?"

"He does." A cough escapes again, a bit of blood in the spittle. "He's not man enough to satisfy her and at the same time likes to watch. Ulysses enjoys being her bitch. Her cuckold husband."

"But if you're an employee and not her bull, who is?"

Say it. Say his name.

"Antonio Alejos." He's grown a bit pallid and sweat forms at his brow.

"Thank you, Mr. Gaytan." I remove my shoe, take a step back, and raise my knife by the very tip of the blade. "Your death is only the beginning."

"Wait!" he yells out suddenly, more panicked than he's been thus far. Maybe it's the delirium from blood loss. Maybe he's afraid to die. "Let me just say goodbye—"

A quick flick of the wrist and I embed the blade three inches deep into the center of his neck, cutting off his nonsense. Alfredo's reaction is automatic, to grip the base, but before he can pull it out, I have my hand on my gun and I'm firing round after round.

I don't stop until his body lies motionless and he's looking back at me with horror in his expression. He's bathing the ground with his life's essence. Paying for his crimes against my family, but I wasn't kidding when I said this is just the beginning.

I'm going for the head of Medusa.

I'm going to break her and then watch the rats try and scatter.

Chapter 21
LUNA

I HAVEN'T SEEN Thiago for more than a few minutes here or there since Saturday night.

Since he dropped me off at home a week ago with a toe-curling kiss that weakened my knees and left me a panting mess when he left. He didn't try to have his way with me. Nor did he come inside my home.

Instead, against my closed door his hips pinned mine while his mouth reaffirmed what I already know is my truth...

I'm his and he is mine.

I am totally failing at this making him chase me thing. I need to be stronger.

"Feeling better, Alejos?" my boss asks, bringing me back to the present and I look up, catching his stern expression. Today, though, behind the serious look, there's a touch of amusement. It looks weird because I don't think I've ever seen my boss so much as smile. "That must've been some virus you caught. Used up all your vacation time this year."

We both know it's a lie. I'm sure the opinions running rampant in this precinct alone placed doubts on my sudden bout of "sickness" as well as reputation. While most officers here treat me with respect— they know who my father and uncle are—I'm still looked at differently. Judged as the ex-girlfriend of a notorious mafia boss and not trusted.

I'm sure that my absence was spoken about, but I just don't care. This isn't my career path for life, just until I find what I came looking for.

"I'm better, sir. Just a small twinge of queasiness left behind."

"You want to be benched today?" he asks, taking a sip from the most hideous mug I've ever seen. It's a toilet. Literally. His daughter gave it to him as a gag gift two years ago on his birthday, and the crotchety old man loves it. Drinks his coffee from it every day.

"Not at all." Sitting back, I keep my expression cool while avoiding the piece of ceramic I wish to smash with a hammer. It's gross. Looks gross. However, I do see the folder in his other hand, the label in the color red that is his way of coding priority levels. Depending on the scene, if first responders tampered with the evidence, and lastly, if we're looking at a case with a fatality. "Whatcha got for me?"

The color he's holding is for fatality.

"Are you sure?" Thompson has never, not even when I came in with a broken index and middle finger from a fall, asked me this. *What's his deal?* "You could help the crew in the back with the phys- ical cataloging of—"

"I'm sure. Not a doubt."

"Fine." The man mumbles the word *stubborn* under his breath. It's low, but I catch it and decide not to question him. "We got a Jane Doe out in Sweetwater. Call came in about fifteen minutes ago." He's watching curiously while extending the file out toward me. As he does this, I catch for the first time since taking this job the sight of a set of numbers tattooed on the inside of his wrist.

I've seen that before. On multiple people. On *his* people.

The hell?

"Sir, what's that on—"

"Are you taking this case, or do I send Walker instead?" My eyes snap back to him and he shakes his head. He's telling me to drop it for now, and I do. *For now* being the operative words.

Someone has some explaining to do.

Someone has been keeping tabs on me.

Someone never stopped taking care of me.

It shouldn't warm my heart, but it does, because it's just another sign that Thiago didn't just leave. That he thought ahead. That he had more faith in me than I had in him.

I never thought twice when the sudden position as a forensic investigator became available for me. When my uncle pretty much walked me inside after graduating and gave me the paperwork to sign, without so much as an interview. At the time, I took it as he spoke highly of me and cleared the pathway I needed without my asking.

He and Natasha are the only two people that knew of my plans. Who knew that I wanted to clear his name and then shoot him myself for the stupidity he pulled.

Because even angry at him—hurting—I needed to help him in any way I could.

There's a lightness in my heart right before it clenches with the disappointment that follows.

I didn't trust him, and yet, my papi knew I'd do this. That I would take the challenge on.

And I've risen to the challenge. Two of the detectives working his case have been fired for tampering. The judge who sentenced him was caught with two prostitutes out on Biscayne Blvd in a seedy motel, pants around his ankles and with his hands dipping into the cookie jar—two street workers whose cases had been dismissed inside his courtroom.

Those pictures hit circulation quickly. Every single local news station played that story at the beginning of each broadcast for weeks and put a giant question mark on all his previous convictions.

And yet, it's still not enough. I'm after the head of this snake, and up until yesterday, I'd been looking in the wrong direction. At the wrong people.

"I'll take it."

"Good. Good." The tension in his shoulders drops a bit. "Officer Alejos will be escorting you, and Natasha is on her way now to handle the written documentation of the scene. It's a gruesome one, and this needs to be handled quickly as it's near an elementary school."

"When do we leave?"

"Now, kid. Let's head out," Uncle Edgar says from behind me and I turn my head, taking in his expression. He looks so much like my father, but that's where the similarities die. He's happy and down to earth, and the only thing he's ever cared about is my and his daughter's well-being. "You ready?"

"Yeah. I'm ready." My equipment is the first thing I prepare after clocking in, and my bag is ready to go. Pushing my chair back, I stand and grab it from the corner of the small desk I use here. We don't talk as we head outside of the building; there's so much to say, but with ears around, it's best to keep our lips shut.

However, that changes once inside his unmarked car. Because while it still belongs to the city and it's loaded with cameras and audio, talking in code is something my family has perfected over the years. He's a cop with a shady past, my father is a city council member with enough sins to ruin his hope of a future governor position, and then, you have me.

The once-almost wife to Thiago De Leon. A known criminal. A known killer.

We're dysfunctional as fuck.

"Missed you at the family dinner on Saturday, Tio." My first words are generic, to be interpreted as an Alejos get together. "Hot date kept you away? Who's the new flavor?"

"Was busy. I *am* seeing someone, but it's a short-term thing." He shrugs, reversing the car and then shifting into drive. The exit is on the other end of the lot, and as he passes a group of rookies standing beside a square car, they all pause to look. At me, not him. "Blind dates usually don't go past that."

In other words he was working, but for Thiago, and blind date means delivery of goods.

"Oh, I know. Your daughter has tried a few times to get me to fall down that rabbit hole and I refuse."

"Has she, now?" He grumbles something under his breath. "Need me to tell her to back off?"

"Not really."

"Are you sure?" His eyes shift over briefly before facing forward, turning right and merging with traffic heading toward the expressway. "I know firsthand how Natasha can be at times."

"After Saturday, Nat got the message loud and clear." My uncle nods, seemingly at ease now, but I'm not done. "Your presence was missed, though. I would've loved to see you there...to hang out like we used to."

Before everything went down, we were all so close. Him, Natasha, and me.

He's who I trusted and came to when my parents were unbearable. When they put down my relationship with someone they see as unworthy. Uncle Edgar has always been in my corner and I took it a bit for granted, gave him crap for picking a side that wasn't mine, when it's the farthest thing from the truth.

And I'll admit that it's my anger that got in the way.

"Hazard of the job, Lunita. You miss important occasions."

"You sounded like your brother just then," I say, trying to crack a joke, but at once I see that it falls flat. His hands tighten around the steering wheel and nostrils flare; the look he gives me alone is one I've never been on the receiving end of.

Before addressing me, I watch discreetly how he elbows the door, giving it one solid thump with his elbow. To the naked eye, it seems that he did it by mistake, but then another sound fills the air— a low buzz, and then as if an old VHS tape slid into a VCR player.

"Look straight ahead and not a word. Understood?"

"Yes."

"Good." A second thump a second or two later, and the whizzing sound picks up in speed. My eyes shift to the passenger side window then, taking in the scenery that in Miami means nothing more than a few thousand vehicles on the road with angry drivers inside. People here drive with a purpose, and mostly a *get out of my way* mentality that very few can handle.

We're special like that. I wouldn't change my home for the world.

And it's also where I truly believe that the expression "road rage" was invented.

It takes about a minute for the whizzing sound to stop and for him to look my way. I can feel his stare and turn to catch his glare.

"What was that?"

"Never compare me to that *asshole,* sobrina," he grits out instead, choking back a curse word or two. "Your father is a self-absorbed cabron that doesn't deserve you as his daughter."

"Tio, I never meant it—" I'm interrupted by the sound of his radio crackling and the operator shooting off a few codes along with the location of a robbery in progress. It's near the Bayside Market-place and all available units are being called in. At once, three other squad cars respond, confirming their location and in route process toward the clothing store.

For a few beats after we stay quiet, listening to the communication between officers and dispatch. His expression says it all, though. There's guilt there and something else that I can't quite identify.

"I'm sorry."

"I'm sorry," we say in unison, and I chuckle. The amusement dies down quickly, though. "I really am, you know. Sorry, that is."

"You did nothing wrong, Luna. Nothing."

"Not for the bad joke, Tio, because that's all it was, but for the last few years. If I ever hurt you or was a jerk, I apologize."

"Not needed, but accepted since I never gave you the chance to pull away."

"You are stubborn."

"Ditto." Edgar chuckles, but that turns into a heavy sigh near the end. "I shouldn't have given you the attitude, Luna. My anger toward my brother shouldn't fall on you." He reaches his right hand out and gives my arm a squeeze. "Mine and Antonio's relationship isn't in a good place at the moment. Let's leave it at that for now."

"Will you two ever be okay?" He shakes his head in the negative at my question and I nod. "Can't say I'm surprised. He's become someone I no longer recognize."

Edgar looks like he wants to add something to that, but a rough exhale escapes instead. "To answer your earlier question; Thiago had this car, and a few others on the force, retrofitted with special blocking devices. Once that goes on, it records the driver for sixty seconds and reports the playback to the department. It'll play in real time and on a constant loop."

"When the hell did he do that?" I play along, dropping a subject I can see plain as day he doesn't want to visit. "The guy has been out for a little over a week."

"This was seven days after his sentencing."

"That makes no sense."

"Doesn't need to." At my incredulous look, he rolls his eyes and waves one hand in the air. "Francisco, the mechanic at the precinct, is on the Leons payroll. You've been around them longer and can fill in the rest better than I can."

"Christ." My emotions are spinning between heartache, confusion, amusement, and lastly...I'm in awe of him. It's getting harder and harder to not let my love for the man dominate me blindly, and while a part of me longs to let go and do just that, his mother's advice still rings true in my ear: he needs to see me as his equal, too.

They've been a constant companion as of late, those words, especially after listening to the recording of him before jail. It's made me think. Made me accept that I too, am to blame. And while I don't agree with his lying, with letting me think the worst of him, I forgot my own promise to him.

To trust him. To know that I am his one and only.

"He's always one step ahead, Luna. Always."

"Funny you say that..." I trail off, turning my attention back to the main road. It's busy and full of loud music—life going on as if nothing's changed—while I'm battling this yo-yoing effect. Inner demons that whisper words of fear, revenge, and love.

"Why is that?"

"Because the more I sit down and think, the more obvious things become, and I feel like an idiot. So many changes, and I never once questioned what was happening around me because truly, it was convenient."

"Sometimes our minds protect us that way."

"Or maybe it was too painful to accept that the man I love more than life itself was close but on the same breath, unreachable." And that sums up my emotions to a T. I'm not an idiot, and yet, I chose to follow blindly without questioning a single move when I damn well could have. To Ivan. To Maritza. To my uncle. To Thiago himself, but I zipped my lips and just kept walking to the tune of someone else's song because I didn't want the truth to hurt worse.

It angers me.

It disappoints me.

It's shifted my outlook a bit from Thiago and more toward myself.

I didn't fight for us; to let me stay by his side. I accepted the apartment without asking about the owner—why do I have the largest one or the entire floor to myself? Why does the unit across from me remain empty after all these years? Why have I seen two men following me at all times when out and not once confronted them because of the tattoo on the inside of one man's wrist? *One just like my uncle. My boss. Like the ones soldiers working for the Leon family all receive when accepted.* Why I am still his emergency contact after all these years according to the police database that I borrowed the login for?

Why?

Why?

Why?

So many questions that I've left as is, and for what? I'm not this woman. I'm not afraid.

"We're here, kid," my uncle says, and I'm pulled back to the present. "You ready?

My head shifts toward him, meeting his eyes from the corner of mine. "I'm sorry, what?"

"We're here."

Chapter 22
LUNA

THE SECOND MY feet meet the asphalt, I'm stopped in my tracks by an uncomfortable feeling. Thoughts of my personal life vanish as a shiver rushes down my spine and the soft, downy hair on my arms stands on end.

There's an eeriness to this crime scene. Ominous. Bone chilling. It grips me—this invisible, crushing weight on my chest that makes me pause with my hand on the door's frame. I've seen things over the years. Know what the depraved side of humanity is capable of.

These are memories that I'll never forget, and yet, this one already feels different.

Haunting.

Darker.

"You okay?" my uncle asks again, from beside me now, and his voice is full of concern. "You're a little pale."

"I'm fine. Just got a weird feeling." I'm looking out toward a small, empty field at the far end of the large parking lot. My unease is coming from that direction, an empty area that's been taped off as a second evidence site. "Ignore me."

"Weird feelings are nothing more than warning signs."

"It'll be okay." Even as I say this, I can't shake the sense of foreboding.

"And I'll be keeping an eye on you. First sign of distress and I'll pull you out."

"Deal." I won't argue his call. He's not being difficult, I know this; it's protocol to pull any department employee—officer or other-wise—if under sudden distress as this can prohibit them from completing their tasks. Some of which could literally mean life or death.

We're inside of one of South Florida's largest outlet malls and behind a popular retail clothing store near the building's center. The entire place opens within a few hours, and yet, I'm concerned about two things: the elementary school nearby, and the morbid onlookers that will try and catch a glimpse of the crime scene.

Because humanity cannot help itself when it comes to death. They all want to see it—experience it—without being the party impacted by the catastrophe. Sadly, curiosity can make an asshole out of the nicest people, and with the rise of social media, people fancy themselves reporters.

As long as they get thousands of likes, they don't care about safety, empathy, or impacting my lighting if the camera picks up a millisecond of flash from their phones.

With the location being a high trafficked one, it's going to be a tight deadline to catalogue, collect, and move the deceased before any interruption can delay everything.

My eyes shift from the back lot to the large white sheets blocking what I can assume is the victim—like a canopy with a makeshift wall—and then the back door of the store. Already we have three employees congregated there, cigarettes in hand as they point and talk. Speculate. Form a twisted version of this poor person's demise.

I need them gone.

"Remove them from the premises. The dumping of ashes could contaminate the scene. It's windy, and I need to secure the integrity of each item before the others collect."

"Go ahead and set up. I'll take care of that." He turns to walk away, but then pauses a mere three steps from me and looks back from over his shoulder. "Something about this call has felt off since it came in. It's why I drove you here. It's what my *boss* asked me to do, and above the badge, I'll protect my family, Luna. If at any moment I say *out*—"

"We out."

"Good." Within a few steps, he's over to the other officers and pointing toward the group of onlookers—yelling something that makes those trying to record run back inside. No one says anything to him, and the louder he becomes, the more proactive the men in blue become.

"Bet you twenty the younger one pees his pants a little?" Natasha says from beside me suddenly and I jump, almost dropping my bag. It droops a bit in my hold, but I reaffirm my grip before glaring at her. "Someone's off her game."

"Should I put a bell on you?"

"Not my fault you're distracted."

"*Not my fault you're distracted,*" I parrot back while she rolls her eyes. "You just have a bad habit."

"Of walking and talking?"

"Shut it." I leave her standing by her father's unmarked vehicle and step under the yellow tape that marks the perimeter containing the body. There's blood all around the victim, a line of red that makes me think she was dragged here. Nat follows me over, in her hand a few items from her own kit. "Young, or?"

"Mid-twenties according to the first responders team, but I've been waiting for you to mark this area. The other site, at the back end, is done and ready for film."

"Anything in particular we need to focus on?"

"My first analysis is inconclusive. I'm needing a second opinion on whether that's the murder scene."

"All right." This is something we've done plenty of times before; it's why we work closely together and often. Natasha has an impeccable eye for evidence. Spots traits others miss, and while I fell into this out of a need to clear Thiago's name, I took to the training Thompson gave me himself rather quickly.

Another thing I haven't questioned until now. And those numbers on his wrist—

"You okay, prima?" The concern in her tone pulls back to the present. "Something up?"

"Just contemplating my approach." I say instead, refocusing myself. This is neither the time nor place. "What's back there?"

Whatever she sees in my expression makes her back down. Nat grimaces and I still myself for her answer. "Her organs."

"*Christ.*"

"Among other things." Nat moves past me and at the end where a small puddle of red sits, she places a plastic marker on the ground with the number thirty-six on it. The numbers prior must be out in the other field. "It's not pretty, Lulu, and watch your step. The small area is contained, but messy. This sick fucker has anger issues that are more than prevalent in his tactic."

"Crime of passion?"

"I'm leaning more toward hate."

"Got it." I don't know which one is worse: passion or hate? They're both extremely powerful emotions that can catapult even the nicest of people to commit horrendous acts of violence. "I'll be back in a bit."

"Take one of my extra-large rulers." She stands then, walking over to a small table set up beside the makeshift structure protecting the corpse. Taking her gloves off, she tosses them inside of a bin for disposing hazardous material and cleans her hands. "With the brightness out..." my cousin calls over her shoulder, "...you might get a clearer reading on camera with it."

"I have two with me, but another never hurts."

"I'll probably toss this one after this scene."

"That bad?"

Walking back after zipping her bag, she holds it out for me. "One of the worst I've ever worked."

"Good morning to us," is all I say and take it, turning around with my own equipment in tow toward the lot with overgrowth. I leave her to it. To set up my shots and get this done as quickly as possible without being neglectful to the most minute detail. It's her strength, while mine has always been capturing what's in front of me through a lens.

From where I am, I can just make out a section that's cleared out except for a lone tree at the center, as if it were placed there for shade when the surroundings are nothing but sandy dirt. The police-standard yellow tape greets me at the edge and as I step under it, the wind carries a wave of putrid—decomposing stench that is unique to flesh, or in this case organs, rotting under the sun for a while.

I don't even need to look at the evidence to know that this isn't a fresh kill.

This poor woman has been deceased for more than twenty-four hours. If not longer.

"Miss Luna Alejos," my name is called from the left and I turn my head toward the voice, ignoring the area where the smell is coming from. It's better this way. I'm disconnected. The voice, though, does have my attention since it's male and unfamiliar. "We're ready for you. Do you need any assistance?"

The badge on his shirt reads "Young" and I quickly run through everyone I've worked with in the past. He isn't one of them. The way he shifts from side to side, right hand shaking, isn't boding well for him, either. Puts me on alert.

How does he know me?

"No." Letting go of my rolling bag's handle, I take out my cell and press the number four. "Who are you?"

"I'm sorry. Maybe I should've introduced myself." Young comes forward with the intention to shake my hand, but I hold up my palm. He's smart enough and stops. "Is something wrong?"

"A few things." No sooner has the last word passed my lips than Edgar rushes over. Ignoring Young for a second, I look over at my uncle before either man speaks. "You know him?"

"He's a transfer from North Carolina. First week on the beat..." Edgar pauses, looking over at him "...and not quite used to how we run things."

"Okay. Fair enough." The others, a few officers that know me, chuckle under their breaths. One glare from me and they turn away quickly. It's one of the few things I took from the De Leons over the years; how effective a single look could be. How it cuts through people's defenses and exposes their weaknesses, because most people don't like confrontation. Those who constantly bark have no bite. "Officer Young, while I appreciate the offer, I'm going to have to decline. As I work to capture this scene, please keep yourself and others at bay. No one other than myself or a forensics specialist is allowed past those lines until we are done. Understood?"

"Of course, Miss Alejos."

"Then do so." I'm being a bitch, I know, but something about him isn't sitting well with me. And as he goes, a forced smile on his face, I hold up a finger toward my uncle. "Check him out," I say, voice very low. "He knew my name without an introduction and my name tag is inside my shirt."

"The others with him know you very well."

"And yet, they don't fidget around me. Avoid? Yes. But their hands don't shake, nor do they shift their weight from foot to foot."

"Say no more. I'll take care of it."

"You calling *him*?"

"Yes."

"Good. I'll start here while you do that." He turns from me then, maybe takes two steps, and then stops. In his hand he has paper, pulled from his pocket and folded in half; I move closer to reach for it. My fingertips grip the single sheet, head down as if looking at it, but I know he wants to say something. "What?"

"You're more like him than you want to admit." Then he's gone, leaving me with that thought and paper in hand. The note is written in Thiago's handwriting and I find myself reading each line over and over again.

A gift for my queen.

Open the left side pocket where you usually keep a set of brushes

to clean your lenses and you'll find a surprise.

Love,

Your King.

"What did you do?" I say under my breath, turning back to my forgotten bag. It's where I left it, and right in the line of sight of the few officers standing guard on the other side of the caution tape.

They're watching me and I don't go for the pocket with the gift —instead, I take out my camera and attach the lens I'll use—a normal with a micro attachment to capture the smaller details.

Camera in hand, I test the shot. My first two are of the view from where I stand toward the mall parking lot where Nat is. The brightness of the morning sun demands that I adjust, and with a small turn of the dial it shifts into complete focus. Clear.

The next one is of Officer Young who looks uncomfortable under the scrutiny of my lens. He should be.

And it's only once I'm done with my test run that I allow myself to look toward the markings on the ground. *Jesus Christ.*

There are no words.

Nothing can describe the image laid out before me.

The blood is the first thing I take in. The amount; dry or coagulated and with flies flying around it. Then, there's the pattern:

Everything that should've been inside the body is in a consciously formed circle. Her organs, now dirty and decomposing, have manually been moved and placed—almost as if it were an artistic expression—and on the direct opposite side of her intestines are two markers.

Two shoe prints.

Two very distinctive shoe prints in varied sizes.

I focus on those first, snapping pictures at different angles before placing my large-numbered ruler beside them. I'm right about them, about the discrepancies, and jot down a quick note to confirm with Nat.

The organs are next and the splatter all around them confirm my suspicion about the body being moved. It also makes me look up where I notice a thick branch—the support used, and a bit of rope looped around it.

"Motherfucker," I whisper, angling my camera up to take in the full scene. This is where this Jane Doe lost her life, only to be dragged across a large parking lot to be left as a display. Looking back over to the men waiting for me to finish, I meet the eyes of the newbie on the force. "Officer Young."

"Yes?" he calls back, not coming across the tape but stepping close enough to clearly hear me.

"We'll be listing this as place of death."

"Are you sure?"

"Yes."

It's sickening.

Sad.

And as I finish, collect my items, and head across the lot back to

Natasha, that sense of foreboding grows tenfold. More so when I catch her and Edgar's expressions as I approach.

The woman on the ground is uncovered and staring at the sky without eyes. Just empty sockets and her mouth parted in what I can only imagine is a silent, horror-filled scream.

However, that's not what shakes me to the core.

It's her resemblance to me.

A Latina at no more than five-foot-two with dark hair; she had my complexion and build. A beauty mark over her upper lip on the right side that I do as well. Our tattoos were different but placed similarly.

This Jane Doe graced me with a glimpse of what my own corpse would look like someday.

Chapter 23
THIAGO

THE BUZZ OF the tattoo machine always seems to lull me into a state of relaxation. It's one I don't indulge in often but I trust him, and after visiting Malcolm in Chicago to drop off my wedding gift personally—a quick trip in which he had his own token of appreciation for me in the shape of Foster's head—I'm back home and find myself needing my friend's assistance.

I've known him for years, and even while locked up, he's the one I had brought into the prison via backdoor entryways to work on the symbol of Luna on my chest.

Talan Cox has done every single piece, the largest being the back one we're finishing today. It's taken two months to complete, hours upon hours of taking a needle to my skin in a very old-fashioned ritual like the warriors of the past would do to get my homage to justice done right.

The large scale sits above the head of its two owners: the devil and his angel. They're both holding the large staff that extends high and distributes the weight evenly. It symbolizes a partnership. How in my world Luna is the good side of me. The one that balances me out and who rules beside me.

The needle digs a little deeper on the curve of my spine and I grit my teeth a bit; it's not that it hurts, but that the area is sensitive and feels as if the flesh is burned. "How's it looking, bro?" I ask Ivan who is also in the room, standing on the opposite side of Talan. He too wants to book in a date after this, has something in mind that when he showed me, I approved of completely. "Think Luna will flip her shit?"

"Most definitely and in a good way."

"She forgave you already?" Talan asks, wiping my back. The paper towel is a little rough on my skin, but at the moment, silk would feel like that. The shading is always worse than the line work. "Cause when I finished the gloves on her neck, my girl was here, and she wasn't cheery at all when it came to you, Leon."

"I'm working on it."

"He's begging her," Ivan and I say in unison, which prompts me to flip him off.

"Can you hurry up," he says, chuckling a bit. I've known the man for years, hung out together as teens, and I've never seen him this far gone for anyone. You can see it on his face just how in love the asshole is. "Maya and I have a bet going and the stakes are high, my friend."

"How high?" Sitting up, I turn toward him with my brow raised. The stretching after being on the table face down for the last two hours without moving is a bit bothersome, but I ignore it. "What will you win?"

"Complete servitude for a month." *This sly motherfucker.* A laugh comes from the reception area just then, very girly and loud. "And that will be her. Guess she's out early."

"Where does she work?"

"School, and working on her Masters," he corrects, smile wide and proud. "Future Mrs. Cox will be a marine biologist."

"How the hell did she end up with a bum like you, Talan?" I ask, fucking with him, but instead, the man just shakes his head and then pounds his chest once.

"Not a fucking clue, but I'll never let my Bitty go."

"Then you'll understand the lengths that we go through to keep them safe and ours."

At my words, he tilts his head to the side, appraising me. "Ask and it's done."

"I'm going to request your presence at my home tomorrow around three in the afternoon. It'll be for an overnight stay."

"With Maya." Not a question, and I nod. Talan and I have a few more things in common than just our appreciation for tattoos. We have a similar build, skin tone, and hair color. With the right clothes and a hat, he could pass as my double for the night. "We'll be there."

"Hands up where I can see them and don't move."

"What the?" Luna shrieks, dropping her handbag and keys. Her head snaps to the left, brown eyes meeting mine from over her shoulder. She goes from worry to pissed within seconds—whirling around to greet my smirk with a scowl. "I should smack you for that."

"Please do." I take a step closer and then another, pushing her back against her driver's side door. "Slap. Bite. Scratch. Anything and everything, my beauty."

"Don't start. Not today."

"So I heard." The smile slips from my face and I focus on why I'm here. "You okay?"

"Not really." Her response is so honest. Her need for my comfort is humbling. But more than anything, the exhaustion she exudes is palpable, and I don't wait another second to do what I came here for.

Before she can protest, I pick her up and turn around. She's in my arms, not the least bit protesting my kidnapping as I walk us away from her building. Instead, she's burrowing against my chest with her nose in the crook of my neck.

Every little puff of breath escaping her feels like a heated caress —reminds me of those gasping breaths between curses for more. Of me. Of the pleasure only I can give.

It's hard to do, especially when her finger plays with the short hairs at the back of my head, but I ignore it. Ignore the throb of my cock and how good she feels—even the scent of whatever chemicals she uses at work couldn't dull her natural sweetness. It makes my mouth water, but what Luna needs right now is love and support, not my cock.

I push my hunger back, lips at her temple while placing a soft kiss or two. "I got you, bebe."

"Thank you." Her voice is low. Barely a whisper.

"Even when you don't see me, I'm there. Please believe that." My car isn't too far from hers and unlocked, making it easy to open the door of the SUV and place her on the passenger's seat. "You're not alone."

Luna gives me a nod and lets me buckle her in, more compliant than I've ever seen her. It worries me. What she saw today will leave a haunting expression that will never be erased.

I saw her pictures; Thompson sent a copy of the file over right after Luna left. And while I hate that she's witnessed humanity at its vilest, I'll never stop her from doing what she feels she needs to.

Because this is her way of doing for me what I do for her: protect.

Before closing the door, I peck her lips once. Just a tiny kiss that pulls a sweet sigh from her lips, and then I get inside myself, pulling out of the parking lot faster than I should and taking the turn down the street that will lead me toward the expressway.

It's a bit busy for the time of day, with the rush-hour traffic at its peak, but I manage to get us back to my home in the La Gorce Island private community within half an hour. She's been quiet beside me as I drive, not caring how close I come to clipping a car or three as I weave in and out of the busy road, but the second I come to a stop at the gated entrance, she looks over.

I've been watching her. Taking in every single breath and the rise of her chest with it. The way her lips, succulent and sweet, thin out as she thinks—contemplates what she saw today. However, what I see now is curiosity in her expression, and I'll take that any day over the sadness. Over her worry or fear.

The motherfucker that did that—stole that young woman's life and scarred my queen—is a dead man. He shouldn't fear the police; I'm his biggest threat. Enemy. My men are looking, and Satan himself will welcome his soul by the time I'm personally through with him.

"Ummm, Thiago?"

"Yes." Lowering my window, I flash a security card in front of the reader. The gates open, but I don't press on the accelerator. I wait for her question with my eyes on her curious face.

"Where are we exactly?"

"Patience." With a grin on my face, I drive through and toward the very opposite end of this island near Miami Beach and park in front of my surprise. It's located near all major points in Miami and with something that is rare to find: a large lot, sitting at over two acres of land and five hundred feet of water-frontage with connections to the ocean and intercoastal waterways. It's private with no neighbors on either side as I bought them out, and the homes will remain as guest houses for family, associates, and friends when needed.

The home itself was large, but outdated, and was taken care of by Hendrix Parker of H.P. Builders. Gutted until the only thing left was the foundation, he brought to life a contemporary-style home with protection being the main focus but without losing its modern appeal my girl loves.

Floor-to-ceiling windows, clean lines, ample natural lighting throughout; the open spaces merge into a large communal space that is perfect for entertaining, while the upstairs is reserved for us.

This home also comes with two hidden rooms that no one will have knowledge of outside of Luna and me.

"Welcome home, baby."

"W-what? I don't...*huh*?"

A chuckle escapes at her adorableness and I turn in my seat, cupping her cheek with my palm. "This is where I plan to grow old with you. Where we'll have babies and become strict parents."

"So cocky." A tinge of pink warms her cheeks and her eyes brighten. For the moment, the sadness is gone and my sassy queen takes her place. "I feel bad for your future daughters."

"*Our* daughters won't be allowed to date until they're at the very least forty."

"What makes you think I'll still be around past—"

"Luna, where you go, I go, and vice versa. This is it for us." A small smile tugs at her lips, and no matter how hard she tries to fight it, it grows until it matches my own. "I'm never leaving you again."

And just like that, the warmth is gone. "You said that once before."

"I did, but back then certain things were out of my control."

"And now they aren't? You have the bull by the balls?" she asks, a weird mixture of incredulousness and worry in her tone. Because even when trying hard to hide them, her emotions have always been easy for me to read. I know her. Her tells. Like now, the way she bites the inside of her cheek when trying to control her facial features.

"More than." I caress her cheek with my thumb. "When I'm done, we'll own the world."

My plans reach far outside of Miami, the state of Florida, or even the United States. What I'm after is a global dominion. To build a worldwide empire.

Imperium.

"What does that even mean, Thiago? What are you up to?"

"All I need from you is to trust me. To know that I'll always come back."

"Like a roach? Those fuckers are persistent." The slick insult is meant to throw me off, but I roll my eyes at the lame attempt. However, I won't call her out on it either. Not today, when I know it's been a rough one.

"I forgot how much of a brat you could be at times." Turning the ignition off, I exit my car and make my way around to her side. My intent is to be a gentleman and open her door, sweep her off her feet, and maybe kiss her breathless at the threshold of our new home, but that doesn't happen. I'm met by the sight of her foot on the pavers and a smirk on her face. "No patience either," I tsk, rolling my eyes.

"But you love me this way."

She takes the hand I extend, letting me pull her out and close the door. One tug and her chest is against mine, my lips hovering over hers. "I adore every single inch of you."

"That's always the right answer."

"It's the truth."

Her bravado slips for the briefest of seconds, and I see the girl in her eyes from five years ago make a small appearance. "I've missed you so much, papi. More than you could ever begin to comprehend."

My arms encircle her small frame and lift her off the ground, feet dangling. "And I love you more than anything in this world. I'd give my life for you without hesitation." She nods, her eyes growing a bit misty, and I carry her up the small set of stairs that lead to the entry-way. The house is unlocked and the food I left cooking on low should be ready to eat by now, but I don't pause to check.

Tonight is about pampering her a bit. Taking care of her needs, and I plan to spoil the fuck out of her.

Our bedroom is up the grand staircase past the foyer and I take them two at a time, not pausing to show her a single room out of the eight or the pictures on the walls. They can wait. Maybe even later tonight if she's feeling better.

The lights come on as I enter our grand master. Her head shifts on my shoulder, just a tiny bit, and I know she's taking the space in —the soothing colors that I chose with her in mind, a stark contrast to the furniture in a dark mahogany. It's white and a shade of grey that I know she likes because of its subtle hint of purple.

There are pillows everywhere, too.

Just how she likes it.

Her kiss on my cheek makes me smile. "You like it?"

"It's beautiful."

"It's ours." Placing her down on the extra-large bed, I take a step back and just take her in. Take in the way she looks there. How right this is. "I'm going to need your nosy butt to stay right where you are for the next few minutes. Can you do that for me?"

"Maybe."

"Get up and I tickle you."

"That's not nice."

"When have I ever played nice?" I ask, a slick smirk on my lips.

Luna licks her own, eyes on my mouth. "With me or the general public?"

"I won't dignify that with an answer, bebe." And just because I'm an asshole without an ounce of shame when it comes to her, I pull my shirt off and toss the thin cotton at her head. "Now, are you ready to get wet for me?" It hits her on the forehead, and still her eyes wander, from my mouth and lower to my chest where her tattoo is. Luna's teeth embed in her lip. "Sweetheart." I get nothing. Not even a *huh*. "Yo, shorty?"

That does it. Her eyes snap to mine and her face pulls into a disgusted expression. "Don't do that. Just no."

"Then stop objectifying me."

"Are you…? Did you just…?"

"Yes. I did." Taking the few steps between us, I crawl over her body, effectively pinning her down. Her chest rises with each harsh breath, lightly pressing over my bare one. The blouse she has on doesn't do much to stop the heat coming off her skin from burning mine. "*Fuck*, I want you. Need you, beautiful."

"Then take me."

"I want to." Lowering my face to hers, I nip her bottom lip and then lick the abused flesh. "God knows I do."

"But?" She drags the word out, a bit breathy at the end. Her sweet breath is a temptation. "Because I feel as though you're about to drop one."

"Maybe…"

"Thiago, I swear—" I silence her with a quick yet harsh kiss. It's lips and teeth with a hint of that desperation that seems to never ebb. She moans into my mouth and my hips buck, spreading her thighs wider apart as I settle between them, her hot core to my throbbing cock. Her little needy noises vibrate against my chest. Slipping a hand beneath her head, I tilt her head back while fisting the long locks—dominate the kiss and steal the very breath from her lungs as our tongues intertwine.

My other hand wanders lower and to the button of her black trousers, popping it open. My hand slips beneath the waistband when a loud buzz comes through the intercom, stopping me in my tracks. It's the alarm I set for the food. *Son of a fucking bitch.*

It hurts to do so, but I move back. "Stay, and don't move."

The way she brings a hand to her lips almost breaks me. "Where are you going? Why are you going?"

"To get your bath ready and then check on dinner."

"You cooked?" It's been a long time since I've done so. It's one of the things I've always enjoyed doing. "I did. Your favorite, too."

"Then go. I'm starving." With her knees, she pushes herself

higher on the bed using my midsection for leverage. Luna doesn't stop her seductive wiggle until she's at the headboard and looking back at me still kneeling on the bed. "What are you waiting for?"

"You will drive me insane one day."

"Good. Because I'm already there."

Chapter 24
LUNA

I'M IN HEAVEN.

In complete and utter bliss as I lay inside the large, free-standing clawfoot tub in the middle of his bathroom. My body has lost the rigidness I've been carrying since working the crime scene a few hours ago when I closed my eyes and let him disrobe me. Since my mother sent me a message to call her or else, right before Thiago picked me up. My troubles stayed at the door as soon as I walked inside—vanishing as my body succumbed to the warm, and sudsy water.

Now, my attention is solely occupied by him.

His presence. What he calls our home. All the troubles he's gone through to make me feel special with something as simple as drawing me a bath after a hard day.

A bathroom that's filled with the soft scent of lavender and honey invading every square inch—every available surface overflowing with flowers and candles. It's sweet and relaxing and decadent; I never want to leave, and more so when the man I love walks back into the room a second later while holding two champagne flutes and a box containing chocolate-dipped strawberries.

He's still bare-chested and I watch with hunger as the ripped muscles of his upper body contract with every single movement. How they flex and show off what years of bulking up behind prison bars can do for a body.

My Thiago has never been skinny or considered small, but this is more. His strength and size are overwhelming me in a way that my breathing becomes a bit labored, chest rising out of the water's edge faster as I wander lower. Down his chest, my tattoo, and then the eight-pack of his stomach. His abdomen tightens under my gaze and one of my hands slips beneath the water.

"Don't." It's a hiss. A warning.

"Don't what, Leon?" My words are a bit breathy. A low whine behind them. "Be more specific."

"If you touch that sweet little cunt, I will spank you." There's no hiding the shiver that rushes through me at his gruff words or the way my skin breaks out in goose bumps. "Now, be a good girl, and hands above the water at all times. I'll take care of you, beauty."

"How do you plan to do that?" A few stray hairs fall from the messy bun my hair is in. Hazel eyes follow each one as they caress my shoulder; he licks his lips. "No answer? Can't?"

No answer to my taunt. Nothing. Instead, the handsome devil doesn't answer.

He takes the remaining steps between us, extending one of the glasses to me once reaching the stone tub. I've never seen one as big as this and so sleek in its design.

His fingers skim mine in an innocent way, and yet, as he hands over the crisp champagne, I feel as though he's touched me everywhere. It heats me from within. It makes me feel delicate and small and fucking protected by his domineering presence.

Setting his own glass and snack down on the low wooden stool beside the tub, he undoes his belt and then drops the leather accessory beside the sparkling wine.

His pants stay on, just become undone at the waist, and his shoes have long been removed. Barefoot and with his chest expanding, he motions for me to scooch up a bit and then slips in behind me. The water rises and overflows, and yet his hands grip my hips roughly and position me over his pant-covered legs, making a larger mess.

Our breathing matches. Our movements are almost desperate as I spread my legs for him, begging silently that he touch me.

"Fuck, Luna. What you do to me, bebe." His hips buck beneath me and I feel him. *Oh God*, I feel him. "You're a temptation I could never deny. A need I could never satiate."

"Please," I whimper, arching my back while sitting upright so I can rub myself over his length. The glass in my hand tips over a bit, the cool drops rolling down the center of my chest as he throbs beneath me, pulsing with the same want I have. For a release. For the connection. "Touch me."

"I've always loved you like this." Strong, calloused hands leave my hips and skim down to the middle of my thighs where he squeezes. His touch borders on painful, but I welcome the sting and the small marks that are sure to be left behind. "Love all the little noises you make."

"Thiago, I—"

He quiets me with a quick nip to my shoulder and then the slow lick that ends at the nape of my neck. "Drink."

"I need to...*fuck*," leaves me on a breathless moan, his teeth digging deeper just below the tattoo there. "Papi, please."

"Drink." One of the hands on my thighs grabs the glass and

brings it up to my lips, holding it against my mouth. "A little sip just for me."

I'm powerless and do as he says, taking the cool refreshment as his other hand cups my core beneath the water. He holds me in his palm, adding pressure over my clit as my body reacts, gyrating against his hand. I swallow, and he parts my slit with a finger before tapping the sensitive bundle twice. Then again. For each sip I take, he rewards me with added pressure—with tight little circles that within seconds have me close. My body contracts in his hold and I move my hips—rub his thick cock with my cheeks as I search for the release I crave.

"How?" That's all I can manage through gasping breaths and the electricity that thrums through my veins. And all because of him. Because of his skin on mine. His touch that with each passing second that ticks on the clock becomes rougher. More. Everything.

"Because I own you." Thiago slips a finger inside of me and pumps a few times. Slowly, almost leisurely, before adding a second. Then third. My body leans back against him, head tipping back when he holds them there and kisses my cheek tenderly. "Because no one in this world will ever be able to satisfy you like I can."

I can't help but close my eyes at his words, and it's when I do that, he tosses the glass onto the floor. It crashes, shards skidding across the floor, but that's not what my attention focuses on.

No. I'm caught by the act of his now empty hand covers the expanse of my neck and tightening its hold. How his chest rumbles behind my back with a loud growl that shakes me to the core.

Thiago has me at his mercy and he knows this. Enjoys it.

"Say it, Luna."

"So close."

He pulls his fingers out and I want to cry. "Say it." Soaking wet fingers land on my clit with force and I shake, walls tightening in search of those delicious digits that now evade my entrance. "Give me what I want." Two passes over the length of my pussy, from clit to just over my other hole and a small tremor rocks me. "Admit who you belong to."

"*You!*" It's a sob of defeat that he rewards by slamming those long fingers in. All it takes is four quick pumps and I fall as another wave of pleasure crashes—makes me lax in his hold. I can't stop the words that tumble past my lips nor the way I reach back, squeezing him through the wet pants that hide nothing from me. "I'll always belong to you."

"Son of a bitch," he hisses, pulsing in my hand the very second after that bit of truth slips past my lips. Thiago comes inside his pants as I ride out every last drop of the relief he pulls from my body, not giving me a second of reprieve as he continues to work me with slower strokes. And as I succumb to my exhaustion of the day, to his power over me, I close my eyes. Time stills as I do, and the noise level around me—his breathing and the open hot water tap—become muffled and low. The last thing I hear makes me smile. It gives me just what I needed to let go entirely. "One day soon, I'll be standing at the end of a long aisle waiting for you. You'll wear white, and I'll put on one of those tuxes I hate but makes you happy. You'll call me handsome, and I won't be able to form words because your beauty always brings me to my knees, but that day, on that blessed day, I'm going to be the happiest son of a bitch as I make you my wife."

I AWAKE to the sound of a stomach rumbling; it's getting louder, and it takes me an extra second or two to realize the sound is coming from me. I haven't eaten since he fed me a few of the chocolate-dipped strawberries before tucking me in hours... *Crap, what time is it?*

There are a few seconds between my eyes adjusting to the darkness and my noticing that Thiago isn't in the room. The sheets are cold beside me and I frown. This is the second time he's done this to me since his release.

"Where are you, jerk?"

"Right here."

I give a small jump at the sound of his voice, eyes snapping toward the direction of the doorway. He's standing there in nothing but low-hung pajamas pants and a smirk. "Quit sneaking up on me!"

"Only when you stop being adorable."

My eyes narrow. "You're up to something. Spill it."

Because I know him. Know his tells.

And right now he's exhibiting the signs of a sexy man with a secret. The seductive grin, the cocky posture, and then there's the heated look he's giving me.

How he takes in my naked form, a bedsheet all that stands between my skin and his sight. Not that the Egyptian cotton does much to hide me.

He too sees me. Sees the way my nipples tighten; the stiff peaks throb for a single lick from his mouth, to feel his lips wrap around the nubs and his tongue to soothe the sting of his bite.

He's my weakness. I'm powerless here.

"What makes you think that I'm up to something?"

"I can always go home."

"Or you can come downstairs with me for a quick bite and then—"

"You did mention something about my favorite meal."

"Your favorite?" He shrugs. "Maybe."

"Did you or did you not make arroz imperial?" Climbing off the bed, I slowly make my way toward him, swinging my hips in an exaggerated manner. "Don't mess with me, Thiago. I'm starving and your mom's recipe is the bomb."

"Follow me and find out for yourself."

"And clothes?"

"Completely unnecessary."

"I don't think so, perv." Turning toward a tall armoire, I open the third drawer from the top and pull out a plain black T-shirt. It's where he's always kept them. The order is always underwear, socks, and then under shirts—every drawer is always the same no matter the piece of furniture. Slipping it over my head, I undo my loose hair bun and fluff the ends a bit. "Now we can go."

"Or maybe we should stay." He pushes off the door's molding and saunters toward me, stopping only when his arms reach me and fingertips grip my hips. They dig in, his touch just shy of painful, and I shiver. Shake in his arms. "What do you say, beautiful? You can crawl back up that bed, lay flat, and spread those thighs so I can eat you instead?"

"What about me?" I bite my bottom lip. "I'm starving."

"I have something to fill that pouty mouth. To stretch…" dipping his head, he kisses me sweetly—teasing the sensitive flesh "…those pretty lips with."

"It's been a while since I've had a taste."

"Too long since I've felt you choke." Thiago turns us slightly, walking us backwards and after a few steps, the back of my legs bump the bed. "What do you say, Luna? Want to play?"

"I do, but—"

"But?" His right brow arches and grip eases. That's how I find my opening, and in a move he doesn't predict, I turn and crawl over the mattress. And maybe it's the sight of my naked cheeks on display as the shirt rides up or the way my hips swing that delays his reaction, but I'm on the other side before he comes to. "The fuck?"

"Maybe later? Feed me first."

"Luna—"

"Thiago…"

"I'm going to enjoy leaving a red handprint across each ass cheek."

"You'd have to catch me first." I take a step toward the door and then another, pausing when I reach the end of the bed. We're an even distance, his longer legs giving him an advantage. "Think you can?"

"Always." He's eyeing me. Letting me advance another two steps without so much as a muscle twitch. "And to prove my point…*run.*

Run, bebe." Mouth twitching, he rubs a few fingers over his lips. "A thirty-second head start is the most I can do."

"What will that prove? I don't know my way around—"

"You won't make it to the stairs before my mouth kisses your pussy."

Chapter 25
LUNA

"**Y**OU LOOK BEAUTIFUL," Thiago says from the bottom of the stairs as I descend a few hours later. I've been holed up inside what he loves to call our bedroom and getting ready after a delicious lunch made by his hands. I was fed the rice dish by his fork, drank sparkling water from his cup, and was then surprised with a large box and a note that demanded I kill him without mercy. Moreover, the way he's staring at me now with those hooded eyes and the kind of smirk that destroys my self-control proves I've done just that. "Simply stunning."

"Thank you." My response is a bit breathy. A bit exposing as I take him in, my own desires plain to see. He's in a three-piece navy suit with a crisp white shirt and a burgundy polka dot tie; the miniature circles are the same shade of blue as his clothes. In the small pocket next to his left lapel, he's tucked in a neatly folded handkerchief and I smile at the old-school touch. Classically handsome from head to toe, Thiago looks like a delicious sin, and the way his eyes roam over me warn of his true intentions. "And you look very handsome, Leon."

He's the predator, and I am his willing meal.

And the way I watch him admits my own defeat.

"Come." He extends a hand out to me, beckoning me closer. And I do; I take the remaining steps slowly, making sure to add a little extra sway to my hips, an exaggerated movement that he follows with undisguised hunger.

The second I reach him, Thiago takes my fingers in his and turns me. He admires every angle of my body, of my exposed skin and the curves hidden beneath a thin layer of fabric. Beautiful and shiny sequins shimmer in the light and highlight the almost indecent cut of this garment.

I don't know where we are going, but I'm succeeding in my quest to drive him past the point of gentle and into the realm of animalistic yearning in an ombre minidress. It's in a golden berry combination with a pair of strappy sandals in the same shade as the bottom half of the skirt, while my makeup is simple: a smoky shadow, winged liner, and nude lips.

I'm not wearing any jewelry except for the thin gold chain with a vintage key pendant that he gave me on our one-year anniversary. His eyes linger on the piece, too, and I see the approval in his expression.

The heat of his stare licks at my exposed skin.

It causes my thighs to clench, and the low groan that follows weakens my knees.

A second turn and then I'm face to face with him, breathing in his masculine scent. "Hi."

"My queen." His lips hover over mine, just a hair's breadth away so as to not ruin matte lipstick, and I wish more than anything that he would do just that. Wreck my makeup. Mark me. "You are a true test to my self-control."

"Ditto." And because I can, I kiss him. Leaning forward just a smidge, I touch my lips to his and hold them there. Just feel him. I enjoy the way he trembles and both hands land on my hips, his hold strong, and my need grows to almost painful as an animalistic growl builds in his chest. It vibrates against my closed mouth.

"We should go. We're going to be late."

"Lead the way."

"Of course."

"Then step back."

"*Fuck.*" One of his hands leaves my hips and grasps the back of my neck, tilting my head to the side. Anchors me to him. "Dangerous fucking creature."

"I—"

"Let's go." A harsh step back and Thiago turns, my hand in his as he walks us out the front door. There's a Rolls-Royce Cullinan in white waiting out at the curb with Miguel standing beside an open door. This is all very formal, nothing I haven't been treated to in the past, but I'm on alert within seconds because he's not alone.

Something's up, and I'm confused by the other occupants in the driveway. *Talan and Maya?*

"What's going on, Thiago?" I ask before they reach us. "Are they coming with us?"

"No." That's all he says because a second later he's shaking hands with our tattoo artist and meeting his girl. "Thank you both for the help tonight. I appreciate it."

"All good." Maya giggles, her mischievous eyes on me. As if she knows something I don't. Since getting the gloves done on my neck, I've been to Cox tattoos a few times with Nat and Amberlyn and even had lunch with Maya twice. She's sweet, studious, and has the kind of attitude that keeps Talan on his toes. I like her, genuinely do, and we're going to have a conversation when I get back as to why she didn't warn a girl on this man's plans. "I'm going to make use of your private stretch of the marina and get some homework done. Do you guys get dolphins out this way? Do they get close to the dock?"

"We haven't lived here long, but they might," Thiago says, his thumb rubbing over my knuckles in a soothing gesture. "It's not something that uncommon."

"Your nerdiness is adorable, but they need to leave." Talan puts his arm around Maya, tucking her against his side, his tone both proud and amused. "Say goodbye and go explore the water, Bitty."

"Bye, guys." Maya elbows Talan's side and steps forward, giving a smiling Thiago a handshake before turning slightly and wrapping her arms around me. Her hug lingers for a moment as she sways me in that way that all women do when excited. "Have fun, girl. The man's gone all out from what I hear," she whispers the latter and then steps back, trying to take a backpack from Talan who grumbles *it's too heavy for you* and hitches it back up his shoulder.

Her eye roll reminds me so much of the ones I've given Thiago in the past, and I laugh. "Men."

"Amen."

"And on that note, we are out. I'll be in contact, Cox." Thiago's large, warm hand settles on the small of my back as he ushers me forward. "The yacht out back is yours for the night."

Talan nods, moving himself and Maya to the side. "Thank you. You two have fun."

A final quick wave is all I have time to do as a second later, I'm inside the car and heading down the long driveway. No one speaks as Miguel drives, nor as he merges onto the expressway and follows the signs that lead us to Kendall. The closer to our destination we get, the more my curiosity is piqued, and when I turn to ask Thiago where we are going, I find myself with some kind of fabric placed over my eyes.

"A surprise?"

"A surprise." He replies before tapping my lips once with his finger, silently telling me to not ask any more questions. And behind the veil of total darkness, I indulge him and sit, waiting as the car speeds up, slows down, turns a few times, and then stops altogether. The drive feels long but at the same time short, and I start to believe we're heading toward Collins Ave. for dinner when two doors open and I feel a soft breeze sweep across my legs.

Then I wait. And wait.

I'm becoming a frustrated ball of energy when once more a door opens, and this time it's on my side. "I've got you, beautiful. Trust me." His scent invades my senses and I can't stop my hum of approval. Neither can I hold back the small squeal that escapes as his arms wrap around my shoulders and thighs right before I'm picked up and carried bridal style toward our next destination. I count the steps. I try to listen for something familiar and I get nothing.

Not a clue.

No music. No people. Nothing...until I feel us ascending a set of stairs and I'm met with the pleasant scent of vanilla right before we're sitting with my body astride his lap.

"Thiago, where are we?"

"Just a little longer. Please."

"You are going to owe me for...what the hell!" I whisper yell as I feel the sudden vibration of a plane's engine. It's not harsh or loud, but the constant thrum causes me to pull the dark sash away from my eyes and meet his before tossing the fabric somewhere across from us. His hands tighten around my midsection, anchoring me to him, and I while I try to find the right words to say without the added curse word thrown in, we begin to taxi down the runway. *I'm going to kill him.*

"Can it be after we get back from a quick trip to New York?"

"What are you...why are we going to New York?" I turn the question around because that I know of, I have nothing there that merits this trip. "Explain."

"You said you wanted to kill me..." his kisses my cheek "...and this is a date."

"A date? In New York?" Christ, everything is happening so fast, but things are slowly beginning to make sense. The phone call from my boss giving me a few days off because of my reaction to the scene, according to my uncle's report. Talan and Maya showing up out of nowhere and the small resemblances between us. We share similar heights and builds; Maya's hair is even dark like mine.

If anyone is checking his house, they'll see a couple at home and think nothing of it.

Girl, pay attention. Your kidnapper is talking.

"I'm sorry, what? Repeat that, Thiago?'

"I said…" his smile widens "…a date and show on Broadway."

"Are you taking me to? Every show is sold out!" I can't hide the excitement in my tone or the smile that breaks free.

"It's a possibility."

"Tell me."

"This is too fun to stop now." Thiago licks his bottom lip and then bites on the plump flesh. "Maybe if you beg prettily."

"Thiago, don't play with my emotions," I hiss out in mock outrage, jabbing a manicured nail into his side and causing the large man to squirm back, a chuckle escaping. "Are you taking me to see Hamilton yes or no?"

"And if I am?" The more he moves while trying to evade my poking, the more my ass wiggles over his quickly hardening cock. I'm not in the least bit of a hurry to move from my place and enjoy watching as the amusement dies and his lust takes over, his always palpable need that feeds into my own. "Do I get a reward?"

We can go from laughing to loving in the blink of an eye.

We can forget the world and its troubles by just locking eyes.

Utterly consumed and powerless to stop it.

"You can have anything you please if the answer is *yes*." I'm taunting him. Pulling the lion's tail while giving in to my own wants. Because it's more than the gesture—the whisking me away for an out-of-state trip with the destination being something I've wanted to do for a few years now. It's because once again, he's showing me that while away, incarcerated and paying for a crime he didn't commit, Thiago was watching. Always paying attention to my wants and needs. "Now will you tell me? Pretty please and with a cherry on top?"

"Be careful, Luna," Thiago grunts, voice husky and dangerous. "That's a very dangerous offer to make a man like me." He punctuates his warning with a thrust of his hips, large hands pinning me in place. I can feel the flexing. How he throbs. "Take it back."

"I have no regrets or concerns on the matter." Goose bumps break out across my skin as I watch his beautiful hazel orbs become hooded. The tick of his jaw as I gyrate—push him just a little bit more. "None whatsoever."

"Welcome, Mr. and Mrs. De Leon. I'm Silvia and I'll be your in-flight server today," a woman suddenly interrupts and we both turn our heads, pausing the conversation. She's older, maybe in her early forties and wearing a very large smile. It's the kind that all people in the service industry—those with years of experience under their belts—perfect over time. "Can I get either of you anything to drink? An aperitif?"

I'm confused by this and it shows on my face. "Aren't you supposed to wait until after takeoff?" Beneath me, Thiago shakes with silent laughter and I poke him once again, digging my fingernails deeper. "Are we not taking off for a while?"

Silvia's smile is indulgent and just shy of amused. "We've been in the air now for fifteen minutes and have reached cruising altitude, Mrs. De Leon."

"What?" I glance toward the window and sure enough, the evening sky is starting to fade as it merges with the endless darkness of a late summer night. *How can I get so lost in him?*

Lord help me. Help us. "This is your fault, Thiago. All on you."

"What is?"

"Distracting me." I'm trying to stand and take the seat beside his, but the man's hold won't allow it. "Once again taking over my world."

"And I'll take full responsibility for that." Tucking me against his chest, Thiago kisses my temple. "I've had a bottle brought on board for this flight. Please serve us each a glass and prepare a charcuterie plate to accompany."

"Of course, sir. I'll be right back with both."

Once she's out of earshot, I tip my face up to him. "You know, this isn't fair to me. What if I get used to you being here, always with me, and then you leave..."

"We don't get much of a choice in this matter."

"How so?" My defenses are low, and I'm fully emerged in the moment. Overwhelmed. Lost. Letting go. And while my mind still tells me in the background to be cautious and not forget so easily, my heart is louder. Reminding me all we were and could be. Of why life is short and could drastically change in the blink of an eye. "How do we not control our present and future?"

Silvia returns then, his requested items on a silver tray. "We're due to land in Teterboro Airport on schedule by seven p.m. where a car will await you on the private landing strip and it will take you onto your next destination." With utmost care, she places the drinks and plate down before pressing a button—a hidden panel within the wall of the jet—and the table begins to shift closer. It's motorized, and when within reach, she lets go and takes a step back. "If you need anything for the remainder of your flight, please press the call button as I will give you both the privacy requested."

"Thank you." Thiago takes a wine glass and hands it to me before grabbing his own. "We appreciate it and will call if need be."

"My pleasure."

The door to the pilot's small cockpit closes and his head turns toward me, lips close. "There's never been a choice because I was made to worship you. There's never been a choice because your heart will always recognize mine." Bringing his glass to my lips, he offers me a sip and I mimic, holding the rim of mine against his mouth. "There's never been a choice because we fight, rise above, and more than anything we love each other through everything. Life will never be perfect, Luna. I'll fuck up and so will you, but it won't diminish how deeply connected we will always be."

"Salud."

"I love you, bebe." Gently, Thiago tips his glass and I do the same. We share the white wine and I'm the one to steal kisses between sips, but more importantly, this feels right. Like this is where I'm supposed to be. Like I've just recovered the part of my heart that died five years ago. "And to answer your earlier question…"

"Quit toying with me," I mock whine. Not that it matters at this point; we could turn around now and go home and it'd still be our best date to date. The thought behind this counts more than the actual trip. He has no idea how much I'm team Thiago already. *That I've always been.*

Chapter 26
THIAGO

WITH MY HAND on the small of her back, I walk us through a private entrance of the Richard Rodgers Theatre in Manhattan. I've purchased every box on either side of us and asked for specific refreshments to be made available on demand. I want her to enjoy the show and not worry about getting up at intermission or be recognized by a nosy theatergoer.

It's something she doesn't fully comprehend yet, but she will. My return and reconnection with her will not go unnoticed by her peers, job, and family. Antonio himself will have a coronary when I make my presence known both publicly and in private.

I want the media to speculate, follow, and confirm.

I want him to choke on his fury when he realizes that I've never truly left her side.

There's a low thrum throughout the building, people finding their seats and excitedly watching the stage. They talk but keep it low so as to not disturb, while a few others look toward the top box where the light of the entrance hall now shines through. They can't see us, as I purchased every other private balcony on this side and across the theater, but I'm scanning the crowd nonetheless and looking for anyone that I might know in attendance.

People fill every area and my eyes settle on another man with his wife taking a seat almost directly below us. He can't see me, not with the darkness of my box, but still looks around as if he feels my eyes on him. Ulysses and Jasmine Senot are in attendance and she looks every bit the whore she is, while he, *he* seems worried. Fidgety. Afraid. Those beady eyes shift around the room while Jasmine is unaffected by her missing bodyguard/lover and the distress clearly visible on her husband's face.

This is something I didn't expect; I thought we'd bump into some kind of reporter or a business associate passing through the city, but never *him*. It comes in handy, though. I'll kill two birds with one stone.

Woo Luna.

Deliver a personal message to the Senot patriarch.

"This place is packed," Luna says while taking her seat, in her hands one of those old-school-looking glasses that I had my cousin Celeste find in a vintage store. It's solid gold and a bit heavy, but my queen got a kick out of the pair. "How long before the show starts?"

Turning my face, I give her my full attention. "Ten minutes or so. Why?"

She smiles. "Because I'm excited and extremely impatient."

"Are you sure you don't need anything, bebe?" We haven't had a heavy meal since this afternoon and the charcuterie plate on the plane was just to tide us over. "Hungry or thirsty? The show starts in a few minutes, and I'll have something sent up if you wish."

"Is that even allowed?" At the look I give her, she rolls her eyes. "Never mind, and the answer is no. We can grab something after."

"We have a reservation at The View for ten tonight."

"Isn't that the place with the revolving view? That makes a full 360-degree turn every hour?"

"It is."

"Very nice, Leon."

I can't help myself and lean over, kissing her lips, nipping her bottom lip once. "And don't worry about being late if you wish to meet anyone from the cast after; they'll hold since it's a private rental."

"Tell me you didn't rent out..." And I lose her. Just like that.

The curtain rises and the first actor steps on the stage; I'm a forgotten thought as she visits another place in time. While she sings along to every song. It's nerdy and cute and I want to bite her, but an hour in and when I am close to taking possession of her mouth, someone else decides to remind me they are here.

From the corner of my eye I catch Ulysses standing and sliding past those in the row with him. He's interrupting, phone in hand, and heading toward the upper exit.

"I'll be right back, Luna."

"Everything all right?" she asks, but her eyes remain on the stage. Riveted. Adorable.

"It's perfect." Standing, I bend and kiss the top of her head before exiting. I follow the corridor that leads here but turn toward the theater's lobby instead of the private entrance. He's just a few steps ahead when I spot him, on his phone and not paying the least bit of attention.

"What do you mean his wife and kids are missing?" he snaps at the person on the other end, gripping the cell phone tight. "Someone has to know. Alfredo wouldn't just leave like this."

Ulysses continues walking right out the front doors and I follow him all the way to the stage door on the left side of the massive building. This is where people gather when waiting for the actors to sign playbills, and other than those specific moments, it's a desolate area. Out of the way and private.

"Claudio, I will not..." my hand shoots out and grips the back of his neck, slamming him face first into the concrete "...the fuck!"

"Long time no see, Senot."

"T-Thiago," he stutters, fear in his tone as the phone slips from his fingers. In the distance, I hear his son asking what's going on and yelling out *Dad* but it just adds to the moment. Let him hear; this will just reaffirm my warning when I caught him in Luna's house demanding something that'll never be his. "What are you doing here? How did you get out of Miami?"

Pulling his face back a bit, I reacquaint him with the wall a second time before turning the piece of shit to face me. His eyes are wide and sweat forms on his brow. "I flew."

"You are breaking the law and I can have you arrested for this." The threat doesn't do what he hopes; I'm not afraid. Unmoved. Smirking as I pull out my Ruger and push it into the dear mayor's neck. "*Please.*"

"Weren't you threatening me a minute ago?"

"Thiago, let's talk. It doesn't have to end like this."

"End?" I take a step back, removing my gun and then tapping his forehead with the barrel. "This is just the beginning."

Limbs shaking and swallowing hard, Ulysses keeps his eyes on mine. "Aren't you going to kill me?"

"No."

"Then..."

"I'm just here to set a date and time for a meeting at your office." The next strike is hard enough to break skin, and blood spills from the wound. "Nothing more."

"Please stop."

"Date and time, Senot."

"A month from now, I have an opening," he says, looking past me and I follow his line of sight. There's a small group standing at the edge of the alley: two men and two women. They're talking. Laughing. Doing everything but paying attention to the assault being committed. Ulysses sees this as an opening and opens his mouth to yell, but I backhand him hard enough to cause his head to snap back. For his teeth to bite down on his tongue hard enough to cut.

"I'm starting to lose my patience." Stepping back, I pull the handkerchief from my breast pocket and wipe my hands. "Date and time."

"I'm going to be out on vacation for two weeks starting Monday." Asshole sounds as if he had a lisp, and I bite back a chuckle. "I won't be back for two weeks, De Leon. Will that work?"

"Perfect." Condescendingly, I pat his cheek and he flinches, almost swaying on his feet when I bend at the waist and pick up his phone, placing it back in his shaking hand. "See you then, and enjoy your holiday."

Then I head back inside just as I exited, making it to my seat as the show comes to an intermission. Luna eyes me with suspicion, more so when a few minutes later we hear the high-pitched voice of the mayor's wife demanding to know where her husband was. Why he looks like—in her words—shit.

It's an unmistakable accent the one Miamian's have. It's Spanglish with a hint of southern and valley girl combined that makes the women of South Florida very unique. Easy to pick out of a crowd.

Luna spots her and doesn't voice her questions aloud but chooses instead to give me a look.

Not a warning, but more of a *you will explain,* and I nod. I'm not hiding anything. This was just a coincidence that I took advantage of.

"Are you enjoying yourself, beauty?"

"Very much so." There's mischief in her eyes as they meet mine. No reproach. "And I have a feeling dinner conversation will be very enlightening?"

"I'd like to think of it as informative."

"Then by all means, Thiago. Blow my mind."

THERE'S a warehouse I own in the city of Hialeah. It's right below the bridge that turns 103rd in the N.W. area into 49th street and is a highly trafficked area with people from both cities rushing back and forth to fulfill different needs: food, shopping, and work. However, more than anything, that stretch right after you cross the bridge is a small industrial area where a lot of textile and automotive shops are located.

There are a lot of abandoned buildings from where businesses have gone belly up or have transferred out of the country. There are junk yards, rental equipment warehouses, and the mom-and-pop shops that service those nearby with everything from dive bars to illegal gambling.

From second-hand items to guns, the latter being my reason for being here.

In the center of this cluster of warehouses is a street desolated and owned by one family: mine. We operate a scrap metal recycling shop that both moves my money and gives customers access to my ghost guns. Here, a client can come and inspect merchandise, buy and load up, then drive off the lot as if they've traded their catalytic converters or clean copper for cash.

This is also where my gift from the gun manufacturer has been for weeks and I'm personally meeting a new potential buyer—an aficionado of artillery who runs a militia in a South American jungle fighting social injustices.

Whatever his reasons are, he comes bearing cash and that's all that matters in my world.

"Thiago, I have what you asked for." Ivan holds a folder out to me a week after my trip to New York, and I lower the Mac-10, placing it back in its individual case. The supplier is very meticulous, clean, and cares about the quality of his product. I appreciate that.

And to think a few weeks back they were nothing but scrap metal in this very yard. "You were right."

"Together or separate?" Taking the folder, I open to the front page and skim down the report, taking in the transcript of the most recent conversation with Jadiel. My free hand tightens into a fist and my veins throb with the ire coursing through them. With the audacity of these three and their aspirations. Two horses in the race and each vies for my queen's hand in marriage, something her father is all too willing to help them obtain for a price, my head being the ultimate goal. "Is this everything from their talk?"

"Separate, and we have audio from both locations. Same day, but four hours apart."

"Eyes on them at all times. I'll listen to this later."

Ivan scratches his jaw. "Each of them has a tail."

"Good." Closing the file, I place it down a second before the large metal doors open and in steps Alejandro Lucas, a decorated military man in his native country of Colombia who now runs an independent military larger than all his neighboring countries combined. His presence is meant to be imposing and the others in the room immediately go on high alert.

A shake of my head holds them back, but I can see the glint of each weapon.

Know their positions and capabilities.

They relax when they see I'm not intimidated in the least.

Alejandro's not alone. Walking just behind him is a group of men wearing camouflage and high-round artillery. Their expressions are emotionless. Their body language is almost robotic.

The perfect killer has both of these attributes.

He stops two steps from me and extends his hand. "Nice to finally meet you, Thiago. I appreciate you meeting me personally and on such short notice."

Taking his hand, I tighten my hold against his firm grip. "I make it a habit to meet all potential buyers."

"That is a smart thing to do. A lot of criminals out there." As he says this, all of his men raise their weapons and point them at me. I don't flinch, but I do release a chuckle. "Something funny, De Leon?"

"Extremely." Because this won't be the first or last time any man stepping through my doors to buy this kind of merchandise attempts to rob me. In this life it's killed or be killed. Take what you want and walk over the corpse of any man standing in your way. But just like him, I come prepared, and my bite is worse than his bark. A quick glance at Ivan and he gives the signal, forty of my own soldiers showing themselves—they're scattered throughout the room and holding the kinds of weapons that he's here to buy. Anything and everything; M1911, M-10, AR-15, Uzi, and the last and most amazing is the military-grade tanker with a functioning missile ready to fire if need be.

Would we all die? Yes.

Would I back down? No.

Instead, I call his bluff and raise a brow. Wait. Watch.

Alejandro's smile grows as the seconds tick by until the asshole is laughing, full on and deep as he releases my hand. "You are one crazy son of a bitch!"

I shrug. "So I've been told."

"It's a quality I admire in those I do business with." His militant employees lower their guns and stand in place, posture rigid and body alert. Alejandro then gestures to the case still open with the Mac-10 inside, silently asking if he may take a closer look and I nod. "As you can imagine, a man in my position needs to surround himself with people unafraid to make difficult decisions."

"Understandable." I take a step back and my men part, lining up in a row on either side of us. "Now, shoot it."

"Do you have somewhere in mind?" His dark eyes, an almost black shade, meet mine as he tests the weight of the piece in his hand. "Is there a range on the premises?"

"Depends on you, Alejandro." He's perplexed by this, and I give Ivan the second signal. There's a door on the far back wall and from that entrance a man is dragged inside beside a movable target that they put in place rather quickly. The paper we give him has ducks on it. It's one Luna would pick whenever we'd go out to a range in the past. "Human or—"

"Let me go!" The man struggles, and my client's face is one of incredulity. This asshole is his right-hand man and the father of his sister's unborn child. He's also a married man, and not to the bright-eyed-eighteen-year-old he seduced with the lies of getting a divorce. He's also someone with a heavy hand who hurts those defenseless against him, and when the wife and his sister confronted him, Chiquito hurt them both.

Separately and in locked rooms, for over twenty-four hours he physically assaulted them, and this is retribution. I will never condone raising a hand to a woman, and when the day comes that I deal with Jasmine Senot, it will be my mother or Luna who decides her fate.

Alejandro doesn't think twice. Face hard and the devil in his expression, he whistles loudly. The sound reverberates throughout the large building and his old friend snaps his head up, giving him the perfect opening. My detainee opens his mouth and mouths *Alejandro* as my client's finger twitches.

One bullet. One intake of breath.

Chiquito Salazar slumps over still in my men's hold, head blown back and brain matter scattered behind them.

"I'll take them all." Alejandro turns to look at me, a smile of satisfaction on his face. "Everything you have."

"You know the price." At this, a lankier man from his entourage comes forward, two briefcases in his hand. He places them atop one of the cargo boxes and flips them open. "There's two million dollars there and eight more if we can triple this order within the month. There's a radical movement growing, and I sit at the helm of this war. My men will need the best to fight."

"Done."

He extends a hand out once more and I shake it, but then he pulls me into a man hug. "I don't know how you knew about him or why he was here, but that son of a bitch has been avoiding my wrath for the last two months. Thank you for this kind gesture. I appreciate this, and you've won my loyalty."

"You're very welcome." Taking a step back, I look him in the eye. "Ivan, have everything loaded and the body of Salazar also on his truck."

"Of course, brother."

"How did you know?" he asks, curiosity getting the best of him.

"I make it my business to know who I am making transactions with, Mr. Lucas. What he did was sick and unacceptable—could not go unpunished—and when I put my men on a search mission, he evaded us too, until appearing at a hotel on South Beach that's owned by my family."

"Hijo de puta," he spits out, accent thick, and I nod. The man was scum. "If you ever need my help, Thiago, it's yours. I mean that."

"And I hope I never have to take you up on that offer." Not because I don't appreciate the offer, but because that means shit's gone south and out of my hands. "Will you be staying in town or leaving immediately?"

There's a look that crosses his face. It softens for a fraction of a second, and I recognize it. "There's someone I need to see first. I may be here for a day or two depending on the outcome."

"Then I say good luck, and enjoy some good food while you're at it. The Cuban Lion on Collins Ave. will hold a table for you for the next few days."

"I might just check them out."

"Tell the chef to make you my favorite." I pat his shoulder twice and then walk out of the building and toward the office I keep on site. Listening to those recordings are my top priority, and I watch Ivan grab them and head this way after giving out orders.

Antonio Alejos is now dead man walking.

Chapter 27
LUNA

I look at the text and my brows scrunch up in confusion. I don't know the number and I'm almost positive that this isn't for me, but then a second message comes through answering my unasked question.

(It's me. Celeste. ~Unknown)

(Did you change your numbers? ~Luna)

But then again, how would I know after communication between us ceased. After Maritza, she shortly followed, and I left it alone. No fight. No questioning. Nada.

Three small dots appear at the bottom of the screen as I'm saving her info into my contacts. They come and go a few times before the reply follows through.

> Yes, silly. Last year at some point. LOL ~Celeste

> Are you hungry? Working? Want to meet up?
> ~Celeste

Do I? Maybe. At the very least to ask her why she ghosted me too.

And besides, technically I am off, having been at the site of an abandoned car that caught fire. Not a huge crime scene as the main item burned to a crisp, but the surroundings held a few interesting facts: footprints, a small water bottle which reeked of fuel, and a bandana with the could-be assailant's bodily fluid. As if he blew his nose and then didn't think that the piece of cloth would survive the fire, so they tossed it carelessly.

Items like that don't magically appear at crimes the likes of arson, and most importantly, not together. That car fire wasn't a coincidence when all three pieces of evidence are found atop a small concrete block to the right of the Honda Accord.

It's also another crime scene where Thiago has somehow managed to sneak a little gift into my equipment bag. Four gifts now that appear out of thin air: an intricate vintage key, a new bracelet, and charms—a baseball, a camera, my age when we met, my age now—a pair of Hermes sunglasses and today…Chapstick and gum.

"He's keeping me on my toes," I mutter low before reading the newest text.

> Are you even off work? ~Celeste

Early morning call means I get off soon. Does one work? ~Luna

Can we make it a girls' lunch? ~Luna

I'm already walking outside the building and almost jogging toward my car, intent on cutting off Natasha who left a few minutes prior. The parking garage isn't far, but it's large, and I cut between two rows before spotting her and Claudio, who's a little closer than I'm comfortable with. While she's walking toward her car, he comes toward me, and I notice then he's not alone.

This puts me on edge. I've known the woman for years, but she's never sought me out or really talked to me. She was always around my father. Talking to him. Laughing at something he said.

Jasmine Senot is looking at me with an annoyed expression. Like I'm beneath her.

Her mere presence puts me on edge, and when her son tries to grab my arm and halt my steps, I hold a hand up. "The answer is no and don't you dare touch me. I have nothing to say to either of you."

"Watch your tone, Luna. Your father wouldn't approve of this."

"I didn't ask, nor do I care."

"Luna, please—" Claudio tries to grab me again, but stops mid-sentence, looking past me and shrinking back. His mother does the same. Then another step; their faces a bit ashen and whoever has spooked them deserves a cookie from me. However, I'm not concerned with them either way. My target is in a hurry and walking way faster than normal.

"Don't come near me again. Next time, I *will* shoot you and claim self-defense."

"This isn't over," Jasmine sneers, pulling her son back another pace. "You will see me again soon enough."

"No. I won't. Back off." I don't stay and chat, hurrying after my cousin.

Natasha's almost at her BMW parked three down from mine, and I place two fingers inside my mouth—the loud whistle rents the air, making her and two other people pause and look back.

"Lunch?" I call out, catching up. "Just got an invite from Celeste."

"Thiago's cousin?"

"Yes."

"Have fun."

"*We* will."

> Sounds perfect. I have some exciting news to
> share. ~Celeste

Turning the screen toward her, I show my stubborn cousin her reply. "See…she has some exciting news!"

"Lulu, I have plans and—"

"With whom?"

"Noneyabusiness." Nat looks away for a second, a small hint of a blush on her cheeks.

"Who?"

"I'm out."

"No, you're not." Looping my arm through hers, I turn us both and all but pull her to my passenger-side door. "Spill."

"Why should—"

My facial expression stops her idiotic reply in its tracks. It's a combination glare/annoyance. "This coming from the woman who blew up my phone the day of Thiago's release, day after, two days after that, and let's not forget the party at his parents' home."

"Which you still haven't given me all the details about." Nat stops and turns to face me, pulling her arm from mine so she can place it on her hip. "Amberlyn and I have been more than patient."

"And last week after our date," I continue as if she hasn't said anything. She's made a fine point, but that doesn't mean I have to acknowledge it.

"Which all I got was…" she holds up a finger to tick items off with "…handsome papi, suit, Hamilton, and hottest kidnapping ever."

"And you want more?"

"Yes." No shame in her *nosy* game.

"What are you offering up in exchange?" At my question, she narrows her eyes. "Come to lunch and I'm willing to share almost all the details. We'll play twenty-nosy-questions after."

"But Ignacio—" She slaps a hand over her mouth and my smile grows. Nat is screwed and knows it.

There are only a handful of Ignacios that we both know and only one is under the age of forty. Moreover, his father and my uncle don't get along for a reason none of us are aware of.

"Ignacio Perez, Natasha? Really?"

"Not now."

"Oh my God! It is!"

"Quit it." She smacks my arm hard. "You know how hard this shit is better than anyone."

Nat's right and I nod, my expression contrite. "Sorry. I'm being a jerk, aren't I?"

"Kind of."

"Forgive me?" I give her my best puppy-dog eyes. "Pretty please, and I'll buy the booze for tonight's sleepover."

"What sleepover? We're not ten anymore."

"The one we are going to have because it seems we're keeping secrets and that's not our thing."

Nat grimaces and nods. "Will it be copious amounts?"

"Do you know any other way?" I ask, giving her the *really* look.

"Then you got yourself a deal."

"…AND then he said I had the prettiest eyes he's ever seen!" Celeste giggles and we all laugh with her. Not in the way she thinks, as if we find everything she's saying is *the cutest anecdote ever* but more of a *what the fuck is going on here* way?

As a matter of fact, I think everyone inside of the busy sushi bar in Coral Gables feels that way. People are whispering, turning to look and slyly pointing while Thiago's cousin is oblivious to it all. And that is the only part of her that hasn't changed; her personality is still the same—sweet and happy—while her outward appearance gives off a different impression.

Celeste has always been beautiful. In all the years I've been with Thiago, she was never one to boast or show off—use her name to her advantage. However, the woman sitting in front of me gives the appearance of something she is not.

Her lips are over plumped, and she's had some unneeded work done.

Her shirt is nearly see-through, and her skirt is too short.

Her laugh is borderline obnoxious with that look-at-me quality that annoys.

What happened to her?

Amberlyn is to the right of me and pinches my arm. "Is she on something?" she whispers this behind her glass of water, keeping up the pretenses by taking a few sips. Because she too had taken Natasha's stance, and the only family member she's kept a relationship with over the years is Ivan. *He's* someone she could never stay away from without a catastrophic reason. "She wasn't like this."

"I wouldn't know." I've finished my tuna roll and I push my plate away, focusing on my iced tea instead. Prior to her text, the only other time I've seen her was at the De Leons house for Thiago's welcome home party, and Celeste avoided me then. One second she was outside, and the next, gone like her father and brother—something that in our teenage years wouldn't have happen.

"That's very sweet, Celeste." Nat does me the favor of engaging her because I'm thrown off by what I'm seeing. "And where did you guys meet?"

"Oh! That's the cutest part!" She waves at someone past us, overeager and smiling from ear to ear. "We met during a family trip to New Jersey."

What the hell were they doing in Jersey?

"And it was love at first sight," a male voice says from beside me, but I don't look back. My eyes are on my cousin's expression and the shock in them. "One minute I was helping one of our servers with a large party, and the next, I was overtaken by her beauty."

"Sergio," Natasha says, dropping her chopsticks. Her eyes flick to mine briefly. "It's been a long time."

"Very." His presence looms behind me for a fraction of a second longer than I am comfortable. Just a minute and internally I'm cringing, letting out a rough exhale when he comes around and stops at Celeste's chair, bending at the waist to kiss her forehead. This is a boy I remember all too well—pushy and obnoxious and conceited—who professed his love to me before my family moved. "Since Luna's freshmen year of high school."

"You mean *our* freshmen year?" I interject, and his eyes settle on me, his look intense. "Last time I saw you was at my cousin's birthday party out on the shore. About two weeks before we moved."

"Sounds about right." Sergio's jaw ticks, and Amberlyn pinches me again. She's picked up on his slight agitation. "Good times."

Bullshit. It wasn't a good time, and I broke his nose with a straight jab to his face when he tried to force a kiss from me. When he threw me back against a wall and tried to pin me with his weight, I was lucky that Natasha walked in at that very moment and shoved him off, adding a second kick to his groin after my own.

"Well, this is pretty cool. You all know each other," Celeste says, her face pinched tight while rubbing her fingers with an ostentatious ring over his casted hand. "What a small world."

"Is this your fiancé?" Both their eyes settle on me, but it's hers that I focus on. I see something in her I've never noticed before: jealousy mixed with fear and worry all in one. *I need to speak with*

Thiago about this. Something just isn't right. How she's moving closer, almost at the edge of her seat and falling in order to cling to his limp arm, throws off warning signals. "Was this your big surprise?"

"Yes." There's a hint of defensiveness in her tone, an almost silent accusation that I don't understand. "Sergio Martinez is my soon-to-be husband and I wanted you to meet under less stressful circumstances. You know how the family is. How your boyfriend can be."

Martinez? Why would he lie about his last name?

"When did you—"

"So, I fell head over heels in love with Celeste and after a week of being unable to be apart, I sold the family business and moved here. I haven't looked back since."

"Wow," I mutter under my breath, but Celeste caught the movement of my lips and I stand, coming around to her enthusiastically before she can question me. "Wow, guys! Congratulations!" Pulling her away from his side, I maneuver us a few steps back and hug her. "I'm so happy for you."

After the female squeal/excitement dance, which I fake to death, Celeste pulls back to look at me. "Do you mean it?" I'm caught off guard by her question. She doesn't know my history with him, and while just being near him gives me the creeps, for all I know he does love her. He's changed. It's plausible even if I doubt it. "Are you happy for me?"

"Of course I am." Behind her Natasha and Amberlyn move toward us, each coming to stand on either side of us. "True love is a beautiful thing."

"It really is, Celeste." Amberlyn kisses her cheek. "We're all so happy for you."

"Thank God." Her reactions don't make a lick of sense, and Celeste continues with her explanation before we can ask. "If you're on my team, maybe you can help me with Thiago? He's not a fan of Sergio...I mean, look at his hand. It's broken, and it's my cousin's fault. *He* sent him out to do grunt work and my hubby got injured."

"Celeste, that's not up to me. You know how the hierarchy works better than I do."

"I know that." Celeste turns her head, looking back at Sergio who's watching us. Something passes between them, and she nods her head minutely before turning back to me. It was a quick shift of her head that the others didn't see, but I do. "I'm not asking for preferential treatment, Luna. Not at all. Just his safety at all times."

The words, *then don't work with the family* sit on the tip of my tongue. I'm so close to calling her out when my phone pings. It's the work ringtone, and Nat follows me as hers does the same.

One unopened message from: Thompson Work

> Mandatory meeting tomorrow. Be here @9 a.m.
> Confirm you received this. ~Thompson Work

"Shit. We need to go, Luna."

"I just saw," I say, following my cousin's lead. "Guess it's going to be a long day."

"Don't tell me you're leaving. I thought you were out for the day." At my raised brow, he tries to backpedal. "At least that's what my baby girl said—I was hoping for a longer reunion."

"My apologies, but unfortunately, work calls." Sliding my cell into my back pocket, I grab my wristlet and walk over to Celeste. "We'll talk more soon, okay? I promise."

She lets out a sigh but offers me a smile. "Maybe dinner later in the week?"

"It's a date, sweetie." From where I am, I look at Sergio and wave. "Nice seeing you again."

It's a lie. Completely and Utterly.

"Likewise, Luna."

The other two say their goodbye and we walk out, not looking back, but I can feel the stares. It makes me as uncomfortable now as it did back then.

"What a creeper," Amberlyn hisses, opening the door so we can walk through. "That guy isn't right. The bad vibes he gives off..."

"He's always been that way." Turning right at the short entrance walkway, we head toward the parking lot. We're almost there, just a few steps from my car which is in the first spot and first row, when I spot someone I'd know anywhere. I stop us, holding out a hand to each and *shhh* them.

Nat's looking at me. "What is it, prima?"

"It's Dad, and he's not alone." Before the last word, Amberlyn whispers *shit* and Nat finds them.

"What the hell is he doing with—"

"I don't know, but I'm sure Thiago doesn't either. Jadiel has no business meeting him." It leaves me on a hiss, and I don't think twice when instead of getting into my car, I cross the street. I'm a few steps behind them, so close to the Mediterranean restaurant, when a black SUV blocks my path. "Watch it, ass...Leon?"

He's driving, smirk on his lips. "Get in, beauty."

"But...my dad...what are you—"

"Trust me to have a handle on everything." His hazel eyes are so beautiful, literally pulling me toward him as if hypnotized. "Get in."

I'm already moving toward him, one hand on the handle, but I pause right before pulling it open. "But my car?"

Thiago looks past me, and Nat takes my keys from my other hand. "Drop the car off later tonight. I'm sure you both have plenty to talk about." My cousin says something that resembles an agreement to my ears, and he laughs, a deep chuckle before locking sights on me again. "Get in."

"But—"

"Get. In." There's heat in his tone. A want that licks at my skin and makes shiver.

And I do just that without another complaint. I'm in his car and buckling in as the girls say goodbye, giggling as they walk away. I'm watching him drive and the world disappears—my mind and body giving in to my desires, but right as we stop at the next red light, I snap back into focus.

"Thiago, my dad was with Jadiel and—"

"I know." He's not upset. Angry.

"You do?"

"Bebe, I think it's time you listen to the recording Carlotta gave us."

Chapter 28
THIAGO

"**A**RE YOU SURE you want to hear the rest," I ask, seeing the distress on her face. The hurt. "We can stop here, and I'll take care of everything."

"Let it play." Luna's voice is strong, and to anyone that doesn't know her, uncaring. But she can't lie to me. Hide from me. "Please, Thiago. I need to hear it all for myself and not get the abbreviated version from a worried boyfriend."

"I'm more than that and you know it." Pressing the play button, I sit back and pull her into my side. I'm here to comfort her. Be everything she needs.

"Those dumbasses have no idea what's coming their way," her father says. You can hear others laughing in the background and water splashing. The music is loud, and very faintly you can hear the moan of a woman. *"Even Luna needs to learn her place, and that's to spread her legs and be bred by who I choose as her owner. Her husband will be beneficial to my campaign, an asset in business, and not that piece-of-shit thug she thinks will be her husband. I'll kill him myself first."*

"I thought that's what Jadiel or that other idiot was for? To kill them all." Senot's wife's voice is now unmistakable. She sounds high. Almost maniacal with a hint of jealousy. *"God knows my son would gladly do it for the little tramp."*

"Watch your mouth, sweetheart. Never speak ill of my daughter." There's a whimper of pain from her and a jumbled *I'm sorry* that sounds as if he's gripping her face—cheeks hard. *"Your son doesn't measure up. Like father, like son. Both are too pussy to take owner-ship of the women they love."*

"Fuck, papi. Mas duro." This time the moan is loud as she asks for it harder. *"Hearing you speak like this is such a turn-on. I need you."*

"Such a cock-hungry whore." The sound of a strike follows, and her squeals quickly turn into cries. Once. Twice. Eighteen times until Jasmine Senot is a blubbering mess and begging for him to fuck her, but all Antonio does is laugh. Taunt. *"You're not worthy of my dick today, Jasmine. At best, I'll let Gaytan fuck you and leave you want-ing. Isn't that right, Alfredo? Tell her you'll never be enough, and I'll let you come inside her used cunt."*

"I'm not enough."

"Again. Louder."

"I'm not enough."

"Good boy."

Her father's laugh makes her shudder in disgust and my girl holds a hand up. "No more. Please…no more."

"I'm sorry, love." Pressing my lips to her temple, I lay a tiny kiss there. And then another. I litter a line from her forehead to cheek with small signs of affection. "I'm so sorry you had to hear that."

"How can he...why?" That's the million-dollar question and I have my theories, but I don't think she wants to hear them. At least, not today. Tomorrow when she's had time to process, I'll tell her exactly what I think. Tonight, though, she needs to mourn a relationship that she still wants—wishes were different. "And my mom? *Jesus Christ*, does she know?"

When I first met Luna, her father was her hero. He was someone she looked up to, that she wanted approval from in every facet of her life. I changed that dynamic. I took away the hooks he's cemented deep with years of bullshit teaching that did nothing but break her mental state and left a young girl behind that needed permission for everything.

To talk on the phone.

Whom she could become friends with.

If she could step a single foot outside her home.

His hold was like a noose, and when I came into the picture, I broke those bonds. Because to men like him, children aren't anything more than pawns to be moved in whatever direction best suits his needs. Antonio Alejos lives in a world where the parent is always right, and his word is the only one that matters.

He doesn't care if she's happy, loved, and cherished—his political career is what matters. The connections to the rich and powerful —the pathway to D.C. he will never have. A motherfucking idiot, because I could've helped him in so many ways.

"I think she knows, Luna, but is in no position to protest. She's made her bed and lies in it because it affords her the life she wants." Her eyes close and she nods, tears escaping. Each one breaks my heart. Makes me want to go out and beat the fuck out of them both for hurting my girl. "There is nothing you can do to change them, bebe. I'm sorry."

"I know." Her sigh is heavy, and she leans further into me. "Are you going to kill them?"

"I can only promise to speak with you before my decision is made."

"That's more than I can hope for after what I just heard. What he's done to—" The words die then as sobs take over. Luna's entire body shakes, the enormity of the situation hitting her hard, and I pick her up. Flipping her to face me, I turn her so she straddles my lap and pull her chest to mine. Her breathing is choppy and face splotchy—tears soaking my shirt—and yet she's the most beautiful thing in my world. Seeing her this distressed doesn't help her father's case.

Instead, it further burns my blood, but I bite back the emotion. This isn't her fault, and the added pressure of my decision will only hurt her. Because his death certificate sits at my desk awaiting my signature.

For her, though, I'll postpone the inevitable. Not forever, but long enough for her to cope.

"It's okay, baby girl. All will be fine…I promise."

"It won't be, Thiago. We both know that." She looks up at me, her eyes so sad. Full of hurt. "This can't end well."

"What would make this easier for you? What can I do to ease your mind?"

"Don't kill him. Anything but that."

"Luna, I can't make a—"

"Just promise me…" she takes in a shuddering breath "…that if it can be avoided and it's not in self-defense, you'll bury him in court or expose him. Let death be the last option on your list."

"I will try." It's the best I can do, and she knows this. Luna nods then and leans forward, placing her lips on mine briefly before burying her face in my neck—letting go of the pain and embarrass-ment this has brought her. And all I can do is hold her. Let her know that I'm here for and will support her in whatever she needs.

"Thank you." That's the last thing my beauty says, because a few minutes later she's asleep. Standing with her in my arms, I walk us to our bedroom and gently lay her down before slipping in behind her, her back to my chest and head nestled beneath my chin.

Her rhythmic breathing lulls me into a semi-calm state, but one thought continues to roam in my head. It worries me that she isn't addressing what Antonio said about her on that tape. How he intends to sell her to the most useful bidder.

Something that will never happen, but has to sting, nonetheless.

THE PHONE RINGS atop the bedside table pulling me from a semi-deep sleep, and I look over at my alarm clock. It reads a little after five in the morning and at once, I'm up and careful not to wake Luna up. Not after our discussion yesterday and having to cancel on Natasha, who seemed more concerned than upset when I gave her a very abbreviated version.

That's Luna's story to tell, and I respect that. She'll share when ready.

Before it rings for a fourth time, I'm pressing the green button and throwing my legs over the edge of the mattress. "Speak."

"S-sir, we have an issue." It's Miguel's son and he sounds scared, his breathing harsh. "They've taken it all."

"Slow down, kid. Who's taken what?"

"The feds. They're all over the port."

"When?" Anger ignites in my veins, my entire being vibrating with ire. "How long ago? Why are you even off the ship?"

He's set to stay aboard for another week before taking some time off to go see his mother in California, something I know Miguel isn't too happy with.

"The guys on the ship sent me out for a food run, and I was on my way back from picking up the order when I almost ran into the commotion. Feds are everywhere, and I was lucky enough to be confused with a delivery boy." There's some kind of commotion around him, but the voice of a man comes through loud and clear: *Get a count and load up this haul. We did good today, boys.* "That's the man in charge, but he's following the lead of another man." He's whispering now, his voice almost shaky. "I'm hiding behind a container from China just to the left of them. I'll send you the picture now."

"Do that and don't get caught. I'm on my way, kid."

"Thank you, sir."

"You did good." I hang up, then and press the number two on my speed dial. It takes three rings, but Ivan answers groggily.

"You okay?"

"Heat at the port." I've already grabbed a pair of sweatpants and t-shirt, slipping them on and then grabbing my Pumas. I'm in a hurry and rush downstairs, slipping them on at the bottom of the stairs. "Meet me in thirty."

My phone vibrates with an incoming text and I pull it away from my ear, looking down at the screen. It's the photo that Junior promised me, and the hijo de puta on the screen isn't a stranger. I've used him in the past to run deliveries for me.

Joel Arroyo is a dead man.

"Motherfucking cocksuckers."

"Something like that." I left my SUV sloppily parked after coming home with Luna and with the key fob inside the cup holder. It's a keypad entry; my pin is the day we met. "Bring a few with you."

"Got it. See you in a bit." He hangs up as I turn the car on, but before I pull out, I send my sleeping girl a text.

Trouble with a delivery at the restaurant. Be home soon. Love you. ~Thiago

Tossing my phone aside, I peel out of my roundabout driveway. At the end of the long entrance stand four men and I roll my window down, pointing at two. "Get in." They do as I say without a word, getting into the back while the other two straighten their postures. "If anyone shows up, you call me. No one is allowed on the property without my or the wife's approval. Understood?"

"Yes, sir."

"Good." I'm a good twenty minutes from the port and as I get out of the community, I make the turn toward I-95 West then South, hitting speeds of over a hundred miles per hour. The motherfucker responsible will not make it off the port. "Guns ready and be stealthy. We're here to pick up and not be seen."

"Yes, sir." These two are a bit new to the family, only a year in, but came with high recommendations from the Perez family. Another prominent family, from the same province in Cuba as my family, and who've made a name for themselves through somewhat legal ventures.

They deal in fraudulent activity: insurance, credit, and hacking. Their son Ignacio is a good guy and does jobs for the family from time to time.

He's in charge of all surveillance equipment at my house. He's also had his eye on Natasha for quite some time.

Biscayne Blvd. is completely empty at this time of the morning and as I pass in front of the Freedom Tower, I make the sign of the cross. I'm proud of my heritage and I know the sacrifices my family made for freedom.

The light turns red up ahead and I slow down, coming to a complete stop as two MDP SUVs blow by the intersection, their lights off and heading toward the American Airlines Arena where they make a sharp turn left.

They're heading for the port. I'd bet money on it.

I also know that taking my car too far inside is a mistake, and after turning on Port Blvd., I park at the farthest lot out and beside a waiting Ivan. Everyone exits the car slowly, careful not to make too much noise, and we take a private side entrance onto the main hub.

There's so much commotion past the door we're standing at; I can just make out the orders being shouted—*check that container* and *tear every last bit apart*—but that's not what stops me. No. Not at all.

What stops me in my tracks is the two men blocking that

entrance. One unconscious, while the other has a gun raised and pointing toward that same door which separates us from the feds.

Junior looks scared, near pissing himself, but holding it down for me. For our family. And while right now isn't the time to ask him the "how," I'm sure it's a very interesting story.

His relief at my presence is palpable; a single snap of my fingers and my men begin to drag the unconscious asshole out. At the same time Ivan is there to help Junior out, the adrenaline of the moment wears out quicker than it arrives, and I take his gun as his arm goes limp.

He's done his father very proud and has earned himself a token of appreciation.

Chapter 29
THIAGO

"WHAT DO YOU mean it was seized?" Casper hisses into the phone, and I can hear the wind rushing past him as if he's pacing. His tone holds anger, but it's not directed at me. I feel him, though. My own need to break something is near overwhelming. Could land me back in jail if I'm not careful. "When did this happen?"

"A few hours ago." My voice sounds gruff to my own ears, thick with sleep as I overlook the main hub and the dying activity. They've done their damage. Took my shipment, and yet they'll never be able to pin it to me. The manifesto is made out to a phantom company.

Nonexistent. Fake office. Fake Florida license. A figment of the imagination.

"*Fucking shit.*" It's grumbled under his breath, and I'm not all that sure he meant to say it aloud.

Seagulls fly overhead, and I squint my eyes. It's barely seven in the morning here and I've been at the Port of Miami since a little before six. "Don't worry. We got the motherfucker responsible, and he's being taken to his room as we speak." I rub my jaw, scratching the stubble there. I'm thinking. Contemplating my options since the merchandise taken had already been sold and my buyer is waiting.

My favorite CEO of a Fortune 500 company has already paid me half of its street value and is expecting delivery to a hidden property he owns in the Bahamas, his yearly orgy with his newest wife and friends.

"I'll be there soon," he says after a minute, his tone more controlled now. I don't think he's alone. Might even be that woman —Mrs. Asher's cousin—that I saw him with at the hotel Malcolm held his reception dinner. I saw them on my way out, but they didn't see me, and it was amusing to watch the self-assured British asshole chasing her around. And had the place not been watched, I would've stayed long enough to give him shit for it.

"Please send a car to take me straight there."

"Not a problem, Jameson." I'm about to say something else, but an unmarked cop car interrupts. It shuts off and the door opens; one of my favorite people steps out. "How's it looking, Officer Alejos?"

"It's hot, Thiago. You shouldn't be anywhere near here, especially if you just got out." He means: *my niece would be so pissed at you.*

"And I'll stay out. Luna will kill me if I go back."

"She talking to you yet?" I almost laugh at his poor acting. He's one of the few that knows the truth; my baby girl loves me. Is back where she belongs.

"Since when have you known your niece to be anything but hard-headed." *She would also knee me if she heard that.*

Edgar laughs at my bullshit, but quiets just as fast when his radio goes off. A woman shoots out a few codes, a robbery in progress and back up is needed. "I'm out, Rivera, but I'll let you know. The initial report should be ready by tonight and it'll show what they know. You'll have the upper hand, but the window is small. Act fast."

Then he's gone and I run a hand down my face. "You heard him? We need to move fast while they'll be preoccupied." Ivan points toward a now sleeping Junior inside my car, silently asking if we wake him up, but I shake my head in the negative. He more than proved himself tonight and deserves the small break. "Question is; how are we replacing? How long will it take?"

"Buy me a few days." A woman's voice comes through Casper's end of the line, soft and low. I can't make out what she says, but his grunt—how he says her name in response—confirms my suspicion. "There's enough in Chicago thanks to a gift from Asher, and it's here in a warehouse. I'll have it driven down."

"Perfect. Shoot me a message with your flight info."

"Will do."

THE INSIDE of this building reeks of rotting flesh, urine, and the pathetic tears of my enemies. And yet, it's so close to the main house where my mother's in the kitchen cooking a large meal for Casper and his entourage.

She's planning to spoil them before they leave and any other day, I'd find it funny. But not today. No, at the moment I'm sitting inside of a building staring at a man whose blood will stain the blade of my knife. *His life for the money lost.*

It's dark and dirty where we keep detainees; here they confess and receive sentencing. They beg and cry and make promises they can't keep before transport to Cuba or the morgue. You either work off your debt or die, but then again, that all depends on the infraction.

On how much you tried to take from me.

If the people of this upscale community knew what happens here, they'd vacate the city. As is, they mostly keep away, and those that lurk close enough eventually scurry off soon enough.

Because fight or flight always kicks in.

"Rise and shine, arsehole," Casper says, kicking the rat on the side of his leg. The bitch stirs, complaining a bit as he comes to, but my British friend has as much patience as I do. The next blow comes from a punch, closed fist, to his jaw. His head snaps back and a tooth falls.

Joel comes to, startled—eyes shifting nervously around the room. Those brown eyes land on Casper first, widening while his mouth drops open. The split on his lip tears a bit more and blood dribbles down his lip and chin.

"What's going on?" Then, that fearful stare lands on me. His body shakes. His sweating becomes profuse—his fingers and legs twitch as if his intent is to flee, but in reality, he can't. Ivan is to the right of him and Callum directly behind; each one is staring at him with the same anger I'm battling with—with the ire rattling the cages of our individual demons. He's surrounded on all sides and tied to a kitchen stool; it's dawning on him just how fucked he is.

"How have you been, Mr. Arroyo?"

"Why am I here?" Bare chested, we have him bound in a way that has him hunching over a bit, hands and feet secured by rope through the wooden legs. Casper sits forward, his face now right in his, however, his eyes keep shifting toward me. My eyes are narrowed and lip curling up at the corner in disgust. Anger. My family has done a favor or two for this piece of shit. When his mother got evicted because of a small kitchen fire in her efficiency and no nursing home would take her in, my mother helped find her a place, threatened the owner into taking her in for free. "What's going on? I—"

He's cut off by Ivan's four-inch blade. A quick flex of his arm and it's embedded deep, the pussy choking on a scream. "Answer Mr. Jameson when he asks you a direct question." My brother pulls the blade out, glaring at Arroyo while cleaning it on the man's bare skin. "Understood?"

"Mr. J-Jameson." The way his voice breaks grates on my nerves. How his limbs begin to shake makes me want to break each one so the nervous twitching stops. "This is a mistake."

"People who usually say that without any prompting or accusations being presented are more than likely guilty." Casper looks toward his cousin, Callum, who does as Ivan did. His puncture is in his back and lower, near the kidneys "Now, let's try this again, shall we?"

"Yes," Arroyo cries out, body fighting to bow into itself but can't. His bindings won't let him. Instead, the jerky movement causes more blood to drip and stain my floor. *Not enough.*

"Good boy." Casper pats his head as one would do a pet, and I hold back a chuckle. "How are you today?"

"Scared. In pain."

"Honest. I like that. Don't you, Thiago?" At his question I grunt in affirmation; I'm not in the mood to talk to the imbecile. "We'll take that as a yes. Now, do you know why you're here?"

"No... *fuck*!" I can't control my reaction to his bullshit any longer and stab him in the thigh, twisting the blade so it tears through the muscle in a very painful way. The cut is jagged and rough. "Okay! Please, I'll tell you what you need to know."

"So speak. Tell me why you snitched to the feds, got our shipment seized, and then cost us a lot of money?" Casper asks, ticking each item off his fingers with the tip of his karambit. "Talk."

"It was to get you out of Chicago." Arroyo's voice is low, almost too low to hear, but we all do, and crystal clear.

"The fuck did you just say?" The concern in Jameson's tone catches me off guard. *The fuck is going on?* "You have ten bloody seconds to explain yourself."

"The Savino family paid me a lot of money to—" He doesn't finish. Casper slits his throat and the next second is rushing out of the room. I catch him just outside the doors to the building, barking orders into the phone, and place my hand on his shoulder. "Not now."

"What's going on?" I ask when he looks back at me, his eyes tormented. "How can we help?"

"They're going after my girl, brother."

"Then we're all going to Chicago, Jameson. Nobody touches family."

WE'RE at a private airstrip in Kendall an hour later, waiting for our jet to be ready when my phone pings. It's been doing this off and on for the last thirty minutes, all incoming messages from Luna who I told in a rushed conversation that I'd be back as soon as I could.

> What's going on? ~My Beauty

> Are you okay? ~My Beauty

> Why are you leaving? ~My Beauty

Looking down at the screen in my hand, I swipe my finger across it and read her latest text.

> Meet me outside by the left side of the building in five. ~My Beauty

What is she doing here?

> Bebe, things are hot right now. Please pull back. ~Thiago

> No. You need to listen to what I have to say. ~My Beauty

"Everything okay, bro?" Ivan asks, stepping in beside me while

Casper paces and Callum barks orders into his cell phone. "If something came up and you need to stay, I'll--"

"Luna is here."

"Oh. Ummm." He doesn't know what to say; her stubbornness in that she's determined to come with me is unbreakable. It's why I lied. I know her and had no choice. "Where?"

"Outside. Says she wants to talk." Casper looks over at me but I shake my head. He nods and continues to walk the length of the room from one end to the other. "I'm going to need a few minutes, and while I'm outside, call Miguel and put everyone on red alert until we come back. Dad will step in. He has his orders, and Miguel needs to oversee that security is on heightened alert at all times."

"And Luna?"

"Two men on her at all times. No one comes within five feet without my knowing."

"Even her own family." Ivan is asking about her parents, not Edgar or Natasha.

"Especially them."

"All right. I'm on it." He pats my shoulders once, already pulling out his phone as he walks away.

Casper looks my way once more and I point to the outside, silently telling him I need a breather. The beginning of a smirk appears at the corner of his lips, but it dies down immediately, and he looks away. It's almost as if he knows, but can't allow himself to feel happy for me when his girl is missing.

She was taken from outside a public parking lot behind a popular Mexican restaurant and in broad daylight.

Casper doesn't want to hear comforting words, and I understand that. In his position, I would've shot anybody that so much as said hello.

Exiting through the automatic doors, I turn left where the sidewalk begins and find Luna already there. She's standing in front of the building as opposed to the side and extending one of her dainty hands out to me. I reach her in a few strides, taking her hand in mine, and it's she who pulls me toward our meeting spot.

We don't talk. No pleasantries exchanged.

Nothing until we turn the corner and then I find myself pressed against the concrete wall, her mouth on mine and legs around my waist. My reaction is instant and full of hunger; the swipe of her tongue across my lips almost blinds me as the ever-present need— that palpable force that thrums when we are close—rages into a near-blinding inferno. But then again, it's always been this way. Our love is both brutal and worshipping. Both giving and selfish.

Before Luna can protest, I flip our positions, forcing her back against the wall. There's a small whimper that escapes her hungry mouth, the sound settling on the tip of my engorged cock that flexes against her core.

I can feel her heat through her short cutoffs she's wearing, and I grind my hips harder. Rub her pretty little pussy and swallow her moans of pleasure. "Luna, love...*motherfuck*, I can't think straight when I have you like this." Another swivel and she throws her head back, lips parting as she takes in a ragged breath. "When you come looking for me, nothing else matters. All I see, hear, and feel is you. Nothing fucking else.

"I'm so weak when it comes to you, Thiago."

"I feel the same. Always have."

"I know." Luna opens her eyes and meets mine. There's some-thing in them, though. A softness I haven't seen in a very long time and my heart thumps harshly inside my chest. "You've always been mine, Thiago."

"I am."

"And I love that." At her words, my hands go from frantic to gentle. From demanding, to rubbing soothing circles against her hips bones with one hand while the other cradles the back of her neck. "I need you to know this, Thiago. I need you to understand that while I'm not happy with how things were handled, *by the two of us*, I've never stopped loving you. It's impossible for me to do so."

"Beauty, what's going on? You know I'll be back, right?" Because I need her to know that I will be back. For her. For us. That my plans far outreach where we are, and I want the dreams of the past to become our future.

Marriage. Kids. Ruling by my side.

"You're your mother's son and that woman is stubborn, papi. There's no doubt in my mind that you'll be back." Bringing her lips to mine, she kisses me again but this time it's softer, slower as she caresses her tongue with mine--tastes me and hums in satisfaction when I bite her bottom lip. "But that's not why I'm here."

"No?"

"No."

My thumb rubs the area where my tattoo is at her nape. "Talk to me, Luna. What's up?"

Her eyes become shiny and her bottom lip trembles. "I love you, Thiago."

"*Christ.*" Her words. They shake me to the core and my hands tighten their grip, the need to keep her where she is overwhelming. "Bebe, I love you more than anything in this world. Would do anything for you."

"We have so much to talk about, Leon. To make up for, but before you go, I needed you to hear those words. To know that I'll be waiting for you to come back so we can begin the next stage of our lives."

My grin is cocky as I nod. "Is this your way of asking me on a date?"

"No."

"Again with the *no,* beautiful."

"That's because I'm not asking, Thiago. I'm telling you." Before stepping back, the brat nips my bottom lip hard. "I'm also quitting my job, too. Just thought you'd like to know."

Chapter 30
THIAGO

WE GO FROM Miami to Chicago to Las Vegas within the span of six hours. Casper's man has located his girl and the shit-for-brains family who's taken her, while we're following a friend and local runner with strong connections to a large Cartel south of the border. Julio Villanueva knows people. He knows this city. And more importantly at the moment, his MC is supplying us with a few unmarked cars and the weapons we need.

"Good to see you, Jameson," he says, pulling Casper into a one-armed hug before holding a fist out for me to bump. We've been

around each other more than a few times before my incarceration—
he's someone I'll call if there's a product I need and fast—and I'm
thankful he's picked up on my need for silence. My boy's girl was
taken and I'm here to do whatever he needs me to, not chit chat.
"Wish it was under better circumstances."

"Me too."

Ignoring the rest of their conversation, I grab a vest and two
Glocks the moment the car's trunk opens. The compartment is
loaded almost to the brim with everything from different sized guns,
bulletproof vests, a machete or two, and to the right side, two ten-
gallon cans of gasoline.

Ivan follows suit and so does Callum, each taking the piece they
want with extra clips and protection. The few men with Julio also
suit up and then everyone steps back to give Casper some space, not
out of fear, but because we understand.

He's the last to reach for anything, and as he grips his weapon of
choice, his phone pings. Dropping the 9mm, he pulls out his phone in
haste and we all watch as he reads the message. Casper's expression
goes from hopeful to full of ire within the span of a second, his hand
tightening around the plastic as he takes in whatever is on the screen.

"Casper?" I ask, worried now that we're too late, but then he
flips the screen around. *Sick motherfuckers.* Aurora's inside of a car
with tear tracks—her fear—clear as day on her face, but that's not
what makes me pause, my own anger growing. What these assholes
have done goes past horrifying; they've put a cheap veil on her head
and a sash that reads *Bride-to-be* over her shirt.

"I know exactly where they are." Julio's standing beside me now,
looking at the picture. "It's fifteen minutes from here and behind a
dingy strip mall away from the main casino area. It's the part of
Vegas most don't see, and the fucker who owns it will marry her
against her will. Suit up. I'll take you."

THE PLACE IS DIRTY: a seedy little strip mall in an area not heavily populated by those traveling to sin city. Exiting the car, I take in the surroundings—the local watchers and the users all trying to act as if they're not watching this unfold. Trying to pretend that we don't see them.

Fucking idiots. No matter who they work for, no one inside that building outside of Aurora will make it out alive. No one.

The chapel at the very end of the street where we park is small, and the neon sign above it barely works. There's also a newer-model Mercedes Benz parked out front with a Prius right beside it that Julio and his men make quick work of. Every tire is slashed, and the gas tank punctured below; the accelerant quickly spreads as it drips, and the broken asphalt absorbs it.

As we leave them to guard the front parking lot, we walk over to the door and listen for noises coming from the inside. There's music playing, a low rendition of the wedding march, and Casper steps aside so Callum can use his silencer to get us in.

We have the upper hand here; they have no idea just how close they are to their deaths, and people react violently when cornered. The last thing we want is Aurora injured.

Two quick shots and Callum pushes the double doors open with his foot, leaving them wide open for everyone to pass. No one's heard us as of yet. There's no screaming or trying to get away, but knowing how fast that can change, Ivan repositions himself with me to take out the runners quickly.

We walk through the small lobby and right into the salon where an old dipshit is playing the organ. He's not good, and the seediness continues as the grimy room and its "witnesses" become my focal point. Casper will get his girl, but the rest of these rats will become nothing more than a game between brothers. Nobody's noticed us as of yet, but that ends rather quickly when an older woman walks in all but dragging Aurora down the aisle.

"Don't do this, Samantha. Let me go!"

"Shut the fuck up, brat. I should've had you disposed of years ago," the dead-woman-walking spits out, her hand raised high as if to strike her, when Casper raises his gun. One bullet and the officiant is dead; a bullet hole to the neck is our signal for the fun to begin.

Now, they all run. Try to scatter, but I unload the first magazine into the upper bodies of three males who almost made it to the door. Their bodies fall and a woman a few steps back screams, the obnoxious sound muted by Ivan's gun.

It's not something we normally do, but when a family member is hurt, normal procedures change.

I'm grateful when the organ player's head slams into the old instrument, his head half missing from the high-caliber round that ended his life. Another woman rushes past me and I don't blink, shooting her quickly in the back and then stepping over her as she bleeds out.

The officiant we thought to be dead shifts on the floor, coughing up blood, and I catch his movement a second before a younger woman, the other Savino sibling, rushes Casper.

She's yelling obscenities. She's crying that he should've picked her, but my friend doesn't spare her a second glance as they exchange bullets. He doesn't miss and she falls to the floor, trying to crawl toward safety, but Casper ends her hopes quickly. A second bullet to the back of the head, and she's dead.

A loud screech rents the air then, and before I end it myself, some idiot rushes me. For a second, I slip, almost falling to the floor, but I manage to flip our positions and land atop of some young thug spitting curses at me.

"You killed my best bitch, asshole."

"It doesn't matter when you won't be alive much longer." Reaffirming my grip on the gun's handle, I bring it down on his head. Once. Twice. Ten times until the bone of his temple cracks and his eyes bulge out of their sockets. And because I'm a nice motherfucker, I stand up and end him before he can take a final breath on his own.

My hands are bloody when I stand and Casper yells out, "Ivan...the mom. Through the door on the left."

"Got it." Ivan takes off and Callum and I focus on ending the last few stragglers wounded and hiding. The entire staff and those sitting down on the shitty pews are dead, and only then do we join Casper, who's staring down Dominic.

Aurora is being held by him, fear in her eyes.

"Let her go."

"I'll kill her," the near pissing man says, his voice shaking.

"No, you won't." Casper focuses on his girl and smiles at her. "Close your eyes and walk toward the sound of my voice, sweetheart." The last word hasn't fully passed my British friend's lips when I change my clip and join Callum in pointing our guns at Dominic. "Trust me, baby. Nothing will happen to you."

"He's got a gun to my back."

"He'll die before a single bullet dislodges from his gun."

"I'm right here, you piece of shit."

I almost laugh when Casper chooses to wink at Aurora instead of acknowledging him. And she smiles back, more so when her stepmother is dragged back inside by my little brother.

"Nico! Baby!"

"Mom!" Dominic yells out, letting Aurora go, who scrambles away as fast as she can. Smartly, she ducks and begins to crawl away —once she's out of the danger zone, we unload every single bullet left in our guns into the man's body. His lifeless body smashes into a mirror behind him a second before Casper has Aurora back in his arms.

The moment is sweet. As sweet as they sometimes come in our world, and I know it's time for me to leave when they begin whispering their promises to one another. I don't regret helping my friend —would do it again in a heartbeat—but I miss my own and after what she said before I left, it's time we lay the cards down on the table.

I want my ring on her finger.

I want her out of her apartment and moved into our home.
I want her by my side always.

Chapter 31
LUNA

"**W**HERE HAVE YOU been, Luna?" This comes from behind me, my key not fully inside the lock after driving back from the airstrip. It was a necessary trip. An exhausting trip for me. Not because I finally allowed myself to say the words back, but because I had to let him go after just getting him back.

Right now, my heart and mind are in sync, and both don't comprehend his having to leave and the possible danger he's putting himself in. Do I understand his need to help Casper? Yes, I do, but that doesn't mean that I don't worry. Because the Lord knows that I care.

Always have and always will.

"Are you even listening to me? I've been calling you for days."

Then, there's the picture I took from the still unsolved case. Jane Doe was found organ-less inside the parking lot of the Sweetwater mall, and I see myself in those vacant eyes. In her hair color, stature, and slim build. There's something about that case that I can't forget and has been nagging at me.

The crime scene was careless and the killer almost taunting the police with his cocky display. How they still haven't identified her after so many days. There's been no missing person's report that fits her characteristics nor loved ones asking about her.

Nada. Not a peep for a Latina whose life was taken much too soon and now sits inside of the morgue awaiting her fate. Either she's claimed within the time limit, or cremated by the state. It's sad, and even in death, her rights have been taken away.

This world is cruel and unforgiving.

"Luna, you have thirty seconds to answer me. Where have you been?" I still don't answer her, something my mother hates, and the accompanied huffs confirm she isn't alone. But then again, this doesn't surprise me. *He* uses her for these types of visits, the unpleasant kind. Dad will rile her up so she'll start running her mouth—nitpicking my life apart—and then come in to mediate the situation as if we are children.

It's manipulation at its finest. A sick game.

And it takes everything inside of me to not open my door, find my gun, and shoot him where he stands. What I heard on that tape is something I've been pushing back—avoiding until I'm ready to face the reality that my father is a vile human being. That he's not the man who took me to the beach on the weekends and came home every night with a treat from my favorite bakery in Jersey.

He's changed, and that hurts. That my mother is a possible accomplice also cuts deep. However, what bothers me isn't the fact that he's a dirty politician or cheating his way to the top; I'd be hypo-critical if I did. No. What hurts is his wanting to use me as a pimp would. That I'm his ticket to finding an idiot to do his bidding, and he could care less about my happiness.

Antonio will try to kill me or Thiago to get his way, and deep down I know that when the time comes, I'll have to accept the outcome. I'll back the De Leons because my father brought this upon himself.

Pushing the door wide open, I step inside and pause right at the entrance to face them. "How can I help you, Mother? And by the way, you've sent me one text. *One.*"

"Niña, don't get smart. Answer me...where have you been?"

"At my *pincha.*"

"That's not our vocabulary," my father spits out like I knew he would, once again showing his disdain for Thiago. This time in his culture. But then again, Antonio Alejos hates anything that isn't prim and proper—fake. I could use the Dominican, Cuban, or Chinese slang word for work, and he'd still have an issue. "You're a college graduate. Act like one."

"I'm tired and don't have time for your rudeness. Mind *your* manners or I'll close the door." My father moves his foot a bit, a minute shift, but I catch it. "I wouldn't do that if I were you, council-man. Unless invited, you will not enter my home."

"Are you kidding me, Luna? I am your father and you will respect—"

"Nothing." Squaring my shoulders, I let my handbag drop to the floor. I'm facing them head on, looking into their eyes so lifeless that it hurts. "I will do nothing."

"Luna, you're out of line. Your father and I—"

"Have no place in my life. Not after our last conversation."

"This again," she hisses, exasperation coloring her features. "He's a criminal! There is no future for you with him that doesn't consist of pain, cheating scandals, and low self-esteem."

"Those are three things that I don't suffer from, Mom."

"You will."

"Do *you*?" I snap, tired of the never-ending go around with them. "Are you projecting on me once again? It was your M.O. when I was a kid—"

"Enough." My father's voice thunders, eyes narrowing on me. "I'm sick and tired of this attitude and the complete disrespect that the De Leon family has instilled in you. I am your father, Luna. Remember that, and life will go much easier for you. Not all men put up with a mouthy woman, and your future husband will knock some sense into you if need be."

"Leave, and don't come back."

"You will regret this, child. Choose your side wisely before it's too late."

"I chose a long time ago, Antonio." My mother gasps at my use of his first name, her eyes showing a hint of fear, but I don't linger on her as my father shoots out his palm toward my face. His intent was to slap me, but I duck back and with my hold on the door firm, look him in the eyes. "Do that again and it'll be my bullet that ends you. Watch yourself."

"Your insolence will cost you highly." His hand grips my mother by her elbow, his fingers digging in to the point that she winces. For the first time, her usual stoic personality is showing emotion. She's scared. "How much do you love him?" my father asks, pulling my attention back to him, a sneer on his face. "Want to keep him safe?"

"Careful, Daddy. Your arrogance might just be your end."

"Luna, please. Stop this." Mom's pleading, trembling. "Family sticks together. We—"

"The next time you want to see me, Mom, come alone."

"Lunita, please stop this. Let's all just—"

"Your mother does as I say." I ignore his idiocy. If my father worries about anything, it's public appearance and she's always been the perfect public wife. He won't give that up, but it doesn't mean that I wouldn't want her to leave him, and I'll find a way to talk to her without him there. Today isn't that day, though. "Something you need to learn and accept. You will do as I say."

"No, I don't. Goodbye." Taking a step back, I slam the door in their faces and bend to grab my phone that's fallen out of my purse. Thiago's busy and I won't bother him, but that doesn't mean I won't let him know what's going on.

> Parents showed up. We fought. Call me when you can, papi. Love you. ~My Beauty

I grab my purse and walk inside the large apartment that feels empty. It feels off. Someone is missing—our home is what I want—and before I chicken out, I pull up his contact info. Thiago gave me his number, asked that I use it for whatever I may need, and my heart stops racing the moment I hit send.

> Miguel, can you please come and take me home? ~Luna

Lips skimming down the center of my back rouse me from sleep. They feel amazing, loving, and I find myself snuggling closer to the body. I know it's Thiago without looking at him.

I know his touch. His scent. His dominating presence that both overwhelms and brings me peace.

"Either you're home early, or I overslept?" My voice is heavy with sleep, yet I've never been more awake. Aware. "Everything okay? Did Casper—"

"Shhhh...later. I'll explain later." The blanket is pulled off me and his warm, just-out-of-the-shower body covers mine. From head to toe, we are one and I part my legs beneath him, spread them as wide as he allows, and lift my ass in offering. "Tell me again. Say the words."

"I love you."

"*Christ*, I'll never tire of hearing you say that." His thick cock flexes, slipping between my slick folds and then pauses at my entrance. Thiago holds himself there while draping himself over me; his lips are at my ear. "I'm nothing without you, Luna. I live for you."

"Papi, I...*oh God*," It's a helpless whimper as he buries himself to the hilt in one smooth thrust. Every single muscle in my body clenches—the pleasurable sting of stretching around his girth feels like heaven. It pulls from me a rush of wetness that soak his cock and my inner thighs.

Thiago doesn't pause or let me adjust. Instead, he pumps his hips without mercy, and I can only fist the sheets below. I'm holding on, trying to meet his thrusts, but can't when he flattens me to the mattress.

This is a claiming. A stamp of ownership.

"*Fuck* you feel good, beautiful. That's it...squeeze me just like that." His thrusts are purposeful—hard—while his hands leave behind an imprint on my flesh that I never want erased. Fingertips dig into my hips, his hold almost painful—it teeters between pleasure and pain and I moan for him. "Show me how much you want this. Who owns that sweet little pussy."

"You. All I want is you." He rewards my needy mewl by moving me up the mattress—my face almost hitting the headboard—with a slam of his hips. My thighs shake and eyes close; I'm already so close. It's building and making it hard to breathe, and I never want him to stop.

Using one hand for leverage, I swivel my hips. And I do it again when he groans above me, when his hand comes between us and he stops, placing his thumb on my clit while smacking my ass cheek with the other.

"Ride my cock." There's a bit of a challenge in his tone, and I look back at him from over my shoulder. Brow raised and smirk on his lips, he rubs my clit in tiny circles and waits. Leaves me on that proverbial edge. "Make yourself come, Luna. I want to feel your pussy flutter around my dick and squeeze me to almost the point of pain."

"No."

"No?" he hisses, and that earns me another smack to the opposite cheek.

"No, papi," I mewl, a needy sound that he enjoys, and use it to my advantage. "I want you to take me. Own me. Make me come so hard that I forget...*yes*."

"Then I apologize ahead of time." Thiago hooks my arms by the elbows with his and pulls me up, forcing my back to arch and bottom to stick out. I'm almost in a sitting position, his lips at my cheek and our breathing ragged. "I love you, Luna."

Then he fucks me. There's no other way to explain the way he takes me.

Every pump of his hips is brutal, a never-ending pleasurable punishment that slams into me with the force of a freight train. His hips slam into me...the *slap slap slap* of skin on skin is the only sound heard inside our room because I can't form a single sound.

My mouth is open, but words don't come out as I'm holding on by a very thin thread.

I can't stop it. Don't want to.

"I will always own you." It's almost an angry snarl as he lets go of one arm and slaps three fingers over my clit. My eyes squeeze shut, and my chest seizes, everything around me disappears as I come for him.

It feels never ending and I know someone is crying out, but I can't stand upright any longer and fall to the mattress. There's a *shhh* sound coming from above me and sweet words that prolong my pleasure as muffled curses follow.

I feel warm and tired and satiated.

I feel sleepy and give in to the feeling.

The last thing I consciously remember hearing is *I was never going to let you go.*

THERE'S something glinting in my face and it's annoying the crap out of me. I move my head, not ready to get up, but it's there and unescapable. Lazily, I swat at it with one hand and I'm met with a chuckle.

"Thiago, stop. I'm tired."

"You said that thirty minutes ago." He sounds amused and the light refocuses right over my right eyelid. *Jerk.* "Time to get up, bebe."

"How about forty more minutes."

"You said *that* over an hour ago." Now I have his mouth on my shoulder, working its way lower and taking the comforter with it. "There's something we need to discuss."

"It can wait," I whine, trying to wiggle away from him. It sucks because my side of the bed is warm and I'm now wiggling toward cold sheets. "Maybe after breakfast."

"How about now?" he says, following me across the bed. This mattress is larger than your standard king, and we both like to sleep on the right side. All night, we were one cocooned mass of limbs and covers with the occasional petting.

"No."

"No? Are we starting the day off like this?"

"Yes."

"Now you want to *yes* me."

"It's too early for you to—" I'm interrupted by the sound of an alarm. It's loud and at once, Thiago's up, slipping into a pair of sweatpants and grabbing his gun from the nightstand. He doesn't so much as look at me, but I do catch the way he points toward the table and I see the second Ruger there. "What's going on?"

"Get dressed." Then he's out of the room and I jump into action, following his orders. There's a pair of yoga pants and a tank top with a built-in bra that I left out for an early morning run. Putting them on, I forgo the shoes and follow the sound of noises downstairs.

No shots have been fired, but at the bottom of the stairs the sight that greets me is my Thiago with a crying man on his knees. The anger on one man's face and the fear in the other. All the guns drawn, including my own, ready to end a life.

And when they notice me, I can't help the shock on my face for two distinct reasons:

There's a large diamond ring on my finger, and it's weight finally registers.

The intruder is someone I recently met and had a bad feeling about.

What the hell? "Officer Young?"

Chapter 32
THIAGO

"N AME?"

"This is all a mistake. Please—" He's cut off by the sharpness of my brass knuckles across his cheek. There's a gash that forms right over the bone, the fourth now on his face. He's bloody. Swollen. A literal mess as we've been at this for an hour now. "No more."

Luna's with me, standing just to the right of us while I interrogate the bastard cocky enough to try and break into my home. She's not speaking, hasn't said a word after identifying him as someone working for the MDP.

"Name?"

"We can cut a deal. I'll—" Another strike, this one to the side of his neck, and he stiffens. The officer chokes from the shock of pain, and then his eyes roll back. The blow was hard enough to hit the Vagus nerve where, I knew it would cause a blackout.

"How long will he be under?" Luna says then and I look over, catching the small smile curling at her lips. She's fingering the ring on her left hand, turning the symbol of my love from side to side. "Because you owe me an explanation."

"Do I?"

"Yes, you do."

"I believe it's self-explanatory." One of the guys who captured him steps forward, offering me a wet hand towel to clean my hands, but I shake my head. Not yet. Not until I end this. "Is Ivan on his way?"

"Should be here within the next fifteen minutes," the guard answers, retaking his place against the wall of my guest house turned temporary jail.

I would've loved a custom-built basement, but it's not feasible on this property. So instead, I had my developer convert this originally four-bedroom guest house into a large open space with two jail-grade cells. There is drainage on the floors, an indoor irrigation system on the roof and walls, and complete soundproofing. No one can hear you from the outside. Not a single peep will pass through.

"Thiago."

"Yes, love?"

"Why is there an engagement ring on my finger?"

While the man in my chair fails to regain consciousness, I take the remaining steps between my girl and me. My hands are filthy and I'm sweaty, but I still lower my face to hers and take her lips in a sweet, soft kiss. Just a few pecks. A little something to hold me over until later, when I make love to my future bride.

Her small hands reach out for me—she tries to pull me in closer, but I shake my head. "Not while I'm like this."

"But...ouch!" Beautiful brown eyes narrow at the harsh nip to her lips. "That was mean."

"That ring is on your finger because it belongs there. Because I plan to make you my wife very soon."

"Would've been nice to have you ask..." she trails off, a slick little grin that matches my cocky one on her plump lips. This crazy, gorgeous, and perfect girl isn't worried about what I'm doing—my breakdown of the intruder—but is focused on her engagement ring.

But then again, she's never judged me.

"I did ask."

"When?"

"At your college graduation a few years back." And I did. Right there in the open field and on one knee after everything was done and the place was empty. At least at the time, we thought it was. In our minds, we were the only two, but two women decided to stay behind and be nosy. I never told anyone, but they smelled blood and captured the private moment. Luna doesn't know this, but I have the pictures inside our office to prove it. "Or did you forget?"

"I remember every single moment of that night." She's looking at me, hands absentmindedly caressing my chest. "You were so handsome in that dark suit and crisp white shirt sans tie."

"Do you remember your answer?"

"I told you then that I'd marry you today, tomorrow, and always." Luna is nodding at me, smiling so big that one would think we were on a romantic getaway and not dealing with a home breach. "Guess this means we're getting married soon?"

"Very soon."

"How much time?"

"Three months to the date and not a second more."

"Okay." Standing on the tips of her toes, she kisses me again. This time with more passion. With a promise of something delicious later. "It's a date."

"Something you two want to share?" Ivan says from the entrance and we look over, my eyes going straight to a box in his hand.

"What's in the box?" Gone is the playfulness and my queen takes note, quickly stepping back and retaking her prior position. Ivan smiles at her and walks over, giving her a quick kiss on the cheek. "Something that will explain who the hell this dumb fuck is, and why the Texas native is roaming the streets of Miami posing as an officer of the law."

"Show me."

The guards in the room spring into action immediately and without my saying, pull over a small table I asked to be put against the wall. Once in place, they step back and Ivan places the items face down atop the wooden surface.

His eyes shift to mine. "Can you promise to keep your cool?" he says this lowly so no one else hears. The question catches me off guard and I tilt my head, appraising him with a cool expression. "Thiago, what's in here is both useful and would piss any real man off. Don't scare her."

"You have my word."

One by one he flips the items collected over: pictures, video-tapes, files with notes and information on the mayor, my father-in-law, Luna, and my family. He's been following them, while my family's information comes from articles: national headlines, local newspapers, and a printout from Wikipedia. Everything is detailed, cataloged by date and holds some very damaging information on the families of some highly regarded city officials and their corruption.

Everything I could ever want and more, but more importantly, his information on Luna is limited and all comes from her job with the forensic department:

Date of birth.

Listed home address, which was still listed as her parents home.

Height.

Weight.

Then, there's a couple of pictures of her doing everyday things. The most recent is of her casual lunch with my cousin and her piece of shit fiancé.

"He gave me bad vibes that day out on the field," Luna says, coming to a stop beside me. Her hand is on my back—scent calming me—as the urge to wake him up and show him what pain really feels like rises to the surface. I've been patient thus far, more level-headed than normal when it comes to her, but only because Ivan is right. She knows me as her man and not the demon my enemies meet. "Even newbies know not to interfere or ask to help the forensic team. We know how to photograph the scene and have very specific ways on how to catalog, then file the evidence. He was too overeager. Seemed almost desperate to help."

"That's because he's not a cop," another male voice interjects, and I find Edgar at the door. Her uncle is furious. Near shaking with rage. "I did some digging of my own after Ivan called me and came across his rap sheet when running a facial scan. Scott 'Young' Rogers is from Houston, and on the run for a litany of crimes. He's wanted for everything from a carjacking, to the homicide of a woman whose crime scene looks very similar to what we found with our Jane Doe."

"Jesus," Luna gasps, hand clutching her chest. "This guy is completely sick in the head."

"Wake him up."

"Yes, sir," both guards answer in unison. The younger of the two drags Young's chair away and toward the farthest corner where a high-pressure spigot sits above his head, while the other man opens the drain and sets the water temperature to ice-cold. There's something about water that always gets the point across in one way or another; be it cold and hard or a tumultuous wave. It makes you calm, but that's the danger within it lurking. Water drowns. A single continuous drop on the same section of flesh can puncture a hole through you.

A single large wave can decimate an entire village and every being in its path.

As my men do this, Ivan grabs everything and puts it away and out the door, only coming back after my evidence is secure.

Then, we all stand across from him, just a few feet apart, and watch as the first jet hits him in the face. Scott sputters, coming to fast and fighting not to drown as the heavy flow soaks him from head to toe. The pressure from the water further opens his gashes, especially the one on his temple and cheek.

"What's going on...*fucking* stop! Help!"

"Why would I do that?" Scott stiffens. You can see the exact moment he remembers just where he is. What he did. He searches for me, following the sound of my voice, but can't keep his eyes open past the water. It's a strong jet the size of my wrist and very cold.

"I'll tell you anything you need to know."

"Will you, now?"

"Yes."

"Okay." Holding a finger up is my signal and the water shuts off. "Now, tell me why you're here, Mr. Rogers. Enlighten me with a story." Coughing, he chokes out a reply I can't quite make out. "Again, louder this time."

"Antonio Alejos hired me to kill you and then deliver his daughter to a property he owns in Tampa."

"That son of a bitch!" Edgar bellows, rushing toward Scott and knocking the tied man to the floor. I don't stop him. No. I feel his anger, his total disgust.

After he's laid a couple of good punches in, I look at Ivan and tilt my head for him to get him off. He resists at first, getting to land an elbow across the bridge of Scott's nose, but stands up after my brother whispers something to him.

Edgar's eyes go to his niece, who is now shaking in my arms. *Take her*, I mouth, and he comes over, pulling her from me—at first, she fights it, but goes after I kiss her temple and rub my thumb over her finger.

"I'll be up in a minute. Go with him."

"Will you be okay?"

"Always, beautiful. I got you."

ELENA M. REYES

"Okay." And it's only after they walk out that I crack my neck and let go. With a quickness that Scott doesn't expect, I flip open a blade I've had in my back pocket and stab him right between the legs. His mouth drops open, the silent scream caught in his throat, but he can't hold it back any longer when I twist the knife.

Then, his scream rents the air. Loud and full of pain and still not enough, so I pull it out and repeat the process five times. Blood soaks his pants and drips onto the already light pink water below.

"How did you get the job?"

"No more. Just no more."

"How did you get the motherfucking job, asshole? Don't make me ask again."

Scott's bottom lip trembles, limbs shaking from the shock trying to set in. "Alejos paid the chief of police to get me in under the pretense that I was a family friend just transferred. It was a favor-for-favor scenario."

"What did the chief receive?"

"A no-holds-barred night with Senot's wife."

Those sick fucks. "Is there proof of this?"

"There's a video at my apartment in Midtown."

"Already have it," Ivan says from behind me. "Everything useful is already in our possession."

"Thank you, brother." Taking the knife out, I bring it to his neck and press it against his Adam's apple. "Why did you collect all that information, Rogers? What was *your* plan in all this?"

"At first, it was money." His crying, the blubbering is getting on my nerves, but I grit my teeth and ignore. His time is almost up. "Alejos offered me a mil and then a way out of the country. But then…"

"Then what? You decided to extort him for more?"

"I decided to kill him and keep his daughter for myself."

Bending a bit, I get right in his face. I let him see the devil that resides within me. "You will never taste her sweetness." The knife goes in with just a small amount of strength from me, slicing right

274

through his neck and causing him to choke. No air. No way of talking. Nothing.

Scott "Young" Rogers will die being the miserable cunt he is. Alone. Without mercy.

He can go ahead and make space for Antonio, because he will be following him shortly.

Chapter 33
THIAGO

SUNDAY'S LUNCH AT my parents home a couple days later is a loud, boisterous affair. People are sitting around a large grouping of tables lined up in a row and talking amongst themselves. I'm at the head with my queen to my right and my parents to the left.

Then there's Ivan, Natasha, Amberlyn, and anyone else we could fit between myself and Jadiel and company, something that I think they're picking up on.

There's fidgeting.

A constant refill of their drink.

Excessive trips to the bathroom.

Even Celeste, who's unaware and blinded by her love for Sergio, looks uncomfortable. But that's on her. I'm a strong believer in self-awareness and being independent, two traits she's missing. The older she gets, the more she's becoming her mother.

It saddens me but doesn't have any weight on my decision. One that's made, and I have the backing of those who matter.

"Who's ready for dessert? I made a huge flan this morning?" Every hand but mine raises, and as they all focus on my mom taking inventory of how many servings she needs, I press play on my phone.

There's a crackling coming from the speakers and the sound of barstools scraping against tile follows—those at this table go quiet.

"Fucking asshole thinks he can treat me like shit," Celeste gasps, listening to her brother spew his true feelings on this recording. Her reaction is to be expected, and I do feel bad for her in this instance, more so as every head turns in his direction. He's pale as a ghost, stiff in his seat. *"I'm going to enjoy putting a bullet in his head, then one in Ivan and tio Orlando. Every fucking male with the last name De Leon needs to die within the next two weeks."*

Jadiel won't meet my eyes.

He's sweating, hands shaking as he grabs his beer.

"Calm down, Ivancito. You'll get your chance to do just that...Alejos paid us a great deal to end his daughter's suffering." They snort a second before a male waiter introduces himself at a sports bar on Biscayne Blvd. It's a place I am familiar with. Know the owner. *"Two Heinekens and a sampler for now. Nachos too."* That comes from my uncle, who thanks the man and then coughs. It's a distinct one. Like someone who's smoked three packs a day for thirty years. *"What's the next step, though? I haven't spoken to Antonio in weeks. Have you?"*

On the tape someone sucks their teeth, a trait my cousin has. Whenever annoyed, he falls back to this habit.

"Yeah, and he's on my ass about this. Something about time

running out and pitching his campaign soon; he wants her married and compliant by then." Their drinks are served, and the waiter tells them the food will be right out. *"Something I agree with. The little bitch has been taunting me for years and I plan to make her pay. Make her my personal fuck doll."*

Beside me Luna grabs her can of Coke, gripping it so hard that it overspills, soaking the white linen cloth. I place my hand atop the table, palm up. An invitation she accepts a few seconds later, intertwining our fingers.

"The broken ones are always fun."

"After Thiago's death, she'll be an easy target."

I press the stop button and bring my beauty's hand to my lips, kissing her soft skin. No one makes a sound, but I do see their intent loud and clear. Some are ready to jump up and grab them, while the two in question are dealing with their fight or flight response.

To run.

To lie.

To kill me for exposing them.

Winking at Luna, I stand and place a hand on my Viejo's shoulder, giving it a squeeze as I make my way around the table. No hurry. No outward display of anger.

I take my time in making my way around the table to Jadiel, reaching him just as he tries to stand. With a hard shove, I sit him back down. "Sit, primo."

"Thiago, that was just me talking shit. I didn't—"

"Silence." My voice thunders, causing him to make a whimpering sound. He's afraid, and the man should be. "I'm only going to make the following offer once, so accept and pray to God that he helps you." Those around the table in the know stand, pushing back their chairs and moving four paces back. "You will be ready at five this upcoming Friday and not ask questions. You will board my cargo ship, get ready in a private room, and meet me in the ring. Two five-minute rounds will decide your fate and mine, Jadiel. Beat me, and the position as head is yours. Nod if you understand." He does, practically squirming in his seat to get away. "Good boy."

And then I leave him there, ignoring his father and sister and the dumbass who I'm coming for next. Everyone standing follows me inside and the sliding glass door closes.

Our position has been made. My offer is valid.

Casualties in this instance can't be avoided, but his sister is the only person I'll welcome back into the family after the chains holding her down are broken.

ULYSSES SENOT's office is closed that Thursday, but we both know that's a lie. The sign is there to deter visitors, me to be precise, but I knew the very moment he stepped foot inside of his floor in the Government Building which holds his office.

Today is the second time he showed up for work since we bumped into each other in New York.

He's been hiding by taking an extended vacation and then faking a bout of sickness upon his return. He's been staying inside and avoiding all types of outdoor activities that require an appearance by the quote-on-quote *good guy*.

What he fails to understand is that while being patient, I've done my homework. That I have eyes everywhere. That I've studied every bit of evidence I'll use to bring them all down, one by one.

Tapes upon tapes of people plotting my family's demise. Our deaths.

Pictures upon pictures of these upstanding citizens doing lines of coke and fucking—sharing what shouldn't be shared and treating this pathetic excuse of a man like a personal punching bag.

And no, this isn't a kink or a mutual agreement between consenting adults. Antonio and Jasmine treat him like shit, beat him, and then laugh at the bruises while he's forced to watch them together.

The only person that still cares for him is his son, and when things come to light, he'll be sitting in a jail cell and serving time for years to come. He'll never see the light of day again—Claudio will carry the burden for his father, I'll make sure of that.

They judge me, but two of those involved who are still alive want to run a sex trafficking ring in the 305 and hide it behind their political personas or affiliations. They have enough pull, know enough corrupt city employees to make that happen. A favor for a favor, and those sick fucks will get away with it because Senot is afraid to say no.

In all of this, Ulysses is the lesser of the scum. An easy target.

But more importantly, my name will be cleared by the end of the day.

I bypass security—a woman whose husband works for me at the port—walking right through the lobby downstairs and right onto the elevators. His office is on the top floor and no one dares to stop me or Ivan, not even the secretary that at the sight of me looks away and pretends we aren't here. This visit is a long time coming, and I warned him years ago to expect me to pass him the bill for my county stay.

"What the—?"

"Hello, Mr. Senot. Might I have a minute or two of your time?"

"Thiago, what are you doing here?" He reaches for the panic button to the right of his leg, but in his nervous haste spills coffee all over himself. "Shit!" His hands grab a wad of Kleenex beside a cup full of pens, dabbing at his desk and the sheet of paper he was reading. "How did you get by security?"

"Just walked right on by." There are two chairs opposite his desk and we take one each. My brother also places our gift atop the table. It's a small box, nondescript and wrapped in black paper.

He eyes the box, his hand trembling as he grabs more tissue and dries the no-longer-there puddle. "How can I help you, Mr. De Leon? I'm a very busy man and—"

"My family would like to extend our deepest condolences on the loss of your long-time employee and wife's fuck toy."

"Thank you. We don't know what...did you just say fuck toy?" Face red and eyes wide, he stares at me with the same horrified expression Gaytan wore right before I ended his life. "What are you talking about? My wife—"

"Is a narcissistic bitch that humiliates you by sleeping around with any willing dick," I finish for him. Beside me Ivan snickers, but rights himself quickly when I look his way from the corner of my eye. What they've done to him is messed up. He is the epitome of an abused husband, but that doesn't negate the fact that he could've said no to attempting to kill someone I love and sending me to jail. That falls on him. "Now, with that being said, I'm here to offer you a one-time-only deal, Senot. Are you listening?"

"I don't make deals with criminals." His self-righteous attitude, that chip on the shoulder that all politicians carry, rises to the surface. He looks downright offended by my words. "We're done. Go."

"Within the next sixty minutes my Luna is delivering two special packages to both the District Attorney's office and the largest media outlet in South Florida. Those two gifts contain pictures of three-somes, foursomes, and your humiliation at Antonio Alejos' hands. Then, there's the audio of backdoor deals being made with my cousin Jadiel—who I've kept out of this to deal with him personally —including my incarceration and the hitman hired to kill my father. I have confession tapes from those parties, given to a now deceased Gaytan as he ordered the hit on your behalf."

"No. NO!"

"Yes." Ivan pushes the box in his direction. "You are implicated in multiple counts of perjury, fraud, illicit activity, and consuming of illegal substances. The same ones you took an oath to combat when you took office. Then, there's the sex ring you're helping to both build and hide for your wife and best friend."

"Thiago, this...how did...don't do this."

"It's already done."

"We can work something—"

"No. We can't." Crossing my leg at the knee, I scratch my jaw. "There is nothing you could do for me that will stop this from happening. And while I may be a criminal, I would never hurt an innocent."

"This is all a misunderstanding. I would've never gone through with it."

"Liars never enter Heaven's gate," Ivan deadpans; it's an old saying my mother would regularly use to try and get us to confess as kids. To scare us into admitting whatever prank or mischief we were up to. Leaning forward, he opens the box and begins to lay out every single item within. The more Ulysses sees, the more he begins to sweat. The more he pulls at the collar of his ugly pinstriped shirt that's seen better days. "Deny it now?"

"I-I—"

"Can't," I end the statement for him. "But here is what you *can* do, Senot."

"Anything."

"Leave."

"What?" he sputters. "What do you mean, leave?"

"I mean grab whatever shit you can fit inside of a duffle bag and get out of Miami." We stand then, and I lean over his desk, placing a single finger atop the picture of Gaytan after his execution. A silent warning and admission from me. "Don't let them drag you down further."

Just as I turn to head to the door, my phone beeps with an incoming text.

> Done. It'll begin playing shortly on media outlets. Once one station grabs a story, they all jump on it.
> ~My Beauty

An arrest warrant is the next step from the DA.
Should be ready within the next 24 hrs. ~My
Beauty

I flip my phone around so that Ulysses can read it. His expression says it all: he's scared.

Thank you, love. ~Thiago

It's not easy on her. I know this.

Her tears on my shoulder two nights ago as she went through each item Ivan collected broke my heart. Loving someone is hard, and more so when they're hurting because you feel their pain—want to take it away and make them smile. You want nothing more than to erase the disappointment and loss.

And while I begged her to let me handle things, Luna once again showed me just how much of my equal she is. Chin jutted out and hand on her hip, I was told she needed to do this. That it's her duty as his daughter to put a stop to his disgusting plans, especially the ones that include her.

"Within the next twenty-four hours your world will implode, Senot. Heed my warning now and disappear because no one outside of your son will miss you."

We leave, and shortly after midday the breaking news headlines begin to appear with the politician scandal. Every news station is reporting. Every name involved is shared. Their long list of charges and the DA's involvement follows—the news of arrest warrants possibly being granted later this afternoon by a judge in the county— are the cherry on my cake.

However, there's a twist in this story come the ten o'clock hour. A breaking news alert that doesn't surprise me as the reporter on the screen begins to deliver the accounts of what's occurred.

Miami Mayor Ulysses Senot is dead after a confrontation in his home tonight. The politician, who's at the center of a huge criminal investigation as of a few hours ago, was shot and killed by his wife, who later turned the gun on herself. At this time the details of this gruesome ending are vague, and we will continue to report on this story as more details emerge.

Chapter 34
THIAGO

I T'S LOUD INSIDE of the cargo ship the following night as people find their seats. Some are drinking. Some are gambling. Some look like they're ready to piss their pants.

The latter being Jadiel who has tried to have my mother intercede twice. She didn't, hanging up the phone and refusing to allow him or his father on her property.

Claudio who tried to run away after the news broke out of Senot's death and then the active warrant for both Antonio and the surviving Senot.

My eyes scan the crowd from my seat on the right side of the

ELENA M. REYES

ring. In the past, when I've fought, it was for fun—sold-out underground fights whose chump change I'd donate to a charity of my
choice.

Tonight, though, there's no fanfare. No bright lights or someone
announcing each fighter. No trash talking, gloves, or the illusion of
protective gear and a clean fight.

I want his blood on my hands.

I want to feel the very moment death takes him when I snap his
neck.

No mercy tonight.

"Will you be okay when all is said and done?" Luna's soft voice
pulls me away from the sight of my uncle trying to pep talk his son.

"Yes."

"Okay." Her lips skim my forehead and down to my ear where
she pauses, her small exhale is sexy. "Come back to me unscathed
and you'll get a reward. Something we both need."

"For me to bend you over and—" She covers my mouth with her
dainty hand, my ring on her finger cool against my lips.

"I was thinking more of a honeymoon."

"That's still a little under three months away, bebe." Too long
when I'm ready to give her my name now. When I want to start
trying for a baby. "We might need to discuss that after. That date is
too far off."

Instead of an admonishment not to rush our special day, my girl
just giggles. "Finish the fight, Leon. Make it quick and trust me
when I say it's in your interest to do so." A bell sounds over the loud-
speakers then and she steps back so I can stand, giving me a sweet
smile when I look over.

"I love you."

"I love you, too."

This ring has no bars, cage, or ropes; a small barrier no higher
than someone's waist is what separates us from the crowd, and I lift
Luna over it so she can take her seat behind me. My mother and
father are there beside her, and so are those closest to me and mine.

Like Ninette and Miguel who sit with Junior; the kid has grown so much since my release and is no longer on the boat. He will begin working with me in two weeks as a personal driver, while studying finance at night at a university nearby.

Ivan appears next to me, a bottle of water in hand. He's laughing at something and when I raise a brow, he shrugs. "I have ten grand on this not going past the minute mark."

"Really? You see him making it that far?"

"I'm hoping for something interesting here." He's lucky he's my brother or I'd toss him off the ship. "Besides, I'm going against Amberlyn, and knowing her, she won't let go of that money easily. I already have a counter offer she can't—"

I shake my head. "Out of the ring and shut it."

"Just help a guy out."

"I'll see what I can do." The second bell sounds and all noises cease. The lights dim all around us and the center stage ones shine brighter. It's just the two of us, looking at the other and focusing on the other's moves.

He's anticipating me to rush him, but I won't. Instead, I begin to stalk forward, my footwork lazy because he is no threat, and I stop two steps from him.

"Hit me."

"Thiago, enough. Let's talk about this."

"Hit me. You get one free shot." Closing my eyes, I relax my stance and lower my guard. "Make it count, Jadiel...it'll be your only opportunity."

"This is a trick." Losing your sight helps you focus on your other senses, and when he moves the waistband of his pants, the material makes a crinkling sound. *Fucking moron.*

His fist connects with the side of my head, the metal barely making contact and he has no weight behind the blow. It's a soft touch with the weapon and I almost feel bad for him.

So much so that I crack my neck and stiffen my jaw. "Again."

I take two more before my eyes snap open and make connection with his. He has a pair of brass knuckles on, a cheap version of mine, and on backwards. The thick metal that should go above each knuckle is inside his palm.

"Even when given a chance, you fuck it up." My hand snaps forward before he can duck, and I grip the base of his neck—squeezing until breathing becomes difficult and his hands begin to claw at my arm.

Sadly, that might be the most damage he causes.

"Okay," he sputters, face turning red. "I've learned my lesson and you've had your fun. I know my place."

It comes out as a bunch of broken garbles with a squeak, but I understand, going as far as to nod and then toss him aside. "Get up."

"Are we good now?" Jadiel is rubbing his neck. "I promise it won't happen again."

"Get up."

"Not until you...fuck!" A single kick hits his midsection and he's crying, curling into himself right before I land another, this one to his head.

I stand back. "Get up and fight or I'll slit your throat right now." His father in the background tries to rush me, but two guards grab him, bringing him to his knees. "Or better yet, I can make you watch as I blow your father's head clean off."

That gets to him. You can see the anger simmering; it overtakes his *pussy-like* qualities and Jadiel stands on wobbly legs, his hands up as if preparing to throw a punch. "Touch him and I'll kill you."

One of the guards strikes my uncle, breaking his nose.

"You were saying?"

"You're a dead man," he screams, rushing forward and connecting with my body. I stumble back a bit but catch my footing and turn us. His body hits the padding below hard and a grunt leaves him, but for once in his miserable life, he doesn't give up.

Jadiel throws an elbow up that connects with my mouth, splitting my bottom lip. I taste the blood and smile, letting him do it again before I fully mount him.

My right leg pins both of his, making it hard for him to move as I take the dominant position. He has no way of defending himself other than those bony elbows, while I position myself to pound his face in.

The first direct hit stuns him. The second makes him cry out.

I use my full force behind each strike, taking pleasure in the way his face begins to swell and break, his blood staining my hands and chest. My elbow comes down on his right eye and I feel the moment the orbital bone breaks. There's a give in the firmness of the bone, the eye moving loosely right before it bulges out.

Jadiel can't focus. He's squinting and fighting to protect his face, but I'm not done and land a second elbow just below the opposite eye. The swelling comes on quickly. His vision looks to be a bit dizzy, and I move into the side guard position. This gives me the space needed to hook his arm, bring my leg over his head, and turn my body.

At once his scream rents the air, the pressure I'm adding creating stress in three places: the elbow and shoulder joint plus the upper arm bone. He's tapping. Begging beneath me. I pull back harder and all three pop; the bone being the last as it breaks in two.

The crowd, who had been quiet until now, begin to stomp the floor, a low chant of *end him* filling the room. It grows louder with each second. The women are louder than the men—they're pissed for more than his betrayal. They're mad because of his plans to hurt my queen, someone everyone in this room loves and respects.

Releasing him, I stand and then fist his hair in my hands, dragging him along behind me toward the center of the ring. People stand. They wait. And when my father calmly walks over and shoots Jadiel's father in the head, he gets a standing ovation.

One down, a few more to go.

My cousin can't quite make out what's happened over the swelling, but I'm kind enough to bend a bit and relay the scene. "My deepest condolences, primo. Your father is dead." His body shakes, his chest caving as a sob bursts forth. I'm not moved, nor do I care.

"You rose against me, Jadiel, that was your first mistake. The second was selling the logistics of my shipments to the feds, helping Arroyo fuck me over. Your cockiness has been your downfall. Believing me stupid enough to not check the video feeds make you an amateur. See you in hell."

Standing to my full height, I tower over him and snap his neck. He's gone in the blink of an eye and falls to the floor, eyes wide open as a group of employees from this cargo ship come into the ring to take the body out. These are the same men that a few weeks ago were goofing around while others were busy loading my gifted guns aboard.

"Let this be a lesson," I say, my voice loud enough to carry over the room. "Betray me and death will be your end. Fail at the job I've entrusted you with and this is your fate. Anything less than respect and loyalty is a direct disrespect to our name and oath."

Chapter 35
LUNA

FORTY-EIGHT HOURS have come and gone since the Senot homicide/suicide. The city is buzzing. It's all anyone can talk about, more so after Claudio's arrest at the airport. He tried and failed to pull a runner after being tied to a third of the crimes committed by our families. And while I am glad that justice is being served, that Thiago's case is being reviewed so those charges are expunged, I'm more concerned at the moment with my mother.

She's not answering her phone which is unusual for her. That damn device is her saving grace and Pinterest is her home. The woman has more boards than anyone I know and hasn't updated a single one since before things went boom.

Mom shares them on her private Facebook and IG almost daily, showing off her ideas for decorating next season. For the changes to her hair she's considering or the DIY bullshit she'll never attempt because it's cute to say you're handy but not so much to actually get dirty.

Her words, not mine.

"Anything yet?" Thiago asks, coming to lie down beside me on the couch. I'm completely moved in now and hanging out atop a monstrosity he had to have for our media room. I won't deny it's plush and comfortable and I sink in like no one's business, but at the moment, I feel off.

Restless.

Worried.

Wondering where the hell my father is hiding and worse, did he do something to my mother. Because bad parent or not, I do love the woman and wouldn't want her harmed. To me she's just as guilty in the sense that she kept her mouth closed and went along with what he said for appearance's sake—accepting the lies and affair with Jasmine Senot—but all physical evidence tied to the crimes shows her noninvolvement.

My phone rings again, and I sigh. It's a local number, the same one trying to get a hold of the daughter of the ex-commissioner since the story broke out.

"Nada." I toss the device aside and turn onto my back, looking up at the ceiling. "It rings three times and sends me to her full voicemail."

"My men are looking for them," he says, voice low while draping an arm over my waist. It's a bit heavy with his muscles, but I don't complain and let him pull me in closer. Breathe me in. "I'll turn this city inside out to find her for you."

"I know you will. I'm probably worried for nothing."

"Intuition is a nagging little voice that makes us rationalize the situation without second guessing or rational explanation. We just know." Turning my face toward his with the tip of a finger, he stares into my eyes. The hazel orbs are full of so much compassion and empathy. "Tell me, bebe. What does yours say?"

"That they're home."

"You think so?"

"Everything in me believes it and I can't explain the why. It's a gut feeling that I can't shake, Leon—"

"Get up and get dressed. We leave in twenty."

"What do you mean? Where are we going?"

"Right where you know we should be."

"But?"

"I'll have Ivan and Edgar meet us there. Let's go."

"Thank you," I whisper, my emotions rising to the surface. He's not making me feel like an idiot or telling me to wait or saying it'll be okay, and he'll take care of it. My papi is validating me with something that most would laugh at and tell me to trust his men, or the police. Our story hasn't been easy, at times painful, but at this very moment I fall in love with him all over again. "I love you, Thiago. Always and forever."

"Always and forever, beautiful." He grabs my hand and leads me up the stairs to our room. There are still a few boxes with my things that need to be put away and my clothes from the night before strewn about, but I've never felt more at home than I do with him. And before I let go of his hand to get dressed, I turn in his arms and rise onto the very tips of my toes so I can reach his lips.

"I want to get married in our backyard thirty days from now."

"My queen deserves—"

"This is just your formal invitation, Mr. De Leon. I've already taken care of everything."

"Have you, now?"

"Yes, now let's go find my mom. I'd really like her to be present at my wedding even if it's bitching the entire way."

THE HOUSE IS EERILY quiet when we arrive around five that evening. There are no cruisers watching the residence or nosy neighbors outside like I expected.

To be honest, I've never seen this street so desolate—empty. *Where is everyone?*

Thiago parks his car behind my mother's silver BMW, leaving the engine running just in case. All the window drapery is open, parted so you can see inside, and I take in the lack of lighting or movement.

I'm the first one out of the car and up to the front—three car doors open and close—their footsteps loud up the paver-lined driveway.

They stand behind me, their support giving me the strength to open the door using a key code combination.

"I think he's here too," Edgar says, and I grip his hand. This is his brother. Flesh and blood. No matter what they've done, how shitty my father is, it still hurts. "I'm thinking—"

"The cottage at the back of the property."

"What cottage?" Ivan asks, walking past me with his weapon drawn. He's followed by my uncle, and Thiago takes the back. I'm surrounded by them as we enter, and the stench inside makes me gag. It's the foul smell of spoiled food, something left out for days, and I follow the smell to the kitchen. The culprit is atop the stove; a large batch of some kind of soup that's turned sour in this heat.

"Christ, that's foul." Thiago's nose scrunches up, and he draws his own weapon, looking at me, so I take mine out as well. He always makes sure I carry, that I'm protected. "Stay vigilant. Safety off."

No A/C has made the house stale too. No electricity running throughout the house means no cameras are running. It's a good thing past this horrible smell; we'll have the element of surprise if they're on the premises.

Nodding, I look back at his brother. "My father built a man cave out back, past this home's property line and in the middle of the undeveloped land behind this lot. It's completely decked out; all utilities working, full living room and bedroom with a functioning bathroom."

"And no one knows about that place?" My brother-in-law's incredulous look would be funny any other day. Not today, and I shrug.

"Those that do are either dead, in this room, or freaking out they don't get involved. As of this morning, two other names have been added to the investigation: the police chief and the judge that sentenced Thiago."

His eyes narrow and he shakes his head. "And we're the fucked-up ones?"

"Hypocrisy is usually wielded by those afraid to look in the mirror. It's easier to cast stones than to accept responsibility."

"Very true, my queen." My fiancé passes me, intertwining our empty hands as he goes. We leave the kitchen and check the den, the family room, and find no sign of life outside of the empty bar. Every liquor bottle is missing. "That's not normal."

"No."

"Should we still check upstairs?" I look at Thiago and shake my head. It's useless and a waste of time. They're not here. "Okay." Looking at Edgar and Ivan, he motions for them to head out back and we follow. No one talks. We just walk as quietly as possibly, not wanting to alert them to our presence.

The lawn is overgrown, and the pool is green—the algae reproduction consuming every inch. Even my mother's hibiscus plants that she loves so much are now dead.

"What the fuck happened back here?" Edgar stops just at the tree line, taking in the density. That, and a small trip wire that glints with the sun's position in the sky. "It's not high. Step over it."

We follow him over and search the ground nearby for more. There isn't any, but we're careful nonetheless as we walk through and find the cottage, a little one-bedroom unit that I hear music coming from and detect the scent of food being cooked.

"You were right, Luna." Thiago lifts his gun, aiming it for the door, and the other two follow him. I stay back. Not because I'm afraid, but because they're more equipped to handle this type of situation than I am.

I'm not looking to let my emotions cause someone harm.

My fiancé raps the ground three times, and on the last, kicks the door in. Three screams follow: two male, and one female. The place is dingy when we rush in, garbage and empty liquor bottles littering the floor, and the people inside reek.

How long have they been back here? This is more than a few days-worth of filth.

I'm taking it all in. Everything. From my father's hate filled eyes as he sits on a tufted blue chair that's seen better days—to Sergio on an ottoman with a crying Celeste holding two plates filled to the brim with hot food.

Her hands shake, spilling what looks to be a pasta dish on Sergio, and his automatic reaction is to lift his hand, swinging it back as if to hit her. Wrong move. Sooner than I can blink, the angry brothers beside me shoot him. They both empty an entire magazine, littering his body with holes from his head to midsection.

It's all happening so fast; one minute he's sitting, and the next slouched on the ground at an odd angle while my father has his hands up and is glaring at his brother.

"You'll pay for this, Edgar. You, and my traitor daughter." There's so much venom in each word. His desire to reach for the shotgun to his left against the wall is plain as day to see. He'd kill us if he could. "Mark my words, you'll both regret the day you chose *them* over your own blood."

"Funny, brother. Because it's hard to draw revenge from six feet below."

"Fuck you," my father hisses out, making a move to stand, and a shot is fired. Just one, and he cries out. It's then that I look over, meeting his eyes the same shade of brown as my own. They're life-less, empty, as blood stains his dirty shirt at the left sleeve and shoul-der. "I'm going to—"

I tune him out for my own sanity. He's not going anywhere, my uncle will make sure of that, and I look over at a furious Thiago. He's keeping it together for me. He's not personally ending my father's life because of the promise he made me. And while the man deserves whatever life throws his way, if it came down to it, I'd rather it's Edgar or myself that pulls the trigger. Something, that I know my papi will understand.

"Check the room down that small hall. My mom..." I trail off as my voice cracks and he walks over, placing a kiss on my forehead.

"Help Celeste, and I'll check the back with Ivan. We'll circle the outside too if we find nothing."

"Thank you." As they head toward the back, I turn my focus to Celeste who hasn't moved an inch. "I'm sorry, sweetie. I got you."

She's a bundle of nerves, the eruption almost violent as shock settles quicker than I can react, and she sways. The plates slip from her fingertips, crashing to the ground and dirtying both our legs. A few shards cut her while my sweatpants have stains, but I jump in without a second thought. Right before she crashes to the ground, I grab her, pulling her into me and away from the bloody scene and food.

There's a small patch of clean flooring to the right and when I can't hold us up any longer, her weight in this state too much, I lower us. "It's going to be okay." I'm rocking us from side to side after placing my gun on the ground, not wanting to freak her out further. "You're safe."

"Am I really?" Her voice is small. Shaky. Timid.

"Yes, we'll take care of you. Help you." Her arm shifts a bit and I ignore the stretch, thinking nothing of it, when time stands still for a second time and my gun is pressed below my chin. My eyes close and I fight the urge to look into her eyes. "Why?"

"Because everything that's gone wrong in my life starts and ends with you." Celeste's hand is shaking. You can tell she's never really held a gun before, much less shot one and I'm not surprised. Not with a sexist father and brother. "All the men in my life have fallen for you, and I've taken the brunt of their frustrations."

"Bebe, she's here!" Thiago calls out, but I don't move or answer. "Did you hear me? She's—"

All eyes are on us now. They see the gun.

My father laughs and then he doesn't. A body crashes to the ground and feet come closer. Multiple bodies surround us, and guns are cocked.

"Celeste, please think this through. This isn't you."

"Prima, don't force my hand."

She ignores Thiago's warning, her tears falling on my shirt. "Because of my brother's obsession with you, Thiago killed him. My father too. I've lost it all, Luna. Every-fucking-body that I loved."

"Drop the gun and step back."

"That's not true. We're all here for you," Leon and I say in unison; I'm calm while I have no doubt in my mind he'll pull the trigger. Something that will break his heart because he does care for her. We all do.

"Dale, Celeste. Stop this...no more blood needs to be shed." Ivan tries to step closer, but I feel her finger shift around the trigger, and I hold a hand up. He stops but doesn't move back.

"I knew about Sergio's obsession with you a week after we met, you know. It's why I told him to change his last name." She pushes the barrel just a little bit deeper, and it's uncomfortable to swallow. "Your father sent him pictures of you from family affairs, gradua-tion...vacations. He fed my love's obsession in hopes that he'd kill Thiago and bring you back under his thumb. You were to be his play-thing, and yet, I was still going to marry him because that's what love is. You accept the other half of your soul with all their baggage and fuckups."

"That's not love, sweetie. You deserve more."

"Shut up!" Her scream at my ear hurts, and I move back,

grimacing—a natural reaction—and it sends my head back and chest away from hers. That slim opening is all Thiago needs, and two shots end her life.

I don't want to see and close my eyes. Her blood is literally on my hands and shirt. So when two masculine hands grab me and pull me off the floor, I fight back.

At that moment my mind goes blank and the world dissolves into loud noises and panic. I can't get air into my lungs.

"Breathe, Luna. Fucking breathe!" The sound of a door opening and closing follows, and then birds in the distance. My feet don't meet the ground, but it's his muscular scent that grounds me. It's what I focus on as his hands grip me tight—encircle me in his hold.

Every breath slowly becomes easier.

Every word he says becomes clearer.

"Breathe, baby. Just like that." Another soothing caress up and down my back, figure eights that begin to relax me. "That's it. Come back to me, love."

"I'm here," I say and it's low, but by his reaction you'd think I would've yelled it.

"Thank God." His lips meet mine. The kiss is sweet—electric, and my shaky hands come up gripping the back of his neck. Behind us, feet approach the cottage at a rapid pace; they pass by and head inside while we stay in this moment.

The kiss calms me. Gives me what I need to lose the tight noose that was slowly choking me.

"Put him in the back of my car. I'm taking him in myself." My uncle's voice registers sharply, though, and I pull back just in time to see Antonio Alejos: unconscious, in handcuffs, and over some man's shoulder. "Ivan, please get Yvette to the main house. She needs medical care and an ambulance will be here in a couple of minutes!"

"What's wrong, Luna?"

"Shit." I'm pushing against him, wiggling in his hold as I fight to get down. "My mom! What's wrong with my mom?"

"Broken leg and a concussion from the looks of it, but—"

"But what?"

"Bebe, Yvette's been doped up pretty hard." At that I gasp, my chest burning from the previous panic. "We found her with a needle in her arm and slumped over. Ivan will ride with her."

"Let me go. I need to—"

"Stop."

"But she needs—"

"Her daughter to not pass out and to meet her in the hospital later. To breathe. To be there for her. To help her in the next stage of her life because everything she's always known is gone." My body becomes languid with his explanation because he's right. Things won't be easy for her, and mending our relationship won't happen overnight...

So much has been said. Done.

"Thank you." And I mean it. Because this man has always been my rock. He looks out for me, loves me, and accepts me as I am. He gives me the world and asks for nothing but my heart in return. And while our love story had a sad intermission, the act that followed has been worth it all. "I love you, Thiago."

He lays his forehead against mine; and his gorgeous hazel eyes have gone soft. "Forever and always."

And while around us chaos ensues, bodies are removed, and the building and everything inside is set on fire, I close my eyes and let him carry me away.

He is mine and I am his.

That's all that matters.

It's how it was always meant to be.

Epilogue 1
THIAGO

ONE MONTH LATER...

"**I** CAN'T BELIEVE you're making me late to my own wedding, papi. Seriously, we need to be...oh *God*!" One stroke and I'm deep inside her tight little pussy, the bottom of her dress being held in one hand while I grip her hip with the other. She's tight and wet and has been begging me to take her like this since late last night.

It's all in the way she moves.

A simple bend at the waist while I'm watching TV, small indecent boy shorts riding up and exposing the new tattoo at her hip. My initials. In my writing. And more provocative is the way she got them.

Sneaky and serving me a dose of my own medicine, Luna asked me to sign a few documents atop her desk because she'd forgotten to send them herself. They were for her new gallery downtown. The contracts for my contractor to start the build for a very detailed and specific darkroom she wanted in the back of the space.

So, I did what all good hubbys do and I signed/initialed whatever she needed me to.

Three days later, this was my surprise.

I also spanked her until the sweet little globes became hot to touch and then fucked her like the bad girl she is. Luna drenched my sheets. Clawed at my back. Met me thrust for thrust while begging in that pretty voice of hers for *more*. Always more.

"Thiago," she mewls, clenching around my girth when I bend my knees a bit, changing the angle. My thrusts are deeper like this. Hitting that tiny spot inside that makes her...*Christ*, Luna flutters all around me and I close my eyes. "Harder...just a little bit *more*."

"So greedy, baby girl." Her exposed back is a temptation I can only withstand for so long, and I bite her. Little nips all over the expanse—wherever I can reach. "But remember that you made me do this. You're the reason we'll be late to our wedding today...all those guests downstairs waiting out on the lawn while the sun begins to set." Each word is followed by a punishing thrust. She clenches, thighs trembling, but I don't slow down. It's the opposite. "They're mingling while I fuck you. They're speculating about our delay while I imbibe of my gift a little early."

The last few weeks have been hard for her. Exhausting, but she took charge like the queen she is and took care of her mother while planning this wedding. I stepped in where I could, when the withdrawals kicked in and Yvette lashed out at her and the hospital staff, but Luna never took it personally. Her empathy knows no bounds and she proved that while making sure her addict mother—a habit forced by her husband, and at time chosen by herself to numb the pain—got the help she needs.

Moreover, while their relationship might never mend—Yvette chose to stay at the treatment center and not celebrate with us today —I know it brings Luna peace of mind to be there just in case. The same cannot be said for Antonio, though. No. Never him.

Edgar has personally seen to the destruction of every asset the man ever had. Their sibling rivalry surpasses what most experience, and we've come to learn that it's because he loved Yvette first. Antonio stole her from Edgar, and when they got married, he made his brother promise to always take care of his family first. His failure to do just that is what finally broke the camel's back.

Antonio Alejos will rot away in his cell before taking a trip to the morgue where they'll cremate, and then bury him in a plot for those who have no family to claim them.

"Please," her hungry little whine makes me tremble, my fingers at her hip digging in to the point she'll have marks on her skin. Always my mark. My love. Me.

"Take it." Another nip, this time to the center of her spine. "You knew exactly what you were doing when you designed this gown."

Her dress is simple in its elegance and fitting of her curves. A long white silk slip gown with minimal beading at her chest and a long train that begins in a ruching detail at her tailbone. The bodice is tight, sexy, while loosening at her hips to give a slight mermaid feel. At the least, that's how she explained it to me the day she gave me the concept. Designers from all over the country were tripping over themselves to design it, but Luna went with a local seamstress and her own original.

One fitting and she knew it was the one. I agree. It's her. It's beautiful.

But more importantly, I'm going to enjoy tearing it from her body tonight.

The six-inch heels on her dainty feet add the perfect height, and I bend over her just a little bit more. Our bathroom, her makeup vanity has the perfect chair for this. A plush mini replica of my throne-like chair on the cargo ship, and it cushions her while I fist the long, curled locks. I pull her head back, arching her against me and kiss her neck. Our eyes meet and in them, I see the same emotions reflected back at me.

Love. Loyalty. A never-satiated hunger.

"I can feel you're close, bebe." I breathe her in, that ever-present scent of lime and coconuts making me throb. Beads of sweat form at my brow and one drop falls to her neck; I follow its descent down her chest, disappearing into the soft fabric of her dress. "Come for me. Mark your husband."

Luna's mouth opens in a silent scream. Not a sound comes out as her entire body goes rigid. She's not breathing, clenching so hard around my cock—a nearly choking grip—and it's exquisite. Almost painful in its beauty, and on the next flutter of her walls, I feel the warmth of her juices doing exactly what I asked her to.

"Son of a bitch," I hiss out through clenched teeth, fighting to keep my eyes on her through the mirror as she milks me. She pulls the come from my heavy balls; it's a perfect mess. I stay buried deep until the very last drop of my release fills her body.

Our breathing is hard. Her hair is a tousled perfection. There's also someone calling our names from the bottom of the stairs because they're not allowed on this floor, and I feel like the luckiest son of a bitch alive.

"Can I marry you now?" Luna giggles from below me, her eyes sparkling in the mirror. "Or do you need a minute to recover." My response comes in the form of a glare and a single swat to her ass cheek before I pull out, tuck myself in, and lower her dress. She can't wear panties with it, and I rather like the idea of her walking toward me with my release coating her thighs. "That stung."

"Then don't be a brat." Turning her around to face me, I pull her into my embrace. Hug her tight to my chest and bend my head to reach her ruby red lips. "I love you, Luna. More than my own life. More than any man has ever loved a woman."

Instantly, she melts against me. Her sassy smirk turns into a soft smile. "Forever and ever and ever?"

"Past this life and the next." Then I kiss her inside of our room, slow and sweet and with more passion that I ever thought possible. "Now, are you ready to sign your life away to the devil himself? To spend two weeks with me on a private beach in Cuba?"

"Would you let me go if I said no?"

"Never."

"And that's why I will. Because even when I'm lost, you stick by me and fight for us."

And that's exactly what she did.

At forty minutes later on the dot, Luna became my wife. My partner in crime. My right hand and the rightful queen of the De Leon Dynasty.

Epilogue 2
THIAGO

THE IMPERIUM...

THIS DAY HAS been a long time coming. Every man within this room rules his domain with an iron fist and loyalty to those they care about. We all bring something different to the table—money, weapons, and the most profitable of all: drugs. An obscene quantity of drugs, that when our resources are pooled together, would overtake every other syndicate fighting for the scraps we leave untouched.

Ninety percent of all production and distribution would go

through us. The De Leons have channels in Cuba and Panama, while the Jameson brothers have Boston Harbor and the U.K. Then you have Malcolm, a cold and calculating man with an empire far reaching what the United States can control.

And yet, he wants more. To control worldwide monetary needs.

All profits would be equally shared.

One family.

One kingdom.

One power.

"Who's in favor of this merger between families?" Malcolm asks, hand held high with a glass of Gin in a toasting manner. We're inside my cargo ship in open water with more men surrounding this vessel than the national guard patrolling nearby knows what to do with. Then again, they wouldn't harass the newest mayor of Miami.

The 305 made a deal with this devil when the residents chose me to clean up their streets. To bring in more jobs and money. And I've done that in my own way. Bringing in businesses funded by myself under fake LLCs that pay its employees well to, not knowingly, launder my money.

A win *win* if you ask me.

"Aye." I don't think about it twice, raising my own. These are men I know and trust—family—and this merger will be beneficial to me and mine. My legacy was cemented a very long time ago, on the day I was born and laid out by my father, but this is different. My two year old son has been born into an opportunity not one criminal organization has yet to accomplish. They've tried—more times than I can count on one hand—and eventually failed because of greed.

Because the need to overthrow your neighbor always comes forth.

Kings cannot rule within the same city or state. Each one of us has an established family and territory with room to grow. Respect is key. Respect is what keeps us in business.

We each understand what it takes on our own, but together we cannot be stopped.

"Aye," Casper and Callum follow in unison, their pints almost gone, but the gesture is there nonetheless. I know Casper's long-term plans, and this fits his need for growth. Lucas will take over Boston eventually and then he has a bigger city in mind. Brighter lights and loud crowds make for a solid investment.

"Aye." The last and to my right is Ivan. He's ready. Has been for over a year since settling on the island. We have plans, and he has a political aspiration to run for president in Cuba. Out with the old and in with freedom, prosperity, and the largest transport channel to the states our U.S. government has ever seen.

"Then it's settled." Malcolm smirks, throwing back what's in his glass. "To the Imperium, gentlemen."

"The Imperium." we chant.

Outtake

LUNA

HOW THEY MET...

"**W**HY WON'T HE stop looking at me?" I whisper to my cousin Natasha, giving her the universal sign for *look but don't look* while passing in front of said boy's desk before exiting the classroom. The same *guy* that hasn't made a single attempt to hide his staring—an annoying habit that's had me on edge since walking into my first class.

It's been like this all day.

Every class inside of this private school. Every single time I look back...

He's there. Watching me.

An expression on his handsome face that I can't quite decipher.

Because there's no denying that he's cute. That I felt my cheeks heat up the second our eyes connected; dark brown on a hazel so vibrant I've never seen before. But more than that, they remind me of a lion's eyes.

The large dominant feline male that you see at the zoo or on a Nat Geo documentary.

For someone my age, there's this hint of something dark behind his stare. Something accentuated by the way people have been flocking to him all day.

I know this because I've been secretly watching too.

Have seen the way the other girls look at him.

How the boys try to constantly engage him in conversation.

He's popular. Respected. A hunter.

But why am I letting him get to me?

"At least he's hot, Lulu." She shrugs, fixing the strap of the over-sized book bag over her right shoulder. "Remember Sergio from down the block?"

At that, another face comes to mind and I pause at an area between the hall of classrooms and the girl's bathroom; the hallways are near empty as most students have taken off for the cafeteria. "Please don't remind me." A shudder of disgust runs through me at the mere thought of that jerk. "It's the only silver lining to our move from Jersey to Miami: no more creepy kid following me around like a lost puppy."

From the moment puberty hit, I became his target. Two years older than me and pushy, he's not my type at all with a pimply face, shorter-than-me stature, and a pompous attitude that screams of enti-tlement. And all that arrogance just because his parents own a local pizza place/arcade that's popular where we lived.

Sergio Martin constantly asked me out on a date that'd never happen, tried to steal a kiss or two and failed—left notes inside my locker declaring a love I wouldn't return. He was a problem I didn't want or need, and it's made moving so far away from my friends a good thing.

It's the only reason I've kept my displeasure to a minimum, well that, and my uncle allowing Natasha to come live with us instead of staying with our grandmother while he handles a business problem in the Dominican Republic.

But now with—

"See, prima. That's called a silver lining."

Rolling my eyes, I slap her arm. "I'm not the only one that had an admirer."

"Mine wasn't so bad." She shrugs, rubbing the spot I just hit. "Kind of sweet actually."

"You say that now!" I whisper yell, taking two steps back while she tries to jam a finger in my stomach. "Quit it."

"Make me."

"I'm ticklish and hate it."

Natasha takes one step forward of her own. "I know."

"Keep at it and I'll trip you."

There's a gleam in her eyes when she comes at me again and I turn, looking over my shoulder to flip her off as I duck out of the way. "You suck—" And that's as far as I get, because while trying to avoid her, I run straight into a hard body.

A body whose scent smacks me in the face and my head becomes light. That causes my knees to weaken, something I always thought to be made up by the Spanish soaps my mother watches.

The reaction's automatic and scary, and I don't understand it. Neither do I hide the small gasp that escapes my throat when I meet a pair of amused hazel ones that have been following me all day.

"Hello, little queen?"

"Little queen?" I squeak, enjoying the way his warm arm feels as he wraps one around my lower back and pulls me in closer. Liking how good I fit against his side—taking in the moment—when I should be pushing him away.

Demanding he let go.

That he leaves me be.

But I don't. Can't. Instead, I once again inhale his masculine scent while biting my bottom lip. I refuse to let out another sound. To show how much he's getting to me.

"Yes, little queen."

"Is that supposed to mean something?"

"One day it will."

"I need more than that." It comes out breathy, and he gives me this tiny little smirk that makes the butterflies in my stomach take off. *I'm in trouble.* "Thiago...that's your name, right?"

"Yes."

"You need to explain—"

This handsome jerk that I don't know, that's been watching me all day, leans in and lets out a low hum of approval while placing a kiss on the shell of my ear. A move that brings a hot flash of want through me. It catches me off guard and I almost miss his whispered words, but when they sink in, my world changes.

"It means one day you'll sit by my side as Mrs. De Leon."

MY SINFUL VALENTINE

The only thing that can crumble a KING is disappointing his QUEEN. So what do my Beautiful Sinners do on Valentine's Day for their women? They spoil and lick and eat...

Worship: Malcolm and London
Say My Name: Casper and Aurora
One More: Thiago and Luna
You've Been Bad: Javier and Mariah
Pretty Doll: Alejandro and Solimar

BUY HERE
https://books2read.com/u/bprv29

NEW DARK ROMANCE

LITTLE LIES
BUY HERE: https://books2read.com/little-lies

I AM DARKNESS.
I AM SIN.
I AM YOURS.

A truth imprinted onto my skin—its sharp vines digging into my flesh as our bond strengthens with each shallow intake of breath my love takes. Her life is intertwined with the devil, a man who hungers for depravity and death, and yet, I bend my knee for her.

Only her. Always her.

She is mine and I will kill to protect. Kill to own her.

BEAUTIFUL SINNER SERIES

ABOUT THE AUTHOR

Elena M. Reyes is the epitome of a Floridian and if she could live in her beloved flip-flops, she would.

As a small child, she was always intrigued by all forms of art: whether it was dancing to island rhythms, or painting with any medium she could get her hands on. Her passion for reading over the years has amassed her with hours of pleasure, but it wasn't until she stumbled upon fanfiction that her thirst to write overtook her world.

She's a short and sassy Latina with an adorable pup, a kiddo that keeps her on her toes, and a husband who claims she'll cause him to go bald prematurely. Lol

Email: Reyes139ff@gmail.com

Elena's Marked Girls.
Come join the naughty fun.
Link: https://www.facebook.com/groups/1710869452526025/

Newsletter Sign-Up:
http://bit.ly/2nHJxTI

facebook.com/AuthorElenaMReyes
x.com/ElenaMReyes
instagram.com/elenar139
bookbub.com/profile/elena-m-reyes

FATE'S BITE SERIES

LITTLE LIES
LITTLE MATE
HALF TRUTHS DUET
HALF TRUTHS: THEN
HALF TRUTHS: NOW
OMISSION PART 1 & 2
COME TO ME (2024)
THE HUNT (2024)
TERO (TBD)

BEAUTIFUL SINNER SERIES
Each book is a standalone.
Now Live!

SIN (#1)
COVET (#2)
MINE (#3)
YOURS (#4)
RISQUE #5
OWN #6
Beautiful Sinner Spin-Off
CORRUPT
MY SINFUL VALENTINE
SAVAGE KISS

ONE RULE
(BOOK #2 LIONEL TBD)

(Marked Series)
Marking Her #1
Marking Him #2

www.ingramcontent.com/pod-product-compliance
Lightning Source LLC
Chambersburg PA
CBHW051332250626
47155CB00007B/2562

* 9 7 8 1 7 3 7 2 4 2 0 4 8 *